Dear Reader,

It's always fun for me to have a book reprinted, but when I found out *The Outlaw and the City Slicker* was to be reissued I was particularly thrilled. This book is a favorite of mine. No, it's not the best I think I've written. After all, it was the third I had published and I would hope I've grown as a writer since then, but something about Sunny and Jesse really captured me. They both seemed so confident and together, yet vulnerable and tentative at the same time.

Sunny especially was a challenge to write. Her twin sister was in another book and Sunny wasn't exactly the "good" twin. We had a few late-night talks trying to get her to soften up. But she pulled through like a champ, a true heroine, and we forever bonded. I hope you enjoy her as much as I did. And Jesse…sigh… what's not to like?

Debbi Rawlins

GREATEST TEXAS LOVE STORIES OF ALL TIME

GREATEST
TEXAS LOVE STORIES
OF ALL TIME

THE OUTLAW
AND THE
CITY SLICKER
Debbi Rawlins

He's a Cowboy!

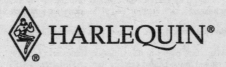

HARLEQUIN®

TORONTO • NEW YORK • LONDON
AMSTERDAM • PARIS • SYDNEY • HAMBURG
STOCKHOLM • ATHENS • TOKYO • MILAN • MADRID
PRAGUE • WARSAW • BUDAPEST • AUCKLAND

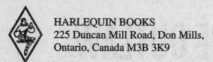

HARLEQUIN BOOKS
225 Duncan Mill Road, Don Mills,
Ontario, Canada M3B 3K9

ISBN 0-373-65226-7

THE OUTLAW AND THE CITY SLICKER

Copyright © 1998 by Debbi Quattrone

This edition published by arrangement with Harlequin Books S.A.

® and TM are trademarks of the publisher. Trademarks indicated with ® are registered in the United States Patent and Trademark Office, the Canadian Trade Marks Office and in other countries.

Visit us at www.eHarlequin.com

Printed in U.S.A.

DEBBI RAWLINS

currently resides with her husband and dog in Las Vegas, Nevada. A native of Hawaii, she married on Maui and has since lived in Cincinnati, Chicago, Tulsa, Houston, Detroit and Durham, North Carolina, during the past twenty years. Now that she's had enough of the gypsy life, it'll take a crane, a bulldozer and a forklift to get her out of her new home. Good thing she doesn't like to gamble. Except maybe on romance.

Books by Debbi Rawlins

Harlequin American Romance

Marriage Incorporated #580
The Cowboy and the Centerfold #618
The Outlaw and the City Slicker #622
Love, Marriage and Other Calamities #675
Marry Me, Baby #691
The Bride To Be...Or Not To Be #730
If Wishes Were...Husbands #741
Stud for Hire? #780
Overnight Father #790
His, Hers and Theirs #808
Loving a Lonesome Cowboy #860
His Royal Prize #881
To Love an Older Man #927
By the Sheikh's Command #933

Harlequin Intrigue

Her Mysterious Stranger #587

Harlequin Love & Laughter

I Saw Daddy Kissing Santa Claus #34

For my parents, Earl and Betty.

Chapter One

"Tell me that isn't her." Jesse Logan watched the taxi driver unload the fifth, sixth and seventh pieces of matching designer luggage. He hadn't actually seen the passenger yet, but taxis in the small west Texas town of Maybe were unheard-of, and Sunny Daye was expected at any moment.

A pair of long, shapely, tanned legs swung from the back seat of the cab. The feet were covered in short, pink leather boots studded with rhinestones.

Jesse's friend Cash cleared his throat. "That's her, all right."

Jesse slowly turned to his longtime buddy. This was going to be a really bad trip. He felt it all the way down to the toes of his own hopelessly scuffed boots. "She does know this is a cattle drive we're going on?"

Cash grinned wryly. "She knows."

"A real, honest-to-goodness, 1800s-style, dusty, hot, four-state cattle drive?"

"She knows," Cash repeated.

Shaking his head in disbelief, Jesse returned his gaze to the pair of legs, which were finding their balance on the rocky ground. Once they were firmly planted, the woman poked her head out of the car. Her long blond hair fanning out in the April breeze, she levered herself from the cab and then towered over the taxi driver as she paid him.

Jesse was too far away to see her face, but he pushed back his Stetson with one finger and squinted against the unusually hot spring sun. What the hell was she wearing? It looked like a skirt, except it was shorter and tighter than any skirt he'd ever seen. He squinted harder at the white strip of fabric that barely covered the tops of her thighs. If they were in New York, he supposed she'd look fashionable. But here in Maybe, they had another word for that getup.

This was going to be worse than a bad trip. This was going to be a damn nightmare. If he didn't need the money from this gig as trail boss, he'd blow off the deal right now, Jesse thought, as he gazed toward the horizon.

Although the sleepy stretch of country stores Maybe called Main Street was right behind them, as far north as Jesse could see there was nothing but pastureland. He knew and loved every desolate inch of it. It had been his home for the past twenty years—ever since his old man had traded their ranch for booze and fast ponies.

Sighing, he slapped at his jeans and watched the dust spray the air as he resigned himself to the fact that no matter what, he was committed to this cattle drive for the next five months.

"Come meet my sister-in-law," Cash said.

Jesse looked at the woman and her adoring taxi driver. The man was shuffling her bags as she stood smiling and pointing. Some men were total idiots when it came to tall, leggy blondes. Jesse shook his head. He should know. In his younger days, he'd been one of them.

But those days were long gone. Just like his rodeo career. Ms. Sunny Daye was in for one hell of a surprise if she thought this was some Disney trip. Or that he was going to baby-sit her throughout this drive. Reluctantly, he pulled off his work gloves and followed his friend toward her.

"Cash." Sunny's face lit up as soon as she saw her brother-in-law. Her large, almond-shaped brown eyes sparkled with pleasure, and her blouse…

"Holy…" Jesse muttered under his breath. As she'd reached up to hug Cash, her cropped fuchsia top rode up to within an inch of her nicely rounded breasts. If she raised her arms just a little higher, he'd see a whole lot more than a wide strip of tantalizing midriff.

He forced his gaze up, then cast a quick glance around. Most of the men had stopped for lunch and had either gone to the town's only diner or had found shade behind the horse trailers. The few stragglers who'd stayed to prepare for tomorrow's departure were too far away to have noticed.

"Sunny, you look terrific." Cash angled back from her, then added, laughing, "But of course I'm biased."

Jesse watched her laugh at his friend's remark and marveled at how much she really did look and sound like Cash's wife. He was almost relieved when she brought her arms to her side, then he glanced at the short skirt and ridiculous boots and shook his head. The twins' similarity obviously ended at their features and voices. It looked like he had a bone to pick with his friend for roping him into letting Sunny stand in for Cash's wife, Rainy.

"How is my sister?" Sunny asked.

"Very pregnant."

"Oh," she said and made a face. "I guess we won't be identical for a while."

Cash looked at her with a raised brow, then glanced at Jesse. "Sunny, meet your copilot."

Jesse forced a half smile.

Sunny looked at him and blinked. "Do they use that term on cattle drives?"

"No." Cash laughed. When he caught Jesse cringing, he said quickly, "I was joking. This is Jesse Logan. Alias Jesse James Logan, alias the Outlaw."

Sunny put out her hand. Her nails were long and scarlet, and Jesse chuckled, wondering how long she expected to keep them that way.

"Hi," she said, her forehead puckered in a frown.

Jesse swiped his gritty palm against his dusty jeans and took her hand. Her eyes met his and widened a fraction. He half expected her to grimace at the residual grime coating his fingers. To her credit, she didn't. She merely looked at him with incredibly sexy brown eyes. And since her palm was quite possibly the softest thing Jesse had ever held, he hung on a moment longer than necessary. "Howdy," he said, finally letting her go.

"Why all the aliases?" she asked. "Are you wanted?"

Jesse and Cash exchanged glances. Then Cash said, "Jesse's a rodeo champ, Sunny. He picked those names up on the circuit."

"Oh." She brought a finger to her rose-tinted lips. "They didn't tell me anything about you."

"Likewise." Jesse sent Cash a meaningful look. This wasn't going to work. She wouldn't last one night on the trail, much less all the way to the Oklahoma border, where she'd hand off her duties to Oklahoma's representative.

"So." Sunny clasped her hands together and looked around. "Where shall I put my things?"

"Cash can pull his truck up and I'll help him load it."

"His truck? That doesn't make sense." She frowned and gestured to the row of designer suitcases that graduated from large to extra-extra large. "Why would we take all this to the ranch, then have to haul it back here tomorrow? I'll just take my overnight bag." She pointed to something that reminded Jesse of a small trunk.

He surveyed the string of pricy luggage, then slid her a side-long glance. She was kidding. He switched his unamused gaze to Cash. Right?

Cash stepped forward. "I agree with Jesse. Let's separate the ones you'll be leaving with us. Rainy's looking forward to your visit after your part of the drive."

"Leaving with you?" Sunny frowned. She turned her confused eyes on the luggage. Jesse got a bad feeling again. Then she smiled. "Oh. You mean the things I brought for the babies." Sunny nodded. "It's that one." She pointed to one of the smaller bags.

"Okay," Jesse said, putting up both hands. "Let's make this easy. Which one are you taking on the drive?"

Sunny blinked several times. "One?"

"One," he repeated with emphasis.

"Don't be silly." She laughed and turned an admiring look on her perfectly matched pieces. "I can't just take one. I'm taking them all."

Jesse put a hand over his mouth and blew for all he was worth. This woman was nuts. If she wasn't Cash's sister-in-law, he'd bounce her shapely butt right back into that cab.

He glanced at a perfect profile of the butt in question and swallowed. If he had a brain in his head, he'd send her back anyway—sister-in-law or not. She and that sweet little fanny both spelled trouble. And trouble was exactly what Jesse needed to avoid.

Cash jumped in again. "Sunny," he said gently. "You're going on a cattle drive. I know you understand. Rainy and I both explained this when we asked you to substitute for her. All you need are a few pairs of jeans, some changes of—"

"Jeans?" She wrinkled her nose. "I won't be wearing jeans." She smoothed down her ridiculously short skirt. "I thought I was publicity director or something."

Jesse snorted. "Something is more like it. All you have to do is deal with local press, set up interviews, pictures... basically, anything I tell you to do." He toed the nearest suitcase. "Starting with weeding out this crap."

He watched her take several deep breaths, her breasts rising and falling hypnotically. Then she lifted her chin and looked him straight in the eyes. "If my things stay, I stay."

"Okay." He lifted a shoulder and started to walk away.

Cash caught his elbow. "Come on, you two. Don't start off like this."

"You heard her." Jesse jerked his head toward Sunny. "She's not going."

Cash narrowed his eyes. "Would you excuse us for a minute?" he asked Sunny, his gaze glued menacingly to Jesse. She stood with her arms crossed and nodded, looking mad enough to spit.

Jesse thought he'd like to see Miss Hoity-Toity do just that. Chuckling, he followed Cash several yards away.

"Stop being a horse's ass, Jesse," Cash said in a low tone.

"Me?" He stared at his friend—the one guy in the world who'd never turned his back on him. But Cash had gotten married…and he'd gotten soft. Jesse had seen the symptoms often enough. As soon as you started needing someone, you lost your edge. Then you got hurt. "She's the one being unreasonable."

"Yeah, but we both know this can be straightened out. She's gonna go on this drive."

"Right." Jesse's eyes strayed to Sunny, her arms still crossed, foot tapping madly. "She doesn't have a prayer of making it."

"I'm surprised at you."

Jesse's attention snapped back at the disappointment in his friend's voice. "Why?"

"I thought you, of all people, wouldn't be so quick to judge someone." Cash headed toward Sunny.

Jesse stared after him. "Damn." Except for Cash, not a single person in Maybe had believed Jesse would amount to anything. They all thought he'd end up a drunk like his old man. He looked at Sunny—from her shimmering blond hair to her perfectly curved hips to the tapping toes of her rhinestone-studded boots—and shook his head. "Damn," he muttered again and took off after Cash.

Jesse caught up just as his friend was about to say something to Sunny. "We came to an agreement," Jesse began, shooting a glance at Cash's canny expression before looking at her. She raised her chin and eyebrows. Jesse gritted his teeth. "You can take two suitcases."

One of her eyebrows shot higher. Cash pursed his lips.

Jesse sighed. "And…" He glanced at the small trunk. "Your overnight bag," he added, although how he managed to force the words through a clenched jaw he didn't know.

Miss Hoity-Toity frowned and started to open her mouth, but Cash grabbed her arm and swung her toward his truck, whispering to her along the way.

As Jesse watched her perfect little backside sway in the opposite direction, a new kind of tension settled in his joints…and places he'd rather not think about at the moment.

He shifted and continued to watch her, mesmerized by the sensual rhythm of her walk. Her tight stretchy skirt molded every curve, and Jesse would bet a month's pay she was as firm as two cantaloupes. He cocked his head slightly to get a different angle and was reminded of an upside-down heart.

"Who's that?" The voice at his elbow made Jesse jump.

"Christ, Hank, what the hell are you sneaking up on me for?" He reluctantly tore his gaze way from Sunny and pinned the younger man with an accusing frown.

"Who's that?" Hank repeated, his mouth hanging open, his wide blue eyes following Sunny.

"My copilot," Jesse answered dryly, handing the man his bandanna as he walked away. The poor guy was drooling like an idiot.

"How AM I supposed to make do with only two suitcases?" Sunny hissed none too softly as Cash guided her toward his pickup. "Much less spend the next month with that arrogant jerk?"

Jesse didn't want her on the drive. That much was clear. She'd seen the reticent looks, heard a couple of snide remarks meant for Cash only. Without knowing her, he'd already judged her. Although Sunny didn't appreciate his narrow-mindedness, she'd be damned if she'd let him get to her.

Cash's eyes glittered with amusement. "I have a feeling you'll give as good as you get." When Sunny grinned in agreement, he added, "But he's right about the suitcases. You don't need that many."

Her smile disappeared. "But, Cash, I'm supposed to be meeting the public, giving interviews. I have to look good."

"Sunny, this is a cattle drive." He glanced at her sparkly boots. "Are those for the kickoff barbecue tonight?"

She looked down, her eyebrows drawing together. "Would they be appropriate?"

He looked somewhat relieved until she added, "I'd hate to be underdressed."

She hid a smile as Cash groaned and opened the truck door. "Let's talk about this later," he said. "Rainy should be home from the doctor's by the time we get to the ranch. We can all discuss it then. Let's go get your things loaded."

Sunny started to shrug. There wasn't anything to talk about. She hadn't packed anything she didn't absolutely need. But, to avoid an argument, she nodded. Then instead of getting in the truck for the short ride to the luggage, she waved Cash on and turned to make the trip on foot.

She didn't see Jesse right away. A younger man with long sandy hair stood staring at her. With as much nonchalance as she could summon, she looked past him toward a mud-splattered RV.

Jesse's dark head was bent over a clipboard near the open door of the vehicle. He was a little too far away for her to see his expression, but several days' growth of beard allowed her to make out the firm set of his strong jaw.

He was really quite attractive in a rough, Neanderthal sort of way. Not her type by any stretch of the imagination, though she could understand why some women might find him appealing. He was tall, quite a bit taller than her five-nine. And his tight, faded jeans made no secret of his lean, muscular thighs. She hadn't gotten a good look at his tush yet, but she had a feeling she wouldn't be disappointed.

She frowned, trying to recall the color of his eyes. His tan Stetson had pretty much shadowed them. Oh, hell, who was she kidding? They were whiskey brown, faintly ringed with gold, and fringed with lashes any self-respecting woman would kill for. So she remembered. Big deal. He was still arrogant and insufferable, and obviously despicably narrow-minded. But the fact that she'd tried to lie to herself, she had to admit, was truly pathetic.

He scratched something on his clipboard, then let the pencil dangle by a string. As if sensing her gaze, he looked up.

Sunny tossed her hair, pointedly scanning the landscape as

she continued to stroll toward the luggage. More horses than she'd ever seen were clustered in some sort of holding pen. Several more were still in horse trailers. Beyond two more RVs stretched acres and acres of flat, lifeless land. The scene didn't look much like the beginnings of a cattle drive, especially since there weren't any cattle around yet. But none of that mattered. For the first time in their lives, her twin had asked for her help. Right now, that was the only thing Sunny cared about. She'd always been the one who needed bailing out. Now that the tables were turned, nothing in this world would stop her from helping Rainy.

She took a deep breath. No one had ever needed her before. The feeling was scary...and heady.

Cash swung his truck around about the time she neared the luggage and the young cowboy. The man hadn't once taken his eyes off her. She tugged at her skirt.

"Hank, make sure everyone's had a lunch break, will you?" Jesse told the man as he strode up behind him.

"Sure, boss." Before ambling off, the man tipped his hat to Sunny, and she smiled.

Cash came around the back of the truck and opened the tailgate. Sunny wrinkled her nose at the loose hay littering the bed and the clumps of dirt packing the corners.

"Do we have to put the bags back here?" she asked.

"Nope," Jesse said, hefting one of the suitcases and grinning. "We can put them up front and you back here."

She gave him a dirty look, then turned to her brother-in-law. "Cash?"

He held up a clean tarp, then hopped on the bed, snapped the canvas open and let it settle over the surface. She smiled and, ignoring Jesse's chuckle, walked over to survey the row of suitcases.

Jesse stood ready to hand Cash the one he had in his hand, then said, "Better decide which bag you wanna leave here."

She knew he was trying to goad her by the singular emphasis, but she merely smirked. If he thought for one moment she had any intention of parting with a single one, he needed a wake-up call.

She waved at two of the largest pieces. "Oh, I'll leave these," she said airily.

Jesse studied the row of matched luggage for a moment, then squinted suspiciously at her. "Don't you wanna check to see what's in them?"

"No," she said. "That won't be necessary."

He frowned but started passing Cash one suitcase after another. When he got to the last one, he paused, dragging the back of his hand across his brow. "What the hell have you got in these things anyway?"

Sunny shrugged. "Clothes, makeup, the usual."

Wordlessly, Jesse raked her body with his gaze.

She tried to ignore him but his inspection was so thorough she finally had to tug at her hem. She unclenched her teeth. Barely. "What?"

"Nothing." He pursed his lips and shook his head, looking so totally innocent that every hair on the back of her neck rose in irritation.

She glared at him, then bent to pick up her overnight bag. She grabbed the handle and stumbled with its weight. What *had* she packed in there? Half dragging it to the truck, she carefully hid her struggle…until it was time to hoist the bag to Cash.

It wouldn't budge.

She tugged harder. The bag still wouldn't budge. And Jesse didn't lift as much as his little finger to help her. And Sunny would be damned if she'd ask him to.

She watched him out of the corner of her eye, lounging against the truck, arms and ankles crossed, an arrogant grin on his face. The man irritated her by merely existing.

She took a deep breath, crouched as low as her tight skirt would allow, grabbed the bag with both hands and hauled it up almost level with the tailgate.

That was as far as it got. She teetered backward slightly, struggling for balance. Just when she thought she'd find out how hard the ground actually was, two strong arms wrapped around her from behind.

Sunny knew who caught her. As soon as his warm, spicy presence invaded her airspace, she realized she'd already committed Jesse's scent to memory.

Her crop top had ridden up, and his tightly muscled forearms pressed into her flesh. His thumb grazed the underside of her left breast before he shifted his hand a breath away. Coarse dark hair tickled the sensitive skin around her ribs and she nearly lost her footing again. Instead, she leaned into his broad, solid chest and breathed a relieved sigh.

Until her fanny connected with something hard around his nether region.

She blinked and straightened. Slowly she turned to look at him.

Jesse stared back, his eyes dark, his pupils dilated. But it was the wild pulse throbbing visibly at his throat that convinced Sunny she hadn't imagined things. She swallowed and fumbled unnecessarily with her purse, before sliding him another furtive look.

He wasn't embarrassed. His expression held no hint of apology. In fact, he looked mad. Then his gaze briefly drifted lower, to her chest, before flickering away, and she realized her nipples had hardened.

Stiffening, she pulled her purse strap across her chest, shielding herself as best she could with her arm and praying the ground would open up and swallow her whole.

"You okay, Sunny?" Cash asked, and she nodded. If he'd noticed the tension between them, he didn't show it. He merely added, "Throw me that bag, will you, Jesse?"

She gladly stepped aside. Without so much as a glance at her, Jesse grabbed the bag she'd abandoned. He passed it to Cash, then dusted his hands together.

He turned to her, his expression bland. "Will there be anything else, your highness?"

She gave him her back and faced her brother-in-law as he

hopped down from the truck. "Cash? Would you help me take these last two suitcases to my trailer?"

Cash frowned. "Your what?"

Behind her, Jesse laughed. A soft, low chuckle that erupted into full-blown hilarity. Ordinarily, she would have found the deep, husky tone attractive. Coming from him, the sound was as welcome as nails scraping a chalkboard.

She clung to her last ounce of patience, refusing him the benefit of her attention, and stared at Cash.

He looked confused. "What trailer?"

"The one I'll be using for the cattle drive."

Cash blanched. "Did Rainy say you'd have a trailer?"

"Well, no. I assumed—"

Jesse laughed louder.

She spun to face him. "What's so damn funny?"

He choked back his amusement. "Well, your highness, it's like this." He dabbed at his eyes before pointing to a spot behind her. "Your carriage has just arrived."

Sunny glared at him until her curiosity and his smug face got the better of her. Slowly she swiveled around.

In the distance, two covered wagons—honest-to-goodness covered wagons—wobbled down the center of Main Street. The once empty sidewalks began filling with excited people pouring out of stores to get a look at the spectacle. To Sunny, it looked like a movie. A bad B-movie.

She turned to Cash. "Tell me I won't be spending the next month in a wagon."

He rubbed his temple. "We did tell you this would be an authentic cattle drive. Remember?"

"Yes, but..." Her thoughts scattered. She turned to the wagons. Why, those things couldn't possibly be air-conditioned.

"Okay, okay," Jesse said, coming to stand beside her. "I admit. I exaggerated."

She slid him a wary sidelong glance, torn between relief and the strong urge to give him one of her famous left hooks. But she'd retired as left-hook champion at age twelve. Now, at the respectable age of twenty-nine, wasn't the time to reclaim the crown.

"Sorry. Didn't mean to mislead you," Jesse said, looking suitably contrite. He gazed at the toe mark he'd made in the dirt and pursed his lips. Then the corners of his mouth twitched and he glanced up, his devil-dark eyes glittering with amusement. "The wagons are for the cooks. All you get is a bedroll."

Her mouth started to open in surprise, then she squinted at him. She had the perfect place for him to put his bedroll, and she was about to tell him so, when Cash grabbed her arm and with a warning look at Jesse steered her toward the trailers. "Let me show you around before we go to the ranch," he said.

Jesse laughed.

Sunny let Cash guide her as she tried to gather her composure and ignore her twelve-year-old inner child, who wanted very badly to connect with Jesse's arrogant face.

Cash and Rainy needed her to go on this cattle drive, she reminded herself. Her sister was in no condition to make the trip now that she was pregnant, and they had a lot of time and money invested in it. Rainy was depending on her. Cash was depending on her. And Sunny owed them both.

She sighed, knowing she had to make this trip, whether she got along with Jesse Logan or not.

Just thinking his name sent a shiver of apprehension down her spine. Why was he giving her so much trouble? Men usually marched to her bidding. Not that she'd ever wanted them to. They just always had.

But not Jesse Logan.

She remembered his annoying laughter and the shiver dissolved. He was a disagreeable jerk, and she was glad she'd discovered that fact early on. Not that she was looking for romance...or that he appealed to her in the least. But falling for jerks had never been her thing. God only knew she met too many of them in her line of work, and knowing that he was a jerk automatically ruled out romantic entanglement she could ill afford.

She gave her hair an extra toss and smiled at Cash, who had

embarked on a dissertation about Texas longhorns. Out of the corner of her eye, she caught sight of Jesse. He'd climbed into the truck with her luggage. Slowly, she turned in his direction. If he so much as touched one...

Her jaw slackened as she watched Jesse draw up the excess tarp and carefully tuck it around her suitcases, shielding them from the harsh west Texas sun.

Chapter Two

The whole town turned out for the barbecue. Or so it seemed to Sunny. Picnic tables, lawn chairs and laughing children crowded the entire Maybe High athletic field and parking lot. A group of men played horseshoes near the startlingly white gymnasium. Beyond that, a line of wooden barrels, doubling as barbecue pits, poured billows of mesquite-scented smoke into the air. Women of varying sizes and ages carried covered dishes from parked cars.

The scene was so Norman Rockwell, it made her nervous. Why had she ever agreed to get involved with this small community and its bid for the brass ring? Especially since she'd spent her life flaunting her independence against small-town narrow-mindedness. These people had spent the better part of last year and most of their town's savings vying for the honor of being the kickoff town for this nationally recognized, experimental cattle drive. She vaguely understood their desire for a place on the map, but what she didn't understand was why she'd agreed to carry their torch.

Then her twin, pregnant with twins herself, waddled toward her, and Sunny knew exactly why she'd agreed to go on the cattle drive—why she had to go. Rainy needed her.

The brand-new feeling still made Sunny dizzy with pleasure. In fact, to some degree, all of Maybe needed her, but that feeling was too overwhelming to take in.

"One more trip to the car ought to do it," Rainy said as she passed her the large, chilled bowl of potato salad.

"I'll do it. You sit down for a while." Sunny finished sealing the plate of deviled eggs with foil and ran her hands down her denim miniskirt.

Rainy laughed. "I'm pregnant. I'm not dying."

Sunny glanced at the cloudless sky.

"It's not the same thing. Trust me," Rainy added.

"I'll have to take your word for it." Sunny made a comical face.

"Someday..." her twin warned.

"Never." Sunny laughed. Her? In Norman Rockwell land? She didn't think so. She reached out and snatched a lime green Frisbee as it whipped past her head. The disk had gotten away from a little girl with long, auburn pigtails. Gently, Sunny sailed the toy to the laughing child.

A strange wistfulness swamped her. She immediately discarded the feeling and turned to Rainy. "I'll go finish unloading the car."

"Wait a minute." Rainy shifted her weight away from the picnic table and took both of Sunny's hands. "I can't tell you how much Cash and I appreciate this."

"You already have." Sunny squeezed her fingers. "Now, I don't want to hear another word about it."

"I know you could be making four times as much by modeling." Rainy hesitated, frowning. "Although you haven't taken many jobs lately, have you?"

Sunny shrugged and looked away. "The usual."

"That *Midnight Fantasy* fiasco is over. You can come out of hibernation."

Sunny grimaced, then bit her lower lip. "No one knows about that, do they? I mean anyone on the drive?"

"No." Rainy clasped her sister's hands tighter, then amended, "Smiley does, of course, but he'd sooner swallow a rattlesnake than say anything."

Sunny's brows shot up as she freed her hands. "Swallow a rattlesnake? You've been living here too long."

Her twin gave her a tight smile. "Please don't worry about the magazine. It's been nearly two years."

"I know." She grinned and managed to make a face at the same time. "Besides, this, uh, camping trip will be far too much fun."

Rainy cringed. "I'm sorry about the mix-up on the trailer. But I promise, you won't be relegated to a bedroll. Jesse was only teasing."

"He was trying to irritate the hell out of me."

"From the tone of your voice, it sounds like he succeeded." Rainy grinned.

"Whose side are you on, anyway?" Sunny put a hand on her hip. "Didn't you just meet him?"

Rainy shook her head. "No, Cash has known Jesse since kindergarten."

"You mean he lives here?" Sunny was surprised. She knew the idea for the drive, as well as the financial backing, had originated in Dallas. Besides, Jesse didn't have that small-town feel about him.

"No. He left when he was sixteen. He hadn't been back since and wouldn't have if it weren't for the cattle drive. But since Cash got involved, he's come back several times during the planning stages. He's a great guy. You'll really like him once you get to know him."

Sunny gave her sister a disbelieving look. Like him? She didn't even like being on the same planet with him.

"In fact, he's really a lot like you," Rainy said, watching her sister's reaction. "He got along here about as well as you got along in Boon. He couldn't wait to get out."

Sunny smoothed the plastic wrap over the potato salad, thinking about their childhood home in Michigan. If it hadn't been for Rainy, she'd have gone out of her mind. She wondered if Jesse had experienced the same claustrophobia she had. Had he blocked out the same whispers, ignored the same censoring stares?

She chased the thought from her mind. The last thing she wanted was to have a blasted thing in common with Jesse Logan. "When are we going to discuss this trip, anyway? I want it made clear exactly what my role is before we set one foot out of Maybe."

"Later. I want Cash and Jesse in on it, so there won't be any misunderstandings." Rainy swiped nervously at her hair. "Although there isn't much to it other than setting up interviews and coordinating festivities with the towns along the route, as I've already explained."

Sunny eyed her sister suspiciously. She wasn't up for any more surprises. Except a few of her own. The thought made her smile. "Okay. I'll get the rest of the stuff out of the car now."

"And I'll help set the main table," Rainy said, smiling. When she caught her twin's frown, she added, "Then I'll get off my feet, Mom."

Sunny laughed delightedly at their role reversal. She liked being the wise adult for a change. All the way across the parking lot to Rainy's station wagon, she smiled thinking about it.

Sunny pulled out two platters of fried chicken, a pan of hush puppies and an apple pie. She placed them on the hood of the car and tried to decide how she would carry them all.

"Need some help?"

Sunny recognized Jesse's voice even before she turned to eye him from his fresh jeans to his blue Western shirt. His dark hair was damp, probably from a shower, and he still hadn't shaved. His teeth were exceptionally white against his tanned face and beard-roughened chin. He looked even better than he had earlier. She wished he'd get lost. "No, thanks," she finally said.

He chuckled and grabbed both platters of chicken.

She started to protest but knew she'd sound petty. Without acknowledging him, she balanced the pie on one palm, snatched the pan of hush puppies and headed for the table.

"You're going to drop that pie," he said as he fell into step beside her. He bowed his head over the plate and sniffed appreciatively. "Hmm, apple and plenty of cinnamon."

"Of course. I always use lots of cinnamon."

He lifted a brow at her. "You made it?"

"Yes." She tossed her hair. "The chicken, too."

"Well, your highness, I'm impressed."

"Ask me if I care."

Jesse slid her an amused glance.

She returned a look that clearly told him to drop dead.

"Okay. For a slice of your pie, I'll quit calling you your highness."

"You can have the whole thing if you stay out of my way."

"Now, now. You know Cash and Rainy expect us to get along."

"Yeah? Well, they don't have to live with you for the next month or so. I do."

"Hmm, that sounds so…" He pursed his lips. "Illicit."

"Illicit?" She gave him a sugary smile. "Now I'm impressed. You managed three whole syllables."

He laughed, a deep throaty sound that made Sunny's steps quicken.

She arrived at the picnic table several seconds ahead of him. Carefully she slid the pie onto the table and set the hush puppies beside it. When Jesse showed up with the chicken, there was barely enough room for both platters on the crowded table. He set one down and frowned.

"Here, I'll take it." She reached out to take the platter, but her hand grabbed his instead. She let go as if she'd received an electric shock.

"Sorry. I don't hold hands on the first date." His eyes crinkled at the corners. "But I am flattered."

She rolled her eyes and pointed to the string of picnic tables where Rainy and several other women were busy arranging the food. "You can take it over there."

"Yes, your—" He stopped himself and grinned. "I'll be right back."

"I can hardly wait."

Jesse's response was a mock salute before he sauntered toward the other women. Sunny watched him go and realized with reluctant interest that he did have a very nice tush. Although his jeans looked fairly new, they were worn in just the right places. Two excellent places that softly molded his muscled buttocks.

She glanced around, and noting that several other young women shared her appreciation, she quickly turned away. She'd be damned if she'd let herself be caught ogling him like they were.

She forced her attention to arranging the food and making sure everything was well wrapped. Several people smiled and said hello as they attended to their own tables. She knew some of them from previous visits to her sister's ranch, and they were for the most part friendly. She still got the odd disapproving look though, probably because of her clothes, but it had been a long time since she'd allowed anyone to manipulate her feelings.

She saw Jesse heading toward her and ducked her head to unnecessarily fuss over a plate of blueberry muffins. When his arrival seemed long overdue, she glanced up to find that he'd been waylaid by a petite redhead. The woman was showing him her tan lines.

Sunny nearly dropped the plate. She could see Jesse's wide grin and white teeth even from here. His easy appreciation of the woman's attributes annoyed the stuffing out of her. And being annoyed irritated her twice as much. Two muffins slid to the ground. Mumbling an appropriate word, she stooped to pick them up.

"Can't believe that boy amounted to anything. Can't say that I even do. How do you feel about him heading this drive, Homer?" The man's voice came from somewhere over Sunny's left shoulder.

She straightened and nonchalantly turned. She didn't know the speaker but his companion, Homer Simms, she remembered, was Maybe's mayor.

"I guess them promoters in Dallas and New York know what they're doing." Homer shook his head. "This drive is gonna make all of them a passel of money, and they got all them corporate sponsors to worry about. They wouldn't hire some no-account to see it through. But I know what you mean. I wouldn't bet a wooden nickel on him. He was a devil as a youngster. Don't know any folks who were sorry to see him go. I sure hope his pa's hankering for booze hasn't rubbed off on him."

"His rodeo career wasn't bad, though," the other man said. "Coulda been way up there in the standings if he'd ever rode the Oklahoma circuit. Can't understand why he never did. That wasn't too smart. I guess when it comes right down to it, none of them Logans are worth a damn."

As Jesse came closer, the men ambled off. Every bone in Sunny's body screamed in indignation. She was two seconds away from telling them to shove this drive. Their petty narrow-mindedness had recalled best-forgotten memories from her childhood. She was tired of people judging others and putting them in boxes because of what they looked like or who their parents were.

So why did she feel so defensive of Jesse? He was just as judgmental as they were. He'd certainly already judged and categorized her. Still, the men's disparaging comments made her curious…and sympathetic. And damn, she did not want to feel sympathetic toward Jesse Logan.

"Mission accomplished," Jesse said, standing across the table from her. He peeled back the corner of a foil wrapping, snitched a hush puppy and popped it into his mouth. He chewed a moment, briefly closed his eyes and licked his lips. At the sight of his tongue, a totally unexpected and inappropriate image floated through Sunny's mind.

The thought shocked her and she felt her eyes widen before she blinked. "Save those for dinner," she snapped.

"Did you make them?" he asked.

"Are you kidding? I never even heard of those things before I helped Rainy cook this afternoon." She wrinkled her nose at the pan of fritters. "They aren't good for you. They're loaded with fat and cholesterol."

"Maybe so, but you better get used to them. We'll be having them most every night along the trail."

"You may be. I'll eat out."

"Out?" He wearily dragged a hand down his face, stopping to rub his jaw. "What do you mean *out?*"

"I'll go to a restaurant."

"Really?" He laughed. Sunny got a sinking feeling she was missing the joke.

Before she could ask for an explanation, Rainy and Cash strolled up arm in arm.

"I hope you two are getting along better," Cash said, looking from Sunny to Jesse.

"Sure," Jesse said, grinning. "Sunny was just telling me how much she loves Southern fried food."

Cash relaxed. "Good. You'll be having a lot of it on the trail."

Sunny exchanged looks with a surprised Rainy, then smiled. Jesse was not going to bait her anymore, Sunny told herself. Not until they left, anyway. Her sister didn't need anything else to worry about.

"Great!" Sunny confirmed, trying to sound enthusiastic while sliding Jesse a warning glance.

"We're about ready to eat." Cash gestured to the large slabs of meat being removed from the barbecue pits. Groups of people were already lining up. "I'll go get the drinks if you all want to get your food."

"What about Smiley and Josh?" Sunny asked. She hadn't seen Cash's foreman or son yet. "Aren't they supposed to meet us here?"

"Smiley should be along shortly. Josh is eating with his girlfriend." Cash looked heavenward. When Jesse laughed, Cash hitched a thumb at him and said, "Wait till you have a teenager."

Jesse looked stunned at the idea. "I'll go get the drinks," he mumbled and headed off before anyone commented.

Sunny watched him until he disappeared into the crowd. She turned to Rainy just in time to see her wink at Cash, and her gaze automatically drifted in Jesse's direction.

JESSE SWEET-TALKED Della Witherspoon out of a large serving tray, balanced an assortment of beer, iced tea and lemonade on it and headed toward the group. Not that sweet-talking Della out of anything was hard to do. Her husband-hunting escapades spanned three counties. Except Jesse figured even Della would know that she'd be barking up the wrong tree when it came to him. He wasn't marriage material. Never had been. Never would be. Not that any of the ladies of Maybe would want to be associated with the town's black sheep, anyway.

Sunny and Rainy were taller than any of the other women there, and he immediately spotted them serving the children at the front of the barbecue line. The twins were both smiling, patting little heads and layering slices of fresh tomato onto the plates of wary-looking tykes.

Only Sunny seemed out of place. While Rainy blended in with the other women, her hair pulled back in a ponytail, a pale pink gloss on her lips, Sunny's long blond hair blew freely in the wind. Artificial color enhanced her high cheekbones, her almond eyes. Her clothes were so tight she looked as though she'd been poured into them.

She didn't belong here. No more than he did.

The thought that they might share even one foot of common ground startled him, and he nearly let two beers slide off the tray. The drinks teetered unsteadily for a moment until he regained his balance. When the sloshing subsided and the paper cups were once again steady, he looked up.

Hank Parsons, one of his young trail hands, had sidled up to Sunny. She had a pair of tongs in one hand, a plate in the other. Hank was bringing a tall, frosted glass up to her lips. She pulled back at first, then took a quick sip and smiled at him.

An earthy word flew from Jesse's lips and the tray slipped from his hands. Ice-cold tea splashed the front of his jeans. Two cups of lemonade splattered on the ground. The beer bounced off a nearby picnic bench and drenched his pant leg. Luckily no one was near enough to share Jesse's fate. Several gasps, however, made him wonder if someone had heard his hasty and ill-chosen epithet. He half grinned apologetically and crouched to clean up the mess.

A raspy chuckle echoed above him, and he looked up to see Smiley Ferguson, Cash's longtime ranch foreman, standing a few feet away. Smiley picked up a battered and now empty lemonade cup.

"What happened to you?" Smiley asked, eyeing the wet blotches on Jesse's jeans.

He stood and automatically darted a look in Sunny's direction. Hank still hovered near her, although she paid him no attention as she continued to serve the children. "Nothing."

Smiley followed his gaze, his black eyes squinting against the waning sun, and chuckled again. "Them two gals sure has got you boys goin'."

Jesse furrowed his brow in studied innocence. "Who?"

Smiley laughed harder.

"Come on and help me with this," Jesse snapped. The old geezer had been around as long as grass. When Smiley worked for Cash's dad, Jesse and Cash, as kids, had never been able to put anything over on him. Since Jesse's father had usually been too drunk to care about the trouble his son got into, he'd always been grateful for Smiley's paternal concern. But right now, Jesse wished Smiley would keep his nose out of things.

The older man bent to pick up the tray, his long black-and-silver braid falling over his shoulder. "She won't be no trouble," he said once he'd straightened.

"Who?"

"I ain't too old to box your ears, boy. Don't go actin' up with me." Smiley speared him with his beady gaze, and Jesse laughed at the line he'd heard for half a lifetime.

"She's not all prissy inside," Smiley continued. "She's been here maybe five times since Cash and Rainy got hitched last year. Always pitches in around the place. Never flirts with the hands, even though they all go followin' her around like a bunch of dang fools. She ain't nothin' like her sister, but she's got a heart as big as Dallas."

"Why are you telling me all this?" Jesse turned his palm up in a show of indifference.

"'Cuz I know you, and you're fixin' to give her a hard time. Just like your buddy Cash done Rainy." Smiley narrowed his shrewd eyes. "And look what happened to him."

That did it. Jesse had heard enough. "You mean like you done Violet Pickford?" he asked, his slow grin adding fuel to the fire.

Smiley's eyes nearly bugged out of his head. "Now, what in the hell made you say a dang-fool thing like that? You fall off one too many broncos or somethin'? Me and Violet have been feudin' since before you was born. You know I can't stand the ol'...the ol' battle ax." Smiley sputtered and Jesse laughed.

The older man gathered his wits and smugly added, "Why do you think I volunteered to go on the cattle drive? To get away from the ol' bat." He slapped the tray. "Now, I'll go replace them drinks you spread all over kingdom come."

Jesse shook his head as he watched Smiley amble away. He often wondered why his old friend hadn't married the lively spinster. Everyone in town seemed to know they pined for each other. Jesse suspected the only reason they competed in the annual chili cook-off was to have at each other, and if it couldn't be under the sheets, then verbal sparring appeared to be the next best thing. Jesse didn't understand that notion at all.

Inexplicably, his gaze drifted to Sunny. He tucked a finger in his shirt collar and loosened it before heading toward her and Rainy.

Sunny looked up as he approached, but he stopped near the barbecue barrels, peering in at the mouth-watering steaks sizzling and hissing over the flames.

"Hey," she called out, "a person could die of thirst around here." Her gaze searched his hands for their refreshments, then rose to meet his.

Yeah, right.

Hank eagerly came forth with the frosted glass. Jesse glared at the younger man. Hank had been around his boss long enough to read him, and he immediately backed off.

"I thought you were getting us something to drink." Her full, cranberry-tinted lips settled into a pout, then her eyes drifted downward, near his hips, and her mouth stretched into a wide, teasing grin.

A lesser man could get an inferiority complex with a look like that, he thought warily as he looked at his jeans. Large, dark splotches moistened his fly and thighs. Slowly he brought his narrowed gaze to meet hers. "Sorry, your highness, they were all out of crystal."

The grin vanished from her lips. "If you think you're getting one bite of my pie, you can kiss my—"

Rainy cleared her throat and cocked her head at the children standing in line, their wide inquiring eyes glued to Sunny.

Jesse mentally finished the sentence and smiled. The idea definitely had merit.

Chapter Three

"Keep it down, Josh," Sunny whispered fiercely, flapping her hand at Rainy's fifteen-year-old stepson.

The boy grimaced and mouthed, "yeah, yeah, yeah," then gingerly let the front door connect with the latch. He dragged two of her suitcases out to the porch with him.

It was close to midnight, and with Smiley still rabble-rousing at the barbecue and Cash and Rainy asleep at the far side of the house, the place was too damn quiet for Sunny. If she pulled this off, it would be a miracle. And as much as she'd hated asking for Josh's help, she knew she'd never smuggle her excess baggage out without him.

"You sure they won't hear the truck?" she whispered as she took the keys from him.

Josh shook his head. "I'm sure. Last time me and Seth snuck—"

Quickly she held up a hand. "Don't tell me. I don't want to know." She took a deep breath. "I'm going to be in enough trouble if your father and Rainy find out I involved you."

"I still think you ought to let me go to the camp with you. You might need a lookout."

Sunny's heart thudded. For a moment, her feet didn't just get cold, they got downright frigid. She didn't want to *need* a lookout. She didn't want to have to sneak around the dark camp while all the men were still partying at the barbecue. But she didn't want to leave a stitch of her clothes or anything else behind, either.

"Thanks anyway, Josh. I'll be okay. When your dad showed me around this afternoon, I staked out the place pretty well." She shook her head. Staked out the place? She felt like a criminal and all she wanted to do was protect her belongings.

This was Jesse's fault, she thought as she helped Josh load the bags onto the back of the truck. Not only was he arrogant, narrow-minded and a big jerk, he was incredibly unreasonable. She gave the final bag such a hard shove, Josh had to shush her. Grinning sheepishly, she gave him a quick hug and said good-night.

With a silent prayer, she started the engine, then steered the monstrous truck down the drive, growing more and more irritated with each hard bounce that befell her fanny.

Ten minutes later she arrived at the pitch-dark campsite. A sliver of moon and a single lamp from a distant RV window gave only enough light to show her the way.

Parking the pickup as close to the chuck wagon as she could, she turned off the engine and grabbed her flashlight. A shiver made all the fine hairs on her arms stand on end, but when she looked around, not a soul was in sight. At dinner she'd overheard Cash and Jesse talking about how they figured the men would stay out late for a last fling. Sunny breathed a sigh of relief because it looked like they were right on target.

Quietly, she began transferring her cargo.

JESSE COULDN'T SLEEP. He was too keyed up over the cattle drive tomorrow. He glanced at his watch and pushed the illumination button. Correction. Today. The drive started in six and a half hours, to be exact.

If he'd had his way, they would have left no later than five, but two news stations were covering their ride from Maybe to the cattle pickup point outside of town, and he'd been forced to delay the start to accommodate them.

Once they were under way, he'd have final say on how this drive went, but corporate sponsors were paying big money to get this project off the ground—hell, they were paying his salary—and he had to sing their tune.

He rubbed the back of his neck with one hand and pushed open the trailer door with the other. Maybe if he'd stayed at Cash and Rainy's for the night, like they'd wanted him to, he could have gotten some sleep.

Ha. Who was he kidding? Her highness would probably have driven him crazy. He thought about what she'd been wearing tonight—a sleeveless top tied up under her breasts and a denim skirt that probably required all of two feet of material. Yeah, she was making him crazy, all right. But only because half his men—the half who'd still been sober—had babbled like idiots around her.

He sure would be glad when they got on the trail and she quit wearing those ridiculous clothes. It was beyond him why she needed so many suitcases. With the things she wore, she could easily pack a two-month supply in just one of those bags.

He thought again about how boisterous the men had gotten tonight. He'd told Cash and Rainy he needed to keep an eye on his crew. That was the reason he'd given for not staying at their place. Except as soon as they'd left with Sunny, he'd had a few words with the men, then left, too. Why, he had no idea. He hadn't gotten a minute of sleep.

He snorted in disgust and let the door close softly behind him. The air was still, the sky cloudless. Even the crickets had quieted down some.

He breathed in the clean country air, looking out over the deserted campground...and spotted the rear of a dark pickup next to the chuck wagon.

Jesse frowned. None of the men had cars with them. They'd either been dropped off or had ridden in the trucks towing the horse trailers. He crept along the shadows, ducked between a trailer and RV and edged his head out for a look.

The truck was still a fair distance away, but he saw the unmistakable McCloud Ranch marking on the driver's door. He exhaled in relief and started to straighten. What could Cash possibly be doing here at this time of night?

A blond head bobbed out of the chuck wagon, looking first left, then right. Stunned, Jesse could only stare for an instant before jerking against the RV and flattening himself to the cold metal.

What the devil was she doing? He took several deep breaths, trying to curb his adrenaline, trying to keep from wringing her neck. After almost a minute, he tentatively stuck his head out again.

And then he saw the suitcase.

He watched her creep alongside the pickup to the open tailgate and wrap both hands around the leather handle. She dragged the suitcase to the edge of the tailgate and pulled it to the ground. She stumbled back with the bag's weight, then half dragged, half carried it to the wagon.

Watching her maneuver her bounty up the rickety steps almost made Jesse blow his cover. Her butt swayed one way, then the other, until it connected so hard with the railing that her muttered curse reached his ears. She glanced over her shoulder before returning her attention to the ridiculously heavy suitcase.

He swallowed a hoot of laughter and, along with it, his anger over her deceit. No wonder she wasn't worried about inventorying the suitcases she'd chosen to take with her.

He shook his head as he watched her move one last bag. Then he ducked through the shadows to his trailer. It was time her highness learned a lesson, and Jesse could hardly wait to provide it.

"SUNNY! SUNNY!" Rainy said close to her ear. Too close.

Sunny swatted at her sister as if she was a fly and snuggled into her pillow.

"I mean it, Sunny. You have to get up." Rainy ripped back the covers and pinched Sunny's thigh. "You're already late."

She yelped and glared at her sister. "You haven't done that since we were fifteen," she muttered before sinking her face into the soft feather pillow. It was far too early to get up, especially since she'd been on a mission half the night.

"I'll make up for lost time if you don't get your fanny out of this bed right now." Rainy threw open the mauve floral curtains. Dawn's muted orange hues failed miserably as a wake-up call. Sunny closed first one eye and then the other as she reached for the quilt.

Rainy tore it off the bed. "Oh, no." Her twin stopped, making Sunny open her eyes. Rainy's face puckered in a frown, and she clutched her stomach. "I think I'm going into labor."

Sunny leaped out of bed, nearly tripping over the discarded quilt. In two seconds flat she was beside her sister.

Rainy's hands dropped from her stomach and she grinned. "And while you're up…" She shoved a towel at Sunny. "Save me some hot water, will you?"

"That was a horrible thing to do, Rainy Ann," Sunny scolded. Then she smiled. "You're starting to act like me."

"Heaven help us." Rainy walked toward the door. "Now, move it. You have to be ready in fifteen minutes." She started to turn away then stopped. "Thanks for bailing me out of this, kiddo. Truthfully, I could have gotten out of going for medical reasons, but Cash and I wanted to make sure we had a firm foothold, especially if this evolves into an annual event."

Sunny's heart soared again at the reminder that Rainy needed her. The feeling was so addictive, it was almost worth getting up early for. She happily told her sister she didn't want to hear another word about it and waved her out of the room.

But ready in fifteen minutes? Sunny tugged down her silk nightie and stuck her head out to make sure the hall was clear before dashing to the guest bathroom. No way would she be ready in fifteen minutes. Her hair alone took longer than that. And then she had to choose today's outfit, do her makeup, check her nails…

JESSE CRUNCHED DOWN too hard on the sprig of hay and it snapped in two, one end dangling from his mouth. He removed them both, muttering a few choice words under his breath. Since he was standing behind one of the wagons and out of sight of the dozen or more news cameras, no one heard him.

He rolled up his shirtsleeves and glanced at his watch for the third time in five minutes. She was late. What a surprise.

The trailers that had delivered the horses to Maybe had already pulled out and were probably halfway to Dallas by now. The men had eaten—the ones who weren't too hung over, anyway—and had packed their saddlebags. The place was crawling with media people waiting for them to mount their horses and ride off. Only the cattle drive's ace PR person hadn't chosen to get her butt here on time.

If he hadn't been so damned terrified of having those television cameras pushed in his face, he'd have been sorely tempted to leave without her. Instead, Jesse hung back and listened to his name being bandied about by reporters in search of interviews.

Several minutes later, Rainy's red station wagon inched through a throng of people and stopped a few yards from the wagon. As much as he wanted to dash out and give Sunny a piece of his mind, he stayed where he was until the media hounds stopped gawking at the twins in favor of interviews with the cowboys.

Jesse strolled over as Sunny stepped out of the car. She stretched, her brief white blouse momentarily displaying a wide strip of tanned skin, then brought one hand to her mouth to cover a yawn.

"Mornin'," she mumbled into her palm.

Jesse grabbed her wrist and dragged her toward the wagon with him. He waved to Rainy, who waited cautiously within shouting distance.

"Just what do you think you're doing?" She glared at him.

He noticed that one of her eyes was significantly more made up than the other. "Not what I'd like to be doing," he muttered and positioned them out of public sight.

Sunny sighed. "First Rainy and now you. I'd better warn you." She narrowed her gaze on him, her mismatched makeup giving her a comical look. "I am not a morning person."

"Does the word *tough* mean anything to you?"

She gave him a dirty look and started to walk away, but he grabbed her arm again and spun her around to face him.

"Listen carefully, Sunny," he said, dipping his head to stare her in the eyes. "This drive will not operate on your schedule. From now on, you will be ready on time. I am not a baby-sitter, and I expect everybody to carry their own load. You tell me right now if you want to be a part of this team."

She blinked. But before she did, he saw a flicker of remorse in her beautiful brown eyes, and his hand loosened on her arm. He'd been harsh with her, but what he'd said needed saying. He glanced past her at the hordes of people milling around the camp. The news cameras were making him edgy.

She had to understand. He needed everyone's cooperation and dedication to make this drive happen. He brought his gaze to hers.

"I'm sorry, I need..." She looked down. "I want to be a part of this team."

Jesse hooked his finger under her chin and raised it. "Okay," he said gently. "Now go give those media guys hell." He felt his lips curve up at her widening eyes.

"Media? As in reporters?" Slowly she turned toward the crowd and stared as if she was seeing it all for the first time. "Local, right?"

He shook his head, peering closely at her, watching fear widen her eyes further. "National," he said and saw the fear slide into panic. Then she blinked the unexpected emotion away. Her expression went blank and he wondered if he'd projected his own feelings onto her.

Surely she couldn't be camera shy. She made her living in front of the one-eyed monster. She should be a pro at this. That was one of the major reasons he'd agreed to have her substitute for Rainy. To take the heat off him. He frowned at the reluctance her entire body was telegraphing.

She drew one hand up the side of her arm and exhaled loudly. "I thought I'd be dealing with local media."

"Once we get started you will. But the sponsors want to milk the kickoff. So does Maybe."

She looked sharply at him. "Do you care about what Maybe wants?"

He shrugged and glanced away for a moment. It was an odd question. One he wasn't sure how to answer. "I care about the person who signs my paycheck. I'm in this strictly for the cash."

She pursed her lips, giving him a strange, pensive look.

"What about you? Why are you here?" he asked.

Her eyebrows drew together, and she stared at him as if she wasn't really seeing him. Then a smile tugged at the corners of her mouth. "Cash, too. And Rainy."

"That's it?"

"That's it," she confirmed and straightened her skirt. Squaring her shoulders, she turned toward the cameras. Her hesitation, however, didn't escape him.

Then he realized what her problem was. The explanation was so simple he felt stupid. With someone like Sunny, the dilemma was obvious. "Okay, you have two minutes to finish your other eye."

"My what?" Her puzzled expression made her look like a clown.

He tapped the cheekbone under his right eye.

She made a face, then burst out laughing. "Oh, brother." She glanced around until she spotted a large metal spoon in the front of the chuck wagon. "Hold this for me, will you?"

She shoved the spoon into his hand, then wrapped her fingers around his and adjusted the height of her makeshift mirror. Jesse felt her silky palm against his knuckles and slowly released a breath. He wondered how that silkiness would feel touching his skin in other places.

"Hold still." She bobbed her head, trying to get a clear shot of her reflection. She removed her hand from his and fished in a pocket he was certain was too snug to accommodate even one of her scarlet nails.

To his surprise, she pulled out a white tissue. To his even greater surprise, she started wiping the color off the already made-up eye.

"Aren't you going about this a little backward?" he asked.

Sunny darted him a glance. "This is faster." She took several more swipes, muting the color until both eyes were reasonably matched. Then she crumpled the tissue and looked around for a place to throw it.

He put out his open palm.

She lifted a shoulder and dropped the tissue in his hand, sending him a bright smile. "Thanks," she said and headed for the cameras.

Jesse stared after her. He couldn't believe she'd simply wiped off the makeup. He never would have guessed that she'd shed her vanity so readily. Not that she had a thing to worry about, he admitted. She looked good even without the cosmetics. In fact, in his opinion, she looked better.

He recalled Cash warning him not to be so quick to judge, and he cringed. His attention caught on the streaks of plum and pink on the white tissue, and he stared in awe at how much junk she'd actually put on her eyes. He'd seen less makeup on rodeo clowns.

He grinned at the thought and told himself he'd have to tease her about that later. His smile slipped away. He was actually looking forward to sparring with her. He thought briefly about how Smiley insisted on antagonizing Violet Pickford, and he crushed the tissue beyond recognition.

Sunny was a contradiction he didn't understand...didn't want to understand. All he needed to focus on was the success and safety of this drive. And then, in five months, he'd be buying his own ranch.

Remembering how close his longtime dream was to becoming a reality relaxed the tension coiling in his gut. Even the echoing pains from years of bronco riding faded for the moment.

He stretched his neck from side to side while he watched Sunny consult with her sister. She looked nervous, and Rainy appeared to be encouraging her.

Something was wrong with this picture. Why wasn't she the big ham he'd expected?

He glanced at his watch. "Come on, Sunny," he muttered under his breath. "Get out there and do your thing."

As if she'd heard him, she looked at him. Not even knowing her that well, he could tell her smile was forced. Rainy patted her arm, and Sunny's gaze flew to her sister. Then she gave her hair that extra familiar toss as she lifted her chin. Without looking back, her shoulders squared, she strolled toward the buzzing crowd.

Immediately Jesse saw a romance in the making. Cameras loved her. Reporters loved her. One of the cowboys had pointed in her direction, and within seconds she was surrounded.

Microphones were shoved in her face, flashes went off left and right. Through it all Sunny smiled and talked with apparent ease. Had he misread her reluctance?

He watched her as closely as he could from his vantage point. Though he was consumed with curiosity about how she was handling the interview, he wasn't willing to risk getting any closer. He had enough to worry about once he crossed the Oklahoma border. He didn't need to court trouble now.

He was only vaguely worried about what she might say. Rainy had rehearsed a speech with her last night, and the Dallas promoters had given out most of the nitty-gritty information through press releases and their own representatives. Still, Sunny seemed so oblivious to the reality of the next month or so that he couldn't help being a little disconcerted.

Starting with the way she was dressed, he thought, shaking his head. He had hoped her choice of clothes would improve once they got under way. But the short skirt she wore, although similar to denim, was stretchy, sort of like the legging material that was so popular. And those boots. He wondered who had labeled those pink things "boots."

Then he thought about how he'd taken care of the clothes problem and grinned.

Jesse was amused for only a moment before he tapped impatiently on the face of his watch. They had to leave within five minutes to meet up with the cattle. Rainy caught his signal, glanced at her watch and intervened with Sunny and the reporters. She and Cash had been great friends to Jesse. Just maybe, he thought wryly, he could eventually forgive them for saddling him with Sunny.

He started toward the trailer to get the rest of his gear when he heard the shriek. Sweat moistened his brow, and he turned in Sunny's direction.

Only she wasn't the shrieker.

Violet Pickford, her face scrunched with annoyance under her unruly red hair and floppy straw hat, marched toward Sunny from the opposite side of the camp. Lengthening her stride, she clutched her baggy white coveralls until the rolled cuffs rode up halfway to her knees. Smiley Ferguson, one bony finger stuck in the air, was hot on her heels.

All heads turned. Cameras and microphones swept toward the odd-looking pair. Sunny and Rainy exchanged glances and shrugged, awaiting Violet's approach.

"You ain't goin' with us, you crazy ol' bat," Smiley bellowed, steadying his hat atop his head as he tried to head her off. "You ain't invited."

Violet ignored him and kept her sights on Sunny. The older woman's chin lifted stubbornly, and she stepped up her pace.

Jesse slipped into the shadow of the wagon and watched the spectacle unfold with a gnawing pain in his gut. The only women besides Sunny on this drive were Maria Vasquez and her sister, and Jesse had only hired them because Maria's husband, Manny, was going and the couple needed the money. He didn't know anything about Violet, and he didn't need this hassle now.

As soon as Violet reached Sunny, the older woman folded her arms across her chest. Jesse again got that sick feeling that this was going to be a really bad trip.

Unlike Smiley, Violet spoke in a low tone. He'd give anything—almost anything—to get closer. He shifted from one foot to the other safe within the shadows and strained to hear what was being said. But it was no use. All he heard was Smiley yell, "It ain't gonna happen."

Violet snapped at him, then turned to Sunny, who shrugged. Rainy held a hand up for order just as Cash returned from inventorying the supplies.

Jesse breathed easier. Whatever the problem was, they'd take care of it. He adjusted his Stetson and started to turn toward the trailer. Suddenly every nerve went on alert as he saw Sunny step toward Violet.

He watched her calm the older woman, and relief swamped him. Maybe she'd end up being good for something. Then Sunny patted Violet's hand, lifted an arm and aimed a finger directly at Jesse.

Camera lenses followed her extended arm. They glared at him, stalked him until they were up close and personal.

Jesse, however, said something other than cheese.

Chapter Four

"I still don't understand what I did wrong," Sunny said fifteen minutes later, her hands planted on her hips.

"Just get in the wagon or I swear to God I'll make you walk." Jesse's patience had gone farther south than the Argentina ranch he'd worked on for two years. His jaw ached from being clenched, and it felt good to give her a tongue-lashing for more than one reason.

The woman was a walking disaster. He'd managed to keep his mug off the news throughout the kickoff festivities, then she showed up and led every camera in Texas right to him. If that wasn't bad enough, she had talked nonstop ever since, trying to explain what had happened with Violet—as if he didn't already know.

"Look, if you'd just listen to me for one minute," she continued. "Violet said that Maria said that Maria's sister was sick and that Maria needed a replacement and—"

"Sunny?" He forced himself to be calm.

Cocking her head, she raised her eyebrows as if she was the damn Queen of Sheba.

"Would you shut up?" He spread his hands. The woman was never going to give it a rest.

"I don't know what you're so uptight about."

He shook his head in exasperation. "Is that at all possible?"

"What?"

He leaned forward, glaring at her, and she edged toward the wagon. "To keep your mouth shut?" he asked.

"If it's worth my while," she snapped and inched closer to the wagon.

"I don't believe it."

"Wanna bet?"

"Name it." He couldn't believe he was bargaining with her.

She stared at him, her eyebrows puckered, clearly at a loss for words. Then a slow grin tugged at her lips. "How long?"

"How long do you have to shut up?" He frowned at first, then returned her grin. "The rest of the day."

"No way."

"Can't do it, huh?" He angled his head back, looked down his nose at her and crossed his arms.

"Sure, I can." She crossed her arms, too. "I just don't think that making you shave is worth a whole day of silence."

Jesse dropped his arms to his side. "Excuse me?"

"Oh, what the heck." She shrugged. "And I get to do the shaving. Got a straight edge?" she asked with the most irritating grin.

He put a hand to his neck, something he rather valued these days. He also valued the six days' growth he felt on his jaw. It was still pretty scruffy, but he was counting on it being nice and full by the time they reached Oklahoma. "You want me to shave?"

Sunny lifted her smug chin.

But it was her obnoxious grin that did it. Jesse answered before he could stop himself. "Deal."

A short, strangled laugh escaped her. "Really?"

Her surprise was so evident, her expression so comical, he wanted to laugh. "Really," he assured her.

"Well, wait a minute. Why don't we say I shut up for half a day and you get to shave yourself?"

"Funny. I'd never have figured you for a welcher."

She narrowed her eyes at him for a moment and he could see her temper glittering from their depths. "Deal," she said and stuck out her hand.

Jesse glanced at the scarlet nails right before he pressed his palm to hers and smiled. Those suckers weren't gonna last long on the trail. Silently, he bid the impractical talons a fond farewell.

But not before he imagined them raking his back.

He dropped her hand like a hot potato. "Right now," he snapped. "The bet starts right now, and I don't want to hear a peep out of you until after seven o'clock."

Sunny rocked on her heels. "Who died and made you king? I say the bet starts in five minutes." She went on to explain why Violet had signed on to the crew.

He sighed, keeping an eye on his watch while he helped her get her overnight bag into the wagon, as she continued to ramble on. This was going to be the longest five minutes of his life. Not only was Miss Chatterbox driving him nuts, but Smiley was threatening to quit on account of Violet signing on for the next week. If he didn't keep those two apart, he'd have a battle on his hands, for sure.

Yet the truth was, as much as he hated the idea of having Violet along, he did need her. Maria Vasquez needed help with the cooking as well as with her young daughter. Jesse knew they both had to stay. The family was desperate for the money. He'd witnessed the devastation of their farm, and no matter how much money he'd tried to give them, or how much of his own sweat and muscle he'd donated to saving their home, fate had had other plans.

So he'd hired Manny as scout and his wife and her sister as cooks. Now with the sister out of commission for the next week or so, Maria would need help with the cooking and little Ana, their six-year-old, giving Jesse little choice.

He sighed. At least his bet was safe. No way would Sunny be able to stifle herself for the whole day. Although as she babbled on, he began to think twelve hours of silence would be worth the price of getting shaved.

Still, he couldn't believe he'd actually agreed to the possibility of her shaving him. What had he been thinking? She had him wound so tight, he was going to blow his cover himself by the time they got to Oklahoma. It was a darn good thing she'd be leaving the drive at the border.

And then another thought occurred to him. Sunny hoisted herself up onto the wagon, and a healthy expanse of smooth silky thigh caught his eye, nearly banishing his new idea to a fleeting memory. He slowly glanced away. But once she'd settled onto the seat next to Maria Vasquez, he tipped his head and peered at Sunny.

"What?" she asked, darting a glance at her watch. "I have forty more seconds."

"If you lose," he said, noting her fat-chance expression, "I want something out of this."

"What did you have in mind?" Her expression was wary.

Good question. As he watched her push nervously at her hair, the deep hue of her fingertips reflected the light, and he suddenly knew what he wanted.

"Your nails," he said, ignoring the confusion gathering in her face. "You'll cut them."

Then he pinched the brim of his Stetson and sauntered toward his horse, his hapless mind struggling against the sensation of his back being raked.

THE MIDMORNING SUN showered the vast assortment of wildflowers with nourishing light. In return, spotty patches of red and yellow lifted the flat, lifeless countryside from total despair. The same sun, however, beat down unmercifully on Sunny's unprotected nose and cheeks.

She looked over her shoulder at nearly five hundred longhorns kicking up half the dust in Texas. She'd never been so hot, so parched and so overwhelmed in her life.

And she couldn't even complain about it.

Things could be worse, she admitted. She could be riding in back of the whole dusty lot of them. Fortunately, the chuck wagon was working on a sizable lead in order to stop and prepare for lunch ahead of everyone.

The wagon rolled over a particularly rocky stretch, and her tender rear end bounced off the hard wooden seat before plopping down with as much dignity as a beached whale. Maria pulled in the reins to slow the horses, but she slid Sunny a look that was anything but sympathetic. When Sunny mouthed a thanks, Maria gave a curt nod, then turned to the business of creating more dust.

Sunny glanced at her watch. Only four hours had passed since she'd made that crazy deal with Jesse. Crazy for more than one reason. She'd been unable to get to know her new traveling companion.

Although the woman couldn't be much older than Sunny, she wore her ebony hair in a severe bun that added years to her age. Her eyes were heavily lidded, inky black and unreadable. Still, Sunny sensed the other woman's disapproval in every appraising glance she received.

Not that she cared. She was used to the stares and whispers, the quick judgments, even when she'd hidden behind sweat suits and baggy jeans. Then one day she'd gotten tired of trying to please people and never succeeding. From then on, the narrower minds grew, the shorter her skirts rose.

A high-pitched hum from the back of the wagon distracted Sunny from the dull roar of unhappy cattle and the distant hoots and hollers of the cowboys, and Sunny grinned over her shoulder. Fortunately, Maria's daughter, Ana, didn't share her mother's biases. She'd helped ease the monotony of the past few hours by alternating between playing in the back of the wagon and sitting on Sunny's lap. Right now, she sat in the back, coloring a book, while singing the latest country-and-western hits in her childish, off-key voice.

Not being able to talk to the little girl was another reason the bet with Jesse had been foolish. The fact that Ana thought it was a cool game to play made Sunny feel small, petty and childish. But she was far too stubborn to give in at this point. Which was a stupid reason to prolong the bet. Because Sunny had no intention of shaving Jesse Logan. Being in the same state as that man was bad enough. She had no intention of sharing the same breathing space. The mere thought reminded her of his spicy scent, and she shivered.

Maria sent her a questioning frown, but said nothing. She'd overheard most of Sunny and Jesse's conversation regarding the wager. Whether from disinterest or attempting to be helpful, she'd so far refrained from idle chatter.

Although Sunny was grateful, the situation left her with too much time to think…like about how foolish she'd been to challenge Jesse.

The bet was asinine, especially since Jesse hadn't been around enough to enjoy her silence. Not that she talked that much, she assured herself. Well, maybe a tad more than most people, and only when she was nervous. But Jesse had only ridden by twice since they'd left Maybe, and only for a few minutes at that. So what was the point?

She didn't care if he shaved or not. Okay, so she was a little curious to see how he looked without the heavy five-o'clock shadow. But she hadn't expected to actually go through with the wager…until he'd threatened her nails.

Sunny held up one hand and looked lovingly at the long, red creations by Gigi. What would her manicurist say if she knew her work of art was under attack?

She noticed Maria's quizzical look and lowered her hand to her lap. Having been a tomboy most of her young life, Sunny had later dreamed of having long, luscious nails à la the early Hollywood starlets. This was only her third stab at realizing her dream. The first two had failed miserably.

Another patch of uneven ground sent her bruised fanny airborne, and she vaguely considered that this drive had not been the best time or place for her third attempt to have glamorous nails. She shifted uncomfortably on the hard bench as Jesse rode up alongside them with Manny.

Jesse looked tired. Lines fanned from his eyes as he squinted against the bright sun. His left jaw was smudged with dirt, his mouth pressed tight against the swirling dust. He pulled the red bandanna from around his neck and wiped his forehead before saying something to Manny.

The other man promptly galloped away, then Jesse motioned

for Maria to slow down and he resumed a steady gait beside the wagon. "Lunch in one hour, okay?"

Maria nodded. "You tell Violet?" she asked, inclining her head toward the second wagon still a good distance behind them. Sunny hadn't heard the woman speak much and was again mildly startled to hear her soft Southern drawl instead of the Spanish accent she had expected.

"Not yet, but I will." He glanced at Sunny before returning his attention to Maria. "Is she talking your ear off yet?"

A brief grin crossed Maria's stern lips. "Not a word. Although why y'all are playing this childish game I'll never know."

"Self-defense, Maria. It's called self-defense."

Maria chuckled, her entire face lighting up in the process, making her look younger and prettier. Even as irritated as Sunny was with him, she couldn't help wondering if Jesse always had this effect on women. The young lady at the barbecue showing him her tan lines came to mind.

Sunny sat up straighter. She didn't respond to his jab. She wouldn't even give him the satisfaction of glaring. She sat with her hands in her lap and stared straight ahead, her chin lifted so high she nearly gave herself whiplash.

"Set your own pace," he told Maria. "Manny's scouting a place now. Just make sure you stay enough ahead of us so you'll have time to fix lunch. Don't worry about being exactly on time. We'll fine-tune things as the days go by."

He pulled on the reins and turned his horse, then raced toward Violet's wagon in a cloud of brown dust. Sunny caught a faceful of the gritty air. She coughed until Maria hit her several times on the back. If the other woman wasn't sitting beside her, Sunny might have thought he'd kicked up the disgusting stuff on purpose.

Rainy had warned her this drive would be no picnic, that the land out here could be harsh and unforgiving. But Sunny had never imagined that so many acres of monotonous prairie still existed. Although she'd been told they were traveling parallel to the highway, few signs of civilization were visible. Not that any of that mattered. If she had the decision to make over again, she'd be here for Rainy in a second. Then for a change, just maybe Sunny could feel like the good twin.

After a brief visit from Manny, then another twenty minutes of watching the tumbleweeds chase each other, Sunny felt the wagon slow to a crawl.

Maria craned her neck. "Looks like the place Manny suggested. What do you think?"

Sunny looked around. More barren ground. She started to shrug, then noticed two small mesquite trees a short distance away. The branches were low and sparse, but they did create a patch of shade. She pointed in their direction.

Maria gave her a bland smile. "If you want to talk, I'm not gonna tell Jesse."

Frowning, Sunny shook her head. She wasn't sure she could trust the woman. She had the feeling Maria, Manny and Jesse went back a long way. Besides, cheating was not a trait Sunny endorsed.

"Okay. But I hope you put a stop to this foolishness. Lord knows Jesse is too stubborn." Maria pulled up the reins and they came to a stop. "I'm gonna get awful tired of talking to myself." She paused, giving Sunny the once-over. "Then again, maybe I ought to get used to it."

Sunny crossed her arms as Maria hopped down from the wagon. She didn't appreciate being eyed as if she had as much substance as a marshmallow. Obviously the woman thought Sunny couldn't cut the outdoor life. Well, she'd bet she'd climbed more trees than Maria had ever thought about climbing. Hell, she'd bet her entire pay that she could stick this drive out longer than anyone.

Then she remembered that she was all bet out for the day and meekly uncrossed her arms. She leaned forward and peered at the trees, confused as to why the woman hadn't gotten closer.

Maria followed her gaze. "I don't think the wagon can make it over there. I'll have to carry what we need. Don't worry," she said dryly. "It's not your job."

Sunny rolled her eyes and ignored the urge to tug at her obviously inappropriate skirt. Inappropriate? It was darn impractical. Tomorrow she'd wear the pair of jeans Rainy had insisted on lending her. The leather miniskirts she'd brought would be better for the festivities along the way.

Pulling a bundle of tarp with her, she jumped down and rolled up her sleeves, ready to pitch in. The uneven ground was scarred, the deep cracks presumably caused by the stifling heat of a thousand summers. She was glad Maria had noticed them. All they needed was a disabled wagon. Jesse would undoubtedly have found a reason to blame it on her.

Maria wiped her brown hands down the front of her baggy jeans, eyeing Sunny, an odd expression on her round face.

"Are we there, Mama?" Little Ana popped her head out of the wagon. Her oversize brown hat with lace trim hung so low that it hid her big black eyes. She pushed the hat back to get a better look, her eager gaze sweeping the area. "Where are we?" Her voice dropped and her mouth settled into a pout.

Maria sighed at her daughter's obvious disappointment. Her gaze strayed to the hat, then flickered to Sunny. "You didn't have to do that. I'm gonna replace the one she lost."

Sunny shrugged and turned to Ana.

After a brief silence, Maria said to her daughter, "We're setting up for lunch. You come help us."

Ana scrambled down the narrow ladder Jesse had devised for the youngster. "Can we skip my lessons today?"

"You know better than that." Maria began hauling large burlap bags from the wagon. Most of them were only half-full, and she hoisted them easily.

As she poked through the supplies, determining what they would need, Sunny picked up one of the bags and carried it along with the tarp toward the shade. Ana followed, toting a large pot, just as Violet pulled up in the other wagon.

In no time Maria, Violet and Sunny had set out a buffet of fried chicken, rolls and corn bread, carrot sticks, apples and oranges. Maria claimed they barely had enough food to feed the thirty-or-so members of the drive, but to Sunny it looked like enough food for all of Maybe.

"Thanks, Sunny." Maria started lining up cup after cup of water as they waited for the first group of hungry cowboys. "You were a lot of help. Today was the easy day but it took longer than I expected."

Sunny's eyes widened in amazement. Easy day? Although the chicken had already been fried and the breads baked, all three of them had really had to scramble to lay out the food, condiments and drinks. She cast a dismal eye on the stack of tin plates. Cleanup wasn't going to be any fun, either.

"You're right." Violet stacked the tin mugs for coffee. "No ready-made stuff after today."

Sunny turned to her, torn between curiosity and dread.

Violet chuckled at her expression. "We have to start grilling our own meat, making biscuits. Especially when we get near towns. This drive has got to look authentic."

Maria passed Sunny a cup of water. Instead of drinking it, Sunny poured half of it over her bandanna, then brought the cool fabric to her hot, sweaty neck and sighed.

The other two women laughed, then greeted the first batch of men.

Jesse had assigned the cowboys to eat in two shifts to make sure the cattle were tended. The women had divided up the chores so that serving and cleanup would require minimal fuss.

Over the protests of the other two, Sunny washed the first set of plates as soon as the men were through. When she began reloading some of the burlap bags, Maria stopped her from filling them to the brim because Jesse was concerned that the women not handle anything too heavy.

Maria's explanation sounded reverent of their fearless leader. And heaven only knew Sunny had already heard enough about how wonderful Uncle Jesse was from Ana.

That was why she was so aware of the fact that he hadn't eaten yet, she told herself. Shading her eyes, she gazed out at the horizon. She couldn't see much because Maria had veered off the trail to set up lunch and the cattle had been halted quite a ways back. She thought about asking one of the men about him, but she didn't want anyone getting the wrong idea.

"You haven't eaten yet," Violet said from behind her.

Sunny dropped her hand and turned to Violet. The older woman peered past her in the direction of the cattle before gazing at Sunny, a curious twinkle in her blue eyes.

Sunny shook her head. She was too hot and tired to be hungry. In fact, she felt slightly queasy as she helped Maria and Violet put out all that food.

"It'll be a long time before supper," Violet said.

Sunny merely smiled and took the drink the woman offered her. She wasn't sure why she didn't just answer. Sunny had already decided the bet wasn't worth winning. After half a day on the trail, she knew her nails would be history soon, anyway. Besides, she had no intention of getting close enough to Jesse Logan to shave a single hair on his face.

"Well, you'd better grab something." Violet dried her hands on the legs of her coveralls as she turned toward the men. "When the second shift is done eating, we'll be packing up pronto. Got to get a head start on finding a place to camp for the night."

Sunny watched her go, then turned in the direction of the distant cattle. But no approaching rider was in sight. Looking at her new pink boots, then at the dry, rocky stretch of barren ground, she frowned. As much of a pain as Jesse was, she didn't want to see him miss lunch or not have something cold to drink. The cup of iced tea Violet had given her felt delightfully cool in her palm. Gingerly, she hopped over a deep crevice, skirted a low prickly bush and headed toward the sound of malcontent cattle.

As good as walking felt after being restricted to the wagon for so many hours, after ten minutes the sun seemed unbearably hot. The ice cubes that had once bobbed at the surface of the tea had melted and the tin cup dripped with condensation. She transferred the tea to her other hand, shoved her hair away from the back of her neck and laid her moist palm across her bare nape. The pleasant sensation lasted all of twenty seconds before the fierce heat again scorched her skin.

Finally, she neared her destination. Although swirling dust obscured her vision, the rumblings of the cattle, the men's loud commanding voices and the horses' pounding hooves echoed in her ears.

Then Jesse's unmistakable dark head and tan Stetson appeared from a cloud of dust. For the briefest of moments her eyes met his startled ones. Then the smell assailed her.

Pungent. Ghastly. Stifling. Sweat mingled with an acrid, beastly odor. Unlike anything Sunny had experienced at Rainy and Cash's ranch, the mass of fumes overwhelmed her. Her stomach rolled, her head spun and she clutched the useless tin cup for support.

She heard Jesse call her name, then everything melted into oblivion.

Chapter Five

Jesse's heart pounded as he ran toward Sunny. He'd seen her sink to the ground, the drink she'd held slicing the air and splashing around her.

Reaching her prone body, he dropped to his knees. Her long hair dragged across one pale cheek and tangled about her neck and shoulder. Gently he pushed the damp locks aside and felt her fevered skin. He let out a grateful breath when he saw the strong pulse at her neck.

Slipping his hand under her nape, he cradled her head in his arm. With his other hand he cupped her warm cheek. "Sunny?" he whispered.

She didn't move. Her lashes lay thick and black against her wan complexion.

"Sunny," he said again, this time more urgently. Although he could see that her pulse still beat strongly, he wrapped his fingers around her wrist to reassure himself. Beneath the silky skin, life surged against his fingers.

God, she was soft. Incredibly soft, like the nose of a kitten. She was fragile, too. Much more fragile than he'd imagined. Her wrist bones were so small and delicate, it frightened him. He loosened his grip.

"Sunny?" He cursed the shakiness in his voice.

She didn't stir.

He shifted, running his gaze down her still form, wondering how he was going to get her to the wagon. Her already short skirt had ridden up dangerously high—enough to give him a peek of something red and lacy.

He yanked his bandanna from around his neck. Barely audible over the din of cattle, he heard a horse approach. He looked up to see Hank headed toward them.

With one hand, Jesse snapped open the cloth and draped it over Sunny's thighs. That was when he noticed the two ugly scratches on the side of her leg.

"What happened?" Hank came to a stop and slid down from his saddle.

"She fainted. Probably from the heat." Jesse reached into his back pocket for another bandanna. "Give me your canteen, will you?"

Hank pulled the container from his saddle, his eyes wide.

Jesse followed the man's gaze. Where the tea had splashed her shirt, the fabric clung to her, molding itself against the lace beneath it and outlining her breast.

Red-hot anger gripped Jesse. He grabbed the canteen from the other man's hand. "Go find my horse and bring him here."

Hank jumped at Jesse's tone. "Don't you want me to help you with her?"

"Get my horse."

The other man frowned, then scurried to his animal. Quickly he mounted and galloped through a spray of dust.

Jesse sank on his haunches while cradling Sunny in one arm. He struggled to open the canteen with the other hand, then spilled some of the tepid water onto the yellow bandanna and laid the cloth across her forehead. Moisture mixed with dust streaked her cheek.

"Sunny, come on, Sunny." He tapped her cheek. He had no idea how he'd get her back without Hank's help, which was hardly his first choice. "Sunny, you gotta wake up."

Her eyelashes fluttered. Jesse's stomach tightened.

"Sunny?" He lifted her head a few more inches and pressed the canteen to her lips. Still, her eyes remained closed. "Come on, honey. Take a sip."

Sunny didn't move…except when Jesse nearly dropped her.

Honey? Where the hell had that come from? Never in his entire life had Jesse Logan used an endearment with a woman, and especially not to a woman as infuriating as Sunny.

"Wake up, damn it," Jesse said through clenched teeth and reached to cover more of her exposed thighs.

Hank rode up with Jesse's horse in tow and tied both animals to a nearby bush. "She say anything yet?"

Turning his back, Jesse shielded her from Hank's stare. "No," Jesse snapped. He gazed at her full lips, slightly parted and looking sexy as hell. And her wet top...

Jesse swallowed and swung his gaze to Hank. The poor guy looked torn between bolting and gawking. Damn, he couldn't fault the guy for looking, but he didn't have to like it. He still hadn't come up with a plan yet, but then the unusually hot April sun beating down on his back and shoulders made the decision for him, and his concern for her welfare won out over her modesty. He covered her long tan legs as well as he could with the flimsy bandanna, but knew she couldn't take much more exposure to the heat.

"Bring my horse here, will you, Hank?" he asked as calmly as he could.

After the younger man did as he was asked, Jesse laid down the canteen and motioned him over. "You take her," he said. "Then after I get on my horse, pass her to me."

Hank's own Adam's apple bobbed a couple of times before he nodded. Slowly, Jesse exchanged places with him, making certain the young man's arm was safely under Sunny's head before he let go.

As soon as he stepped away, emptiness swamped him, blocked the light, polluted the air he fought to breathe. The feeling was so real, so physical, he nearly staggered. Gulping in several quick breaths, he felt his Adam's apple do a two-step as he swung into the saddle.

There he waited, his heart pounding double time, as Hank gathered Sunny in his arms and brought her to him.

"She'll be all right, won't she?" Hank whispered. He stumbled a little under her inert body. It wasn't that she weighed much, but she was tall, nearly as tall as Hank.

Jesse instantly hooked an arm around her waist and assumed most of the burden. Not that he considered her a burden, he realized, looking into her peaceful face, smudged with dirt and a trace of leftover makeup. At least not when she wasn't yakking, he thought wryly and smiled.

"She wake up?" Hank pushed his hat back with his free hand. The other he used to steady Sunny's left hip.

Jesse lost the smile. "No." He drew her the rest of the way across his lap until Hank no longer needed to brace her. Her head slumped against Jesse's chest. "I'll take her to the wagon and meet up with you."

He didn't wait for Hank to respond. He turned his horse toward the camp and set off at a gentle gait. When she slipped a little, he tightened his arms around her and was reminded again of how incredibly soft she was.

Her hair smelled of vanilla and almonds and he took big, greedy whiffs of it. She stirred as his chest expanded, but instead of rousing, she snuggled more soundly against him.

The action made him want her. And that made him angry.

He cursed under his breath. This cattle drive had been in the making for over two years. The salary he was earning for heading it would finally allow him to buy his own ranch and settle down. He couldn't afford to get distracted. And here he was hoping this short ride to the wagons would never end.

Damn her. He spurred his horse and rode as fast as safety would permit.

But not before he allowed himself one last helping of vanilla and almonds.

SUNNY COULDN'T REMEMBER the last time she'd had so many dreams. Some pleasant, some dreadful, some downright erotic.

She rolled over on the unfamiliar mattress. It was harder and lumpier than normal. And her room was far too hot. Her eyes barely drifted open. What was all that canvas overhead? Her eyes closed again and she snuggled deeper to bask in the residual sensation of the more sensual dreams that had graced her sleep.

Sunny could almost feel the strong arms that had held her in her dreams, feel the crisp chest hairs beneath her curling fingers, the taut stomach, the hard...

The room grew hotter still, and she kicked off the coverlet.

She ought to get up, she told herself. Even with her eyes closed, she knew it was getting light outside. And Rainy was expecting her. Wasn't today the day Rainy needed her in Maybe?

She'd have to get up in a few minutes. No doubt about it, Sunny thought, yawning.

And she would have, if exhaustion had not clamped her within its jaws.

"MISS CHATTERBOX back to her old self yet?" Jesse asked Maria as he passed her two dirty dinner plates and held his breath. As far as he knew, Sunny had slept the entire afternoon, and he was getting worried.

"You could at least show some sympathy." Maria dunked the plates in the soapy water. "She's fine. Only tired. Don't worry about her."

"I'm not worried. I've enjoyed the peace and quiet."

Maria gave him a bland look. "Is that why you ate only two bites of your dinner?"

Jesse sighed. "Has she woken up or not?"

"Violet heard her a little while ago, but when she went to check, she was still disoriented so we let her go back to sleep."

He frowned. "Do you think that's a good idea?"

"For heaven's sake, Jess." Her hands covered with suds, Maria used her forearm to push back the dark curling hair at her temple. "We've both seen this kind of thing before. The heat and excitement got to her. Let her sleep it off."

"Yeah, you're right." He passed her another plate and strolled away. As soon as he was out of Maria's sight, he doubled back to the second wagon, where he'd taken Sunny hours ago. He hadn't liked Maria needling him earlier today and decided she didn't need to know he wanted to check on her himself.

The privacy curtain at the back of the wagon had been left partially open and he could tell that Sunny was still lying down. Quietly he hopped up and parted the curtain further.

Sunny lay on her side, hugging a pillow, a coverlet pulled up to her waist, with only a narrow strip of tanned flesh showing between the cover and her blouse. Her hair was spread wildly about and her features were in full repose. Even when he shifted closer and the wagon creaked, she didn't make the slightest move.

He knew she was exhausted. Hell, most of the men had eaten a hasty dinner in hopes of getting an early night's sleep. And they hadn't been dragging luggage around until early this morning. He smiled at the reminder, only slightly sorry for the surprise awaiting her after all her trouble last night.

Rubbing his jaw, he gazed at her, wondering if he should wake her. Rough stubble scratched his fingertips, and he remembered their bet.

Damnation. She was going to win. Unfair as it was—he glanced at his watch—in five minutes, she'd win.

What a crazy bet that had been. He hadn't been around enough to enjoy her silence, and there was no way he'd trust her with a razor in the vicinity of his person.

He dragged his fingertips from his jaw down his throat. However, it wasn't the touch of a blade he was imagining. His gaze slowly fell on Sunny's hand splayed across her midriff, those glossy red fingernails lying innocently against the ivory coverlet and the strip of bare skin.

His body tightened.

His thoughts scattered.

Okay, he admitted, so it wasn't the blade he was worried about. He looked at his watch again. Three more minutes. He could wake her, startle her into saying something.

Then she'd lose.

But so would he…unless he let her sleep.

He muttered a succinct and earthy word, disgusted with himself for even thinking along those destructive lines. How many of these prima donna types would it take before he wised up? Hadn't he learned anything? Hadn't he had his fill of flighty rodeo queens whose self-serving attitudes had confirmed what he'd always known? Those women weren't interested in the long haul, in owning up to responsibility. Once they smelled blood, they swooped in for the kill. Then they left you to bleed. Better men than he had been shattered in their wake. So had little boys…

Sunny stirred, drawing his attention to her…and a long, ugly scratch on the side of her left hand. What had she been doing wandering out in the bush, anyway? When she stirred, raising her hand to her face, Jesse automatically glanced at his watch. Only one more minute. She opened one eye, then the other, widened them on him, then blinked.

Fifty-two more seconds.

She raised her head slightly. Her lips quivered in surprise, then parted, about to speak.

Jesse's gaze held helplessly to her mouth before he muttered a curse, leaned down and kissed her.

At first her lips were soft, pliant with surprise. Then, as she seemed to gather her wits, he felt her mouth stiffen. But that only lasted a second, and he followed her down as she lowered her head against the pillow.

She shifted and he sank to the edge of the makeshift bed, nibbling her lips, teasing them with his tongue.

The alarm on his watch beeped, signaling the end of the bet. But he didn't stop. This had nothing to do with the bet, and everything to do with need—the need to touch her.

He called himself a damned fool, but continued to taste her, trailing tiny kisses down her neck, absorbing her softness as his hands tunneled through her hair. She arched her neck and he worked his way up her throat, along her jaw until his lips met her unbelievably soft ones. He caught her lower lip gently between his teeth, and when he felt it quiver, he pulled back.

Her eyes were unfocused, dazed, and he pulled back even further. Immediately she flattened her hands against his chest and curled her fingers into his cotton shirt, searing his flesh beneath.

Lust bloomed in Jesse's groin and he had to take deep, even breaths to clear his brain, his vision. She still looked confused and he wanted to be certain she knew what she was doing. He wanted her alert. He wanted there to be no doubt that she knew who she was kissing. Hell, he wanted her...period.

And that made him the biggest damn fool of all. He let out a harsh, unsteady breath and shifted away.

Sunny allowed her shaky hands to fall from Jesse's chest and she shoved the hair away from her face. She lowered her lashes for an instant, scrambling for composure. When she looked at him, he'd moved away slightly and was staring at her with such a blank expression it made her want to scream...except that her vocal cords were about as useless as the rest of her at the moment.

Surely this was one of those dreams again. Maybe if she pinched herself, she'd realize this wasn't really happening. Her fingers moved at the suggestion, only they ended up on her tender lips. If this was a dream, she wasn't sure she wanted it to end.

For a brief moment, Jesse's impassive eyes softened and he reached over to cover her fingers with his. Gently he stroked the corner of her mouth. "Sorry about the whisker burn," he whispered.

Automatically she pressed her cheek into his soothing touch.

Then she stiffened. This was no dream.

Jesse's hand fell away. His eyes went blank again.

"What the hell do you think you're doing?" Sunny scooted back and narrowed her accusing gaze on him.

Slowly Jesse rose from the cot, his lips pressed into a thin line. "Giving you, your highness, more than you deserve."

She fisted the coverlet beneath her hand, propping herself up on one elbow, her indignation burning her already hot cheeks. "Excuse me?"

"You won." He cocked his head arrogantly, sticking his

hands in his back pockets. Only the action tightened the front of his jeans, making something perfectly clear to Sunny.

She swallowed and quickly forced her gaze to the conceited angle of his chin. "Won?"

"Our bet." He stroked his jaw.

Unconsciously, she rubbed hers, too. Where he'd branded her with his roughened chin.

His hand paused and he blinked away a hint of regret before his gaze skimmed her mouth, her eyes…her mouth.

And then she realized what he was saying.

She'd won their bet? Jerking her wrist, she stared at her watch. Then her eyes drifted to him.

This was one of the few times she'd seen him without his hat. His hair was longer than most of the other men's, dark curls licking at the collar of his cotton shirt. One more button than usual was undone, exposing a wedge of tan chest. Black curls swirled there, too. Her pulse skidded and she wondered if she'd been the one who had undone that button.

Good God, she hadn't wanted to win this bet.

"Look…" She levered herself up. "We'll scratch the bet. It wasn't fair."

Jesse raised his eyebrows. "Sure it was."

"No, really." She started to swing her legs off the cot while tugging her skirt down under the coverlet. Then something occurred to her, something almost too dreadful to contemplate. She hesitated, one bare leg exposed to the thigh.

"How did I get here?" Her mind fumbled through the afternoon's hazy events.

"You fainted."

"I remember that," she snapped. Which wasn't exactly true. She recalled taking the iced tea out to him, remembered the hot sun pelting her arms, the dust clogging her throat, the awful smell. Her stomach rolled again.

Jesse edged forward, ducking his head to look at her. "Are you okay?"

"Fine. Now, how did I get here?"

His gaze slipped to her exposed thigh. "Me."

Sunny swallowed and shifted the coverlet over her leg. "How?"

"I threw you over my shoulder."

Her eyes felt as wide as large pizzas. Reflexively she tugged down her skirt and hoped like hell she had no rips in her underwear. Her mother's early warnings rang in her ears.

Jesse burst out laughing.

Her eyes narrowed to threatening slits.

"Actually, I brought you on my horse." He pressed back a grin. "You rode sidesaddle." She felt her shoulders relax. "Across my lap," he added, one side of his mouth beginning to lift.

She raised her chin and started to stand, careful that her skirt slid down to its proper place, which, she admitted to herself, was not proper enough.

"Hank passed you up to me. But he was a gentleman," he added.

"I don't need any more details." She stood only a scant foot from him. A woodsy smell drifted from his skin and whispered across her overwrought nerves. He'd recently had a bath. And right now she'd kill for one. She only hoped he'd already arranged for a motel room for her, as well. That was absolutely the only thing on her mind as she took another whiff before she tried to sidestep him.

Except he wouldn't move out of her way. His broad shoulders blocked most of the light, and his dark eyes roamed her face. "Aren't you forgetting something?" he asked.

She ran a hand through her tangled hair. Remembering that his fingers had recently followed the same course, she clasped her hands in front of her. "I don't—" She started to shrug, then sighed, feeling like an ungrateful twit. "Thank you," she murmured. "Thanks for bringing me back."

"That's not what I was looking for." He moved closer.

Sunny shifted and forced herself to maintain eye contact. No easy task with his devil-dark eyes so close they seemed to read her every secret and his breath tickling her cheeks as he leaned ever so slightly forward. He was going to kiss her again. Any second. She was certain of it.

"What I want," he said, inching still closer, "is for you..." He was so close she could almost count the fine lines fanning from his eyes. In two seconds their lips would meet.

Jesse slid his hand between their faces and stroked his jaw. The backside of his fingers grazed her lips. "To tell me when I'll get that shave." The fan lines crinkled, deep and taunting.

"When hell freezes over." Sunny put a hand up to his chest and gave him a hard shove. Then reached for her overnight bag. "I'm going to my room now," she said through gritted teeth. "And don't you dare disturb me."

Jesse recovered from the unexpected shove, the grin faltering on his mouth as he blinked at her in obvious but inexplicable confusion. "To your—"

Then the grin returned full force...right before his hearty laugh shook the entire wagon.

Chapter Six

There was no motel. Only acres and acres of flat, dry, dusty, desolate land and clusters of cowboys setting out bedrolls.

Sunny dropped her overnight bag beside the wagon with a thud.

She thought she had awoken. Instead, she found herself in the middle of a nightmare.

As hot as the day had grown, the late-evening air was unexpectedly brisk. Rainy had warned her about how unpredictable spring nights could be, she remembered as she rubbed the chill from her arms. In fact, Rainy had warned her about a lot of things. Only Sunny hadn't listened. She'd been too damned excited about playing the unfamiliar role of rescuer.

But now, Rainy's cautionary words filled her head as Sunny warily scanned the camp. Primitive, her sister had said. Rough, pioneer, authentic. A shiver that had nothing to do with the chilly air stinging her arms and legs racked her, and she sank onto the overnight bag, stretching her legs out in front of her.

She didn't want to be cold and hot and dusty all in the same day. Or to rough it out under the stars. She didn't want to play at being some damn pioneer. In her opinion, a hotel without room service was roughing it enough. Her stomach rumbled at the thought of a silver cart being wheeled toward her, a plate of grilled salmon and steamed vegetables waiting under a silver dome.

Sunny sighed heavily. She wanted a hot shower. She wanted a tropical drink with a paper umbrella in it.

A cherry. She sighed again. A cherry would be nice, too.

Then she caught sight of Maria dumping a large barrel of murky water, the suds few and far between, and Sunny felt a smidgeon of guilt for not having helped with dinner.

The feeling lasted all of three seconds.

She hadn't been hired to make dinner for a bunch of wild cowboys…especially one in particular.

An image of Jesse choked her senses, his eyes dark and taunting, his smile slightly lopsided…right after he'd kissed her. Sunny gulped a lungful of the cold night air and felt the burn all the way to her stomach.

She'd actually responded to his kiss…his tender, demanding, expert kiss. And like some silly schoolgirl, no less. Shaking her head, she brought her knees up to hug them. He had caught her off guard, that was all. She would never have responded if she'd been fully awake and not hazy with sleep…dreaming of him.

"Argh!" She voiced her disgust as she bounded to her feet and dusted her bottom.

"Problem, your highness?" Jesse's amused voice came from behind, elevating her irritation to new heights.

When she turned a haughty look on him, she noticed that he watched her dusting with far too much interest. She took a hard and final swat, but he'd already shifted his eye level to hers.

"You mean, besides you?" she asked with a sweet smile.

"Me?" His eyebrows shot up in practiced innocence. "And here I was going to show you to your bath."

"A bath?" Sunny's mood cautiously lightened. She looked around, but saw nothing beyond the two wagons. Had they brought in a trailer?

"Yup. Care to follow me?" His voice dipped low, teasing, seductive.

Not in a million years, was the response on the tip of her tongue. She settled for giving him a dirty look instead, then bent to pick up her bag.

Jesse scooped it up before she could touch the handle. "Come on," he said. "Before it gets too dark."

Still wondering where the trailer was, she nodded and fell into place beside him.

Some distance away, the cattle—and their horrendous odor—had been settled in for the night. Their sporadic moos drifted across the prairie, and in the dusky twilight she made out the silhouettes of several men on horseback tending them. Mesquite sprouted haphazardly, most of the trees puny in comparison to their well-fed urban counterparts. Other than that, there was absolutely nothing but sparse clumps of shriveled vegetation emerging from the ground.

Her feet slowed and she'd started to question Jesse when she heard the sound.

It was muted at first, a tiny echo of her own fantasy. Then the unmistakable gush of water filled her ears. She picked up her pace, passing Jesse, squinting into the fading light.

She stopped. "Where is it?"

"Another couple dozen yards and you would have had your bath and your clothes washed at the same time."

She started to pivot toward him, a sinking feeling weighing her movement, but he came up beside her, looking at her with a wry twist of his mouth.

"What is it?" she asked, proud of her deceptively cool voice.

"A natural spring."

"And you expect me to bathe in there?" The water even sounded cold.

"Actually, I really didn't," he drawled.

Sunny took a deep, silent breath. She hated his pompous tone. Given the choice, of course she wouldn't use these dubious facilities, but she didn't have that luxury.

"Well?" Jesse asked when she'd been too busy mentally devising ways to inflict pain on him to respond. "We haven't got all night."

"We?"

"I'll be your lookout."

His words inspired a new realization and she frowned in the direction of the pool. "There's not a shred of privacy." She slanted him a suspicious glance. He was putting her on. Surely Maria and Violet hadn't stripped, then traipsed into this public bath. She'd been too trusting a couple of years ago and she'd paid with her reputation. She wasn't about to make that mistake again. She took a deep breath to calm her sudden edginess.

"Stick close to that mesquite." He pointed to a short, squat tree, its gnarled branches low to the ground. "It'll block you from two directions. I'll take care of the other two."

Sunny rolled her eyes.

"Suit yourself." Jesse shrugged, a mischievous gleam entering his eyes. "Unless you need me to scrub your back."

She raised her eyebrows and angled her head until she was looking down her nose at him.

He grinned. "Of course I could do that while you shave me."

An erotic image popped into her mind of herself naked and breast level with his devilish face. She jerked her chin down to accommodate a painful, dry swallow, verging on a cough.

He laughed, putting a hand to her back.

She shrugged away from him. "I'll wait until tomorrow."

"Just as well," he said, starting toward the camp. "I wasn't up for a shave tonight."

"Forget it, Logan. It was a stupid bet. You keep your pathetic excuse for a beard. I'll keep my nails."

"Nope," he said seriously. His brow furrowed and his hand strayed to self-consciously rub his jaw. With a sense of triumph, Sunny knew her defenseless jab had dented his fat ego. Then he glanced at her nails and grinned again.

Okay, so it was a matter of time before Gigi's creations would be history. Big deal. She already knew that. She turned and hurried away from the spring.

"The thing is," he called, "a bet is a bet in my book. I won't feel right until it's finished."

He'd been baiting her and she'd fallen for it. She gave him

a quick, dismissive glance over her shoulder as she left him in her dust. "Fine. Make sure the razor is sharp."

His laughter followed her until she raced far enough ahead that his annoying joviality blended with sounds of the distant cattle and the nearby crickets. Although it was now almost dark, the light of the waning campfire guided her to camp, and she realized the spring wasn't so far away.

The distance had fooled her earlier, she figured, because she had been with *him*. It had then seemed like a hundred miles away. She let out a loud sound of disgust. He was the most unbearable, aggravating man she had ever run across. And confusing, she admitted. She couldn't figure out why he gave her such a hard time. It was a new experience. She normally had the opposite problem with men, and for that reason alone she ought to be grateful for Jesse.

Many of the cowboys appeared to have bedded down. Maria, however, was still poking around the chuck wagon. It occurred to Sunny that she still had no idea where she was supposed to sleep, but if sprawling under the stars meant wiping that self-satisfied grin off Jesse's face, she'd do it in a heartbeat. Then a night chill chased up her spine and her bravado faltered…her memory stirred. She'd left her bag at the spring.

Sighing, she rubbed her arms and continued toward Maria. Remnant dinner aromas tickled Sunny's nose as she got closer, and she was suddenly so starved she couldn't see straight.

"You all right?" Maria glanced up from the dough she was kneading.

"Great," she replied a little sheepishly. "I suppose that's for tomorrow's breakfast?"

Maria nodded and continued kneading.

"Since I'm not likely to be sleepy anytime soon, I'll help," Sunny said dryly.

"Jesse probably wants to see you."

"Yeah, he already did."

Maria looked up sharply at Sunny's sarcastic tone. "He was worried about you."

"Sure he was." Sunny tossed her hair. Worried, nothing.

They all might be wowed by him, but she had his number. In her business she'd met men like him before. Men who viewed women as objects for their amusement. Men who cared about nothing and no one but themselves.

Maria's lips thinned in disapproval, but when Sunny's stomach rumbled noisily, she inclined her head toward a spot closer to the wagon and said, "Your dinner is over there."

It was then Sunny noticed the large bundle of foil balanced on a spit over a soft orange glow.

"It should still be warm," Maria said. "Those are fairly fresh coals."

Sunny smiled gratefully. She knew dinner must have been over for some time. "Thanks," she said. "You shouldn't have gone to the trouble."

"I didn't." Maria raised her black, expressionless eyes. "Jesse did."

JESSE RODE BACK from taking his shift with the cattle well before sunup. Most of the men were still sacked out. Yesterday had been a long, hard ride and the uncharacteristically hot weather hadn't helped, either. It had felt more like a July sun rather than an April one beating down unrelentingly. Although many of the cowboys Jesse had hired were used to hard, physical work and extreme heat, there were equal numbers who weren't. But they were men who had been out of work for a long spell. Jesse had known most of them for years and he hadn't had the heart to turn them down. He knew too well how the rodeo circuit could use a man up and spit him out, then leave him in the cold to face the rest of his life.

He knew all the men would eventually pull their weight. And if there was a little extra work for him to cover in the meantime, he could handle it. What he couldn't handle was four or five weeks of Sunny.

His gaze automatically fixed on the supply wagon, where he'd given her a cot to use last night. The same cot where he'd awakened her yesterday...with a very foolish kiss.

Jesse ground his teeth at the memory. Damn it. He shouldn't

have kissed her. It had felt good. Too good. She was soft and sweet, and she made him want to forget what a poor investment a city slicker like her would be. Plus, she was Cash's sister-in-law, for God's sake. That alone put her off-limits for a casual roll in the hay.

Besides, the drive was too important. It deserved all of his attention. If he screwed up, he'd have to kiss off the bonus the promoters had promised him upon completion. And that meant kissing off his plans to own a ranch. It was bad enough that he'd already made concessions for her...concessions he didn't want her to know about. Because Jesse knew about her kind. They always wanted more. Until they bled a man dry.

With the exception of a campfire several yards beyond the chuck wagon, the camp was still pretty dark. He saw Violet settling a pot over the flames and knew coffee would be ready soon. Maria sat closer to the wagon, her hands buried in a large bowl. Groups of cowboys huddled in bedrolls dotted the site. All was peaceful and quiet.

Then Jesse saw a flash of light dart around the inside of the supply wagon where Sunny was supposed to be asleep. The beam whipped down the length of the canvas dome, then bounced around for almost a minute before disappearing altogether. In seconds the light dawned again to zip around frantically.

Jesse smiled. He knew exactly what was happening.

THE SECOND LONG, cherished red fingernail in two minutes snapped off as Sunny wedged her hand between two bags of flour. The word she let fly surprised even her.

She sank back on her haunches. "I can't believe this," she said aloud to the partial darkness. The flashlight slipped from her hand and rolled away. She wasn't worried. It couldn't get too far. The darn wagon was packed tighter than one of her leather skirts. Which, she had almost convinced herself, she was never going to find.

"What the hell could've happened to my luggage?" She shook her head and once more plowed her hands between the rough burlap bags of dried beans. Prying the bags apart as far as she could, she peeked behind them. Nothing.

Not that she expected one of her suitcases to magically appear, since she'd already combed the place. But it was just so darn baffling. She was sure she remembered each of her four hiding places. And it wasn't like the wagon was that big.

Frowning, she nibbled on one of her butchered nails. Could her bags be in the other wagon? No. Could someone have found them? She doubted it. She'd had it on the best authority that the wagons had been ready to go before she'd hidden her stuff beneath the provisions. Besides, if someone had found the suitcases, she would've heard about it by now. She had, in fact, been prepared for that likely event. She'd only hoped that the discovery wouldn't be made until after they were well on the trail.

Her chin sank onto her palm. Something wasn't right, that much was certain. Had someone unwittingly moved the bags?

Whistling, coming from right outside the wagon, ricocheted through the still, early-morning air. It was a cheerful yet eerie sound, and intuitively she knew that whatever had happened to her luggage had been on purpose. And she knew exactly who was behind it.

Without a doubt, the culprit had to be Jesse.

How had he known where she'd hidden the suitcases? When had he sneaked them out? Well, he had messed with her for the last time.

She jumped up and ripped back the privacy curtain—ready to ambush him—and came face-to-face with his smug, knowing expression.

"Good morning," he said cheerfully, his eyes glittering with amusement. "Sleep well?" His gaze lingered on her as he dismounted his horse with a grin.

In that moment, Sunny knew she wouldn't give him the satisfaction of watching her come unglued. "Great." She calmly pushed back her unbrushed hair.

Oh, God. My hot rollers. Gone.

Her fingers snagged on a tangle.

My curling iron!

She jerked her finger free, then forced a smile. *I'm going to tear your heart out.* "And you? Sleep well?"

"Great." His grin widened. "If you still want that bath, I'd grab it now." His gaze slipped to the bare shoulder exposed by her oversize T-shirt and she yanked it up. "The men will be waking any minute."

"Thank you for reminding me," she said with excessive politeness and jerked the privacy curtain into place. Then she reached for her overnight bag...the one that he'd returned to her last night. The same bag he'd innocently suggested she might need. She bit back a ripe comment. It would be a cold day in a place a whole lot farther south than Texas before she'd show him any reaction.

She listened for a minute to see if he'd taken the hint and gotten lost, but she heard nothing. So she sifted through the meager supply of clothes she'd stuffed into the bag at the last minute. Unfortunately, her first preference, the jeans Rainy had loaned her, were among the items missing in action, as were the baggy, comfortable shorts Sunny would now give her eye-teeth for.

After she settled for a totally unsuitable skirt and blouse, she pulled out a pastel floral exercise bra and slipped it on before replacing her T-shirt over it. No way was she going to bathe in the raw, no matter how dark it was. She rooted around for several more moments, still hoping Jesse had gotten her message.

When she climbed out of the wagon, taking only soap, a towel, her clothes and the flashlight, her wish had come true. He was gone. Only his horse remained. She slipped the towel around her shoulders in deference to the slight morning chill, which was in no way going to discourage her from having her bath. She was surprised that the air didn't seem as brisk as it had last night, which made absolutely no sense to her. But, she admitted, nothing much had in the last two days.

Never had she allowed a man to get to her as Jesse had. From now on, just like the cold, the heat, the pesky critters buzzing around her ears, she was going to ignore him…and his hot, seductive kisses. She shuddered, causing the flashlight beam to shimmy, and she stumbled over a clump of dried twigs. Snorting in aggravation, she righted herself and fixed her attention on the unpredictable ground.

The sky was just barely beginning to lighten, so she stopped by the campfire to tell Maria where she was going.

Maria looked tired. Her bun drooped at the back of her head. She had not yet tucked in her faded, plaid shirt. Sunny opened her mouth to assure her that she'd be back in time to help with breakfast, but then stopped herself. She didn't need to explain herself to anyone. Her job was public relations, meeting with people in participating towns along the way, coordinating their festivities. Not cooking. She started to continue toward the spring, but not before she saw Maria heave a weary sigh. The woman could only have gotten a few hours' sleep.

Sunny caught at her lower lip. *I'm such a wimp.* "I won't be long," she told the woman. "Then I'll be at your disposal."

"Sure," Maria said, a grin blossoming on her lips. She darted a look toward the spring before turning back to forming the pasty white biscuit dough.

Sunny frowned as she swung the flashlight beam ahead of her and continued on, wondering what that was all about. The woman was probably just getting punchy, Sunny figured, and concentrated on not tripping over the rocky ground.

Walking to the spring alone, in the dark, made the trip a whole lot more unnerving than it had been last night. Critters chirped and squeaked in the scruffy knots of shrubbery, and Sunny swore she saw something dart out in front of her. But she convinced herself it was only a rabbit, something small and fluffy and cute like Thumper, and tried to steady her hand so the light beam would guide her safely down the narrow path.

The short, gnarly mesquite guarding the spring provided a good landmark. She made out its lumpy outline against the dawn's early glow. The familiar and comforting sounds of chirping birds displaying their zest for the new day subdued her zinging nerves.

A minute later, she heard the faint sound of water and hurried toward the promise of a long-awaited bath.

Several feet from the edge of the spring, the ground softened beneath Sunny's sneakers. The bank dipped toward the still water, which lay before her like a sheet of glass. Not even a ripple marred its crystal perfection.

Only she knew darn well it was going to be downright cold, and she shivered in anticipation. She dropped her towel on a patch of grass and carefully set her clean clothes atop it. She laid her flashlight there, too, no longer really needing it as the sky's inkiness ebbed into gray.

This had better be worth it, she thought, eyeing the water with a touch of dread.

"I'd jump in right away if I were you." Jesse's voice came from somewhere near the tree. "That'll ease the shock."

Chapter Seven

Sunny froze, her arms crossed in front of her, her hands gripping the hem of her T-shirt, ready to yank it over her head. She let the fabric fall from her fingers and spun toward his voice.

Bare-chested, water scarcely reaching his navel, he cruised away from a low-slung branch that arched over the spring.

The water receded an inch or two as he moved, making Sunny wonder if he was wearing anything below the waist. She felt heat germinate in her tightened chest before crawling into her face.

Confident it was still dark enough that he wouldn't notice her discomfort, she tossed her hair—her poor, sorry, tangled hair—and lanced him with her best glare. "What do you think you're doing?"

"The same as you, probably." He shrugged, and her gaze settled on his well-developed shoulders. Wet, dark hair swirled on his tanned chest...around his nipples. She could almost see them, but it was still too dark, and he was a little too far away....

She realized she'd taken a step forward and stopped, appalled, disgusted with herself. She planted her hands on her hips with so much enthusiasm, she teetered forward a little. Sinking back on her heels, she said, "You were peeping at me."

"Oh, no, you don't." He cupped some water and scooped

it behind him but made no other move. "Accusation not accepted. I purposely spoke up before you took your clothes off. Even though I wasn't sure you hadn't already seen me."

She gasped. "You've got to be kidding. You're either conceited or delusional. I don't know which." She stooped to pick up her things. "And I don't care."

"Sunny, wait a minute." He pushed laboriously through the water toward her, the water level slipping as he progressed.

Her eyes widened a moment, then she whipped her gaze away from him, turning her back before she got an eyeful of something she wasn't quite ready to handle. "Jesse Logan, you stop right where you are."

Silence greeted her heated ears. No water splashing, no talking. Even the squawking of birds seemed to recede as Sunny stared straight ahead, away from him, toward the still camp, the endless sky.

Then from behind, Jesse's low, rumbling chuckle set the world back in motion.

Sunny seethed.

"You can turn around now," he said after a moment.

She didn't trust him. Not for two seconds. But she wouldn't allow herself to stomp off without her bath—or her pride. Slowly she faced him.

Looking directly and purposely into his eyes, she released her pent-up breath. In her peripheral vision, she caught something black-and-white, lower, near his hips.

His eyes narrowed on her for an instant. "You surprise me." He looked away to scoop up his towel.

As he scrubbed his face with it, Sunny noted that he wore a pair of swim trunks. Then she scoped out his muscular thighs.

"Why do I surprise you?" She cocked her head. "Because I didn't throw myself at you?"

"Hell, no." He laughed, then his face settled into a pensive frown. "You think women throw themselves at me?"

"Don't they?"

He grinned. "Only sometimes."

She glared. If that wasn't his explanation then there was only one left. Sunny's glower faltered as hurt pricked her heart. As annoying as Jesse was, she thought maybe he, of all people, understood her just a little. But obviously he wasn't immune to narrow-mindedness, and she wasn't about to explain to him that flaunting her independence didn't mean she was easy.

"What I meant," he continued, his voice closer, "was that you can look like you stepped off the page of a calendar one minute and the next, well…" He lifted a particularly tangled lock of hair off her shoulder, his gaze wandering down her large T-shirt and scruffy sweatpants.

He hadn't come anywhere near her scalp, yet Sunny could feel tiny prickles all over her head and down her spine. His spicy fragrance whipped through her feeble senses, and she felt her eyes widen in reaction.

He grimaced. "I'm getting myself in trouble, aren't I?" He quickly dropped the thick lock and shoved his hand through his hair.

What? Her thoughts scattered briefly before she realized that he'd probably just verged on insulting her. She hid a smile, inordinately happy that he wasn't like the rest of the men she often came into contact with in modeling. But he didn't have to know that. "I don't understand." She pouted as prettily as she could, considering the mile-long sleep lines she knew creased her face.

"I'd hurry with my bath, if I were you," he said gruffly.

"Why? Do you think I look that bad?" She ignored the threatening grin and perfected the pout.

He peered suspiciously at her, then said, "Not at all." He stepped closer. His chest was within touching distance, the crisp black hairs already drying. The muscle above his left nipple jumped as he started to raise a hand. "Want me to demonstrate what I think?"

Sunny forgot to breathe as she sidestepped him. "What I want is for you to leave." She strolled to the water's edge, slipped off her sneakers and stuck her toe in for a test. It wasn't cold shower, but nevertheless it had an amazing effect.

She heard him moving behind her and hoped he was collecting his things. She lingered, kicking at the water, trying to adjust to the temperature, waiting to hear him leave.

Finally, when she couldn't wait any longer, she turned around.

He was still nearby, though he had moved closer to the tree, where his clothes were heaped over his boots. He'd draped a towel around his neck, but other than that, he still wore only the swim trunks. After rummaging through his things, he straightened and held up something she couldn't quite make out.

"It's not a straightedge," he said, grinning. "But you can still flick my Bic."

Sunny started and nearly lost her balance. Only a small miracle saved her from skidding into the water, though she came close enough that mud oozed between her toes. She looked at the disgusting brown gunk, then raised her eyes to spear him with a haughty look. "I've already told you. The bet is off."

"No," Jesse drawled, shaking his head. "You see, we could've called it off if the bet was still in progress. But I'm not about to accept your charity now." He held up the razor again. "You won fair and square."

"What if I don't want to claim my prize?" She wiggled her muddy foot in the icy water, then backed up and casually glanced at him.

"Then I'd wonder what you're so afraid of."

"Me? Afraid?" Sunny was glad she'd already backed out of harm's way. The low, serious tone of his voice took her by such surprise, she would surely have ended up with something worse than muddy toes. "What an absurd thing to say."

"Is it?" He pulled the towel from around his neck and rubbed his arms and thighs with the white terry cloth. His chest muscles bunched and relaxed with the motion. His biceps swelled to well-defined mounds, and Sunny had to admit to herself that he might have a point.

But she'd be damned if she'd show it. "I'm not afraid of you or anything you can dish out."

"Good." He scratched his jaw, his fingers grating against

the beard-roughened skin. "It was getting kinda itchy, anyway."

Sunny couldn't tell if he was teasing her or not. Did he really expect her to shave him? She padded back to her clothes. "Now if you'll kindly remove your obnoxious hide, I'll have my bath."

He chuckled. "I'll make sure you have your privacy. But keep it short. I suspect the men will start getting down here in the next half hour."

"Fine."

"Call if you need your back scrubbed."

"You'll be the first to know."

He laughed again as he gathered his things and disappeared behind some shrubbery. "I'll be within shouting distance."

She resisted the urge to make him promise not to peek. But even the thought sounded juvenile. Besides, she figured wryly, after the magazine incident nearly two years ago, the idea that she should be so concerned was almost laughable.

Except she was worried. Because Jesse had been right. At some deep level she couldn't quite understand, he scared her half to death.

JESSE WAS SCARING himself. What the devil was he doing messing around here with Sunny when he had nearly five hundred head of cattle to worry about moving out today?

Until he'd seen her this morning, he'd had no intention of taking another bath. He'd already had one last evening, and within two hours he'd be so covered with dust and grime that this bath, a very cold bath, at that, would be no more than a bad memory. Bad because he was courting trouble. Big trouble.

He rubbed his body with the towel until his skin tingled. Not because he was still wet, but because now that he'd had time to think about it, he was freezing. Interestingly, when he'd been with Sunny, he hadn't noticed how cold it was. She was doing strange things to his brain, not to mention someplace a little farther south.

Grimacing, he yanked down the wet swim trunks, toweled

himself dry and pulled on boxers and jeans. He was angry with himself. He knew better than to let lust interfere with work. He'd already been there, done that...and he had two scars to show for it.

Unconsciously, he rubbed the puckered skin above his left shoulder blade, one of the reminders of his wilder, younger days when, just like the song, he'd foolishly looked for love in all the wrong places.

And not once had he found even a shadow of the emotion.

So why, when he damn well knew better, was he playing hide-and-seek with Sunny?

Sure, she was beautiful, but so were the dozens of rodeo queens he'd dated in his younger days and resisted in more recent years. Except Sunny didn't play on her beauty as so many of them had. Hell, he'd never woken up with a woman who hadn't already painted her face for the day. Well, maybe once or twice, but they'd just about dropkicked him out of bed in embarrassment.

He sure couldn't imagine Sunny kicking him out for that reason. But she'd no doubt kick him out for some reason or other, he thought wryly. Then he smiled. He did like her sassy mouth. No coy stuff for her. In fact, she could be a downright fireball.

So why had he startled the daylights out of her earlier? More important, why the devil was he having this conversation with himself? She was off-limits, too much trouble, and in approximately five weeks, she'd be someone else's problem.

And he'd be one step closer to owning his own spread and just maybe a grain of respectability...the respectability his father had lost.

He finished getting dressed, though he left his shirt unbuttoned in anticipation of the shave he'd have Sunny give him. For practical reasons, like not having a mirror, he needed her to fulfill her part of the wager. Yet as he replayed in his mind the brief but panicked look on her face a few minutes ago, he knew that his motives went deeper. Somehow he had spooked her, and if that was how he could keep her at arm's length, then so be it.

Five minutes later, Jesse stuffed a fresh towel, razor and soap into the scuffed leather bag that had seen more towns than most people saw in a lifetime. Then he walked over to the path leading to the spring and listened. He couldn't hear water splashing so he cupped a hand around his mouth and called, "Are you about done?"

"Count to twenty."

Jesse smiled and did as he was told. Twenty-five seconds later, he emerged from the sun-scorched shrubbery and saw her crouched over her things. Instead of changing into the clothes she'd brought with her, she'd slipped into the large white T-shirt, which, although dry, clung to something damp and colorful beneath it around her breasts. The same old gray sweatpants covered her legs.

She looked up as he approached, her hair hanging in long wet ropes around her face. She smiled tentatively as she stood, and he saw that her teeth were chattering.

Without thinking he reached out and cupped her upper arms with his hands. He ran his palms down her bare arms and back up, snuggling under her sleeves against the soft, toned flesh... What the hell was he doing?

He stepped away and threw her the fresh towel. With wide, astonished eyes, she caught it and clasped it to her breasts. "Put that around your shoulders," he said gruffly.

She did as he suggested, her chin lifting in the process.

"You should have changed," he said, "It's too cold to stay wet." He held out the razor.

She eyed the piece of blue plastic for several long seconds, the expression on her face telling him plainly that she was considering bolting. Then she shrugged and said, "Okay, it's your face." As she plucked the razor from his hand, the corners of her mouth turned up.

"No funny stuff," he warned, twisting around to grab a tin pan he'd left near the tree. "We'll use this to catch the soapy water. No use polluting the spring any more than we have to."

"You're the boss."

Yeah. Right. He slid her a glance as he dipped the pan into the water. She was smiling. He didn't like it. But he made no comment as he carried the pan to a couple of stumps near the tree. He kicked at first one stump, then another. Once he was assured that one was sturdy enough to hold him, he sat down and spread his legs.

"Come here," he said, patting one thigh. He was pleased to see her smile waver.

She gave her head an extra-hard toss, but her hair was wet and didn't move far. He grinned, while pretending to steady the pan of water on his leg.

"How are we supposed to do this?" Sunny hung back, eyeing the setup with obvious misgiving.

"You stand right here." He pointed to the spot between his legs. "That should put you at about the right level." His gaze briefly skittered to her T-shirt where it clung to the wet bra beneath it. He cleared his throat. "Hurry up. We haven't got all day." He plunged the bar of soap into the water and savagely lathered his face.

She huffed in irritation and, squaring her shoulders, stepped forward. But not before she gave one quick, hopeful glance toward the path. Jesse half wished someone else would show up, too. He was setting himself up, he realized, under the guise of pushing her away.

But here she was, stepping into his personal space, and he'd be damned if he'd give up the heady sensation her nearness was causing. He tilted his head, presenting her with his chin and fixing his stare safely above her right shoulder.

Her soft fingers hesitated as she touched his jaw and angled his face to a better position so she could reach his neck. "I've never done this before," she whispered.

"Just stroke upward," he said.

When he tilted his head farther to accommodate her, his eyes met hers. She blinked, then lowered her gaze to his mouth. When he smiled, she blinked again and jerked the razor up the length of his throat.

"Ouch!"

"Sorry," she mumbled.

"Try to make it a straight sweep, will you?"

"If you don't like the way I do it, you can do it yourself."

"Now, now. I bet you don't shave your legs like this."

"My legs don't feel like buffalo hide." She shook the razor in the water, letting soap and water fly all over his jeans.

He grinned. "Felt up many buffalo, have you?"

"Don't move...or I may slip."

"Don't be such a poor sport."

"Poor sport? I won the bet, so why do I feel like the loser?"

"I don't know. You're the one who wanted to see how I looked shaved."

Gaping at him, Sunny stepped back and dropped the hand holding the razor to her side. "I never said... I don't care how you... I merely said..."

"Come on." Jesse wrapped an arm around her thighs and pulled her closer again. "No breaks until you're finished."

She stumbled forward under the unexpected pressure of his grasp and caught his shoulder with one hand. Once she was steady, she leaned down and took another swipe at his chin.

"Ouch! Would you be careful?"

"I'm doing the best I can."

Sure she was. He squinted at her smug smile. "Let me show you." He closed a hand over hers and gently stroked the razor under his chin. Her hand felt small, fragile, especially for someone as tall as she was. The wariness was back in her eyes, the same wariness he'd seen earlier when she thought he was naked.

"Okay, I got it." She stubbornly stilled her hand.

He ignored her protest and guided her through another motion up the underside of his chin. "It's all in the angle and the amount of pressure you use." His thumb glided along her wrist. "The length of the stroke."

Her eyes met his and widened slightly. Her lower lip quivered and drooped open. Then her mouth scrunched up and her eyes narrowed to angry slits. "All right, that does it." She jumped back so fast, Jesse had to tighten his hold on her wrist to keep from falling off the stump.

"What?" He grimaced as a wave splashed over the side of the pan onto his crotch.

"Let go of me."

"Not until you tell me what's wrong."

"You know damn well what's—" She sighed. "I need to go help Maria and Violet with breakfast, Jesse. Can't you do this yourself?"

He'd never heard her say his name before. Sure, in a fit of temper she'd said Jesse Logan all in one breath. But he'd never heard her say just his first name, all soft and breathless. Nor had he seen the way her lips pursed around the *J,* like she was getting ready to kiss him.

He released her. "Go ahead. Get out of here."

She hesitated, rubbing the wrist he'd dropped. "Jesse?"

His gaze darted away from her mouth. "Yeah?" He stood, concentrating on balancing the pan of water on the stump.

"I don't want to fight with you."

He shrugged and slid her a quick glance. "Who's fighting?"

Her mouth twisted wryly. "Okay. But I don't want anything else, either."

"Such as?"

She took a step back, one shoulder rising slightly. "Any complications."

"You've lost me."

She made an exasperated sound, as if she thought he was being deliberately obtuse. Which, of course, he was. He wanted her to spell out what she thought was happening, because he sure as hell didn't know. None of his actions made sense. He knew better, yet here he was flirting with trouble.

When he didn't elaborate, she said, "I need to make this trip. Rainy and Cash have a huge stake in the outcome."

"You think I don't know that? Everyone involved has a big stake. I have a big stake. Besides, Cash is my friend."

Sunny shook her head. "I'm not discounting that. But Rainy needs me." Her face lit up. "She needs me to do this for her.

They're banking on this drive being a success and becoming an annual event. Rainy thinks then maybe Cash—'' She looked away. ''Rainy needs me and I'm not letting her down.''

Jesse watched as steely determination darkened her eyes. She didn't look so flaky right now. Beneath the artificial fluff, he saw an earnest young woman with beautiful brown eyes, long wet hair and a fierce loyalty that Jesse would never be gifted with in this lifetime.

He stooped, scooped up her things, then shoved them at her. ''Get out of here, Sunny. Right now.''

Chapter Eight

After three days on the trail, Sunny was on her last change of clothes. She'd nearly torn both wagons apart looking for her suitcases and had finally accepted the fact that someone dumped them before the drive began.

And from the strategic and irritating smirks on Jesse's face, she had little doubt just who the responsible party was.

Each morning at breakfast, he'd given her the once-over, and that same smile would blossom to the size of a sunflower. Yet she'd not said a word to him. In fact, after their encounter at the spring three mornings ago, she'd stayed away from him as best she could. Which had been pretty easy to do, because he seemed to be doing his best to ignore her, too.

She still wasn't sure what had happened that day. Although at the time she'd thought he might have been coming on to her, the minute she'd walked away she wasn't so sure. She met so many jerks in her line of work, she could be horribly cynical at times. And then again, she admitted wryly, it could have been her overwrought hormones giving her the wrong idea. The man definitely had appeal. For women who liked that type, anyway.

Definitely not her. She was happy to stay clear of him. Although a couple of times in desperation she had been tempted to ask him about her luggage. She was so tired of the short, impractical skirts she'd been forced to wear, she could scream.

She glanced at the denim-and-spandex number she wore today and sighed. Why had she allowed her so-called friends to help outfit her? They were all a bunch of Yankee models, for heaven's sake. What did they know about a cattle drive? Hell, what did she know?

"You gonna sigh all the way to Sparks, or are you gonna keep me company?" Maria turned to her. While the woman's attention was diverted from the trail, the wagon bumped over a bed of rocks.

Every bone in Sunny's body rattled as she bounced out of her seat. When she settled down, her skirt edged up an inch higher on her thigh. A pale strip of skin showed just below the hem. The rest of her legs looked red in comparison—and heaven only knew where her sunscreen was.

Maria's gaze traveled from Sunny's legs to her face. "You better get back in the wagon again. You're starting to burn. Your cheeks are red, too."

"I'm okay," she said, even though she could feel the sting. She studied the other woman's brown, weathered face. Not even a hint of pink, although today the sky was totally cloudless. "Doesn't the sun bother you?"

"Nah. Though I do plan to buy some sunscreen for Ana when we get to Sparks." She glanced at Sunny. "And a hat. In fact…" She kept her eyes on the trail but leaned toward the interior of the wagon. "Hey, Ana, give Ms. Daye the hat while you're in there."

Ana poked her head out. She pulled the hat from her head and plunked it on Sunny's. The hat dipped low over Sunny's eyes and Ana laughed.

"You think that's funny." Sunny slowly twisted around. She gave Ana a menacing look then started walking two fingers toward the child, who shrieked in anticipation. When Sunny tickled her, Ana squealed with laughter, kicking and writhing until she ended up sprawled across Sunny's lap. She cried uncle as Sunny had taught her to do two days ago and Sunny finally let up.

"When's dinner?" Ana asked, reclining into a comfortable position against her new friend.

"When we get to Sparks," Maria said.

Ana groaned. "When's that?"

Sunny lifted the hat off her head and returned it to Ana's. "In about two hours." She turned her wrist so that her watch faced the child. "What time will that be?"

While Ana frowned in concentration, Maria smiled. "You're good with kids."

"Me?" Sunny pulled a face, then poked Ana gently in the back, making a buzzing sound. "Time's up."

Ana giggled. "Six-thirty."

Sunny whooped, whistled and stomped her feet. "Right on the button."

Ana dissolved into a fresh round of giggles. "Mama, can I have a watch when we get to Sparks?"

Maria's expression tightened. "No, Ana. I need to buy you a hat."

"Can't I have a watch, too?" She stuck out her chin. "I need a watch since I know how to tell time now."

"No, Ana. You can't." Maria snapped the reins.

Sunny didn't say anything. She wasn't certain, but from what she'd gathered, Maria and her husband were strapped for money. Maybe she shouldn't have taught Ana how to tell time. What did she know about children? She should have minded her own business.

After several minutes of Maria's silence and Ana's sulking, Sunny said, "Aren't you excited about being in a real town tonight?"

"I guess so," Ana said without enthusiasm.

"I'm glad we don't have to cook," Maria said, sounding more eager.

Sunny grinned. Trying not to disturb Ana, she reached into the wagon and pulled a piece of paper out of her bag. She unfolded it, then scanned the page. "The town-sponsored barbecue is tonight. Tomorrow morning I give an interview to the local paper. Then the rodeo is scheduled to begin at ten." She stopped and sighed with delight. "Can you believe it? Two whole days without hearing…" She lowered her voice and her chin, furrowing her brow in a deep frown. "Head 'em up and move 'em out."

She did such an accurate imitation of Jesse that both Ana and Maria burst into laughter.

"You're so funny," Ana said and proceeded to mimic Sunny mimicking Jesse. After she got the desired laugh out of both women she said, "I bet Uncle Jesse could copy you good." She stuck a bony finger at Sunny's chest.

"Why?" Sunny wiggled her finger under Ana's arm.

Ana squirmed and giggled and between breaths said, "Because he's always watching you."

Maria and Sunny exchanged quick glances. But neither woman joined the laughing child.

JESSE PULLED the bandanna up from around his neck to cover his mouth. He'd hate to see an X ray of his lungs at the moment. Not only was today a scorcher, but a warm wind had whipped up from the west and was playing havoc with the dirt being kicked up by the longhorns.

He didn't think anyone on this drive was going to enjoy a real shower tonight more than he would. Then he remembered Sunny…as if he could have forgotten her in the first place.

He'd made a point of staying away from her for the past few days, but that didn't mean he could steer his thoughts clear of her. He even attributed the crazy dream he'd had last night to Sunny. He wasn't quite sure how it related to her, except he hadn't dreamed of his family's ranch in over a decade. And now, of all times, the depressing dreams were recurring…after he'd spent an hour staring up at the black, star-studded sky, thinking of her.

Although the wagons had no need to maintain a lead in order to set up for dinner, Jesse had told them to stay ahead of the herd to escape any unnecessary dust. He could barely see them and decided to go tell them to slow down. They needed to arrive in Sparks all at the same time.

The women sat in stony silence as he rode up alongside them. He'd hoped Maria would get along better with their PR person. He slipped the bandanna from his mouth to around his neck and asked, "How's it going?"

"Okay." Maria nodded. "We figure we'll be arriving in town in about an hour."

"Yeah. We're making good time today. Everyone must be anxious for a real bed to sleep in."

Sunny, who'd ignored him until now, sat up straighter and stared at him. "A real bed?"

He grinned. Then he noticed the red staining her cheeks and nose, and his lips thinned. "Where the hell is your hat?" He'd tried so hard to ignore her in the past few days that he couldn't remember if he'd ever seen her with one. Though they had been traveling with the sun behind them until today. "Didn't Rainy tell you to bring a hat?"

"What do you mean real bed?"

"In fact, don't you have enough sense to wear one?" Jesse asked.

Maria opened her mouth to speak, but Sunny laid a hand on her arm. "I'll take care of it when we get to Sparks."

"So, you didn't have enough sense." Angrily, he shook his head.

"If I thought it was any of your business, you'd be the first to know," Sunny said breezily, though he could tell she was simmering below the surface. "Now tell me about the bed."

"If you get sun poisoning and require medical treatment, you don't think that would be my business?"

She rolled her eyes. "I'm not going to get sun poisoning."

The longer he looked at her, the redder her face seemed to get. Then he noticed her legs. They were red, too. Painfully red, unless he missed his guess. "You didn't even bring sunscreen, did you?"

"Would you lower your voice? You're going to wake Ana." She scowled at him.

"A hat is simple enough, Sunny." He looked at the loose topknot and the flyaway blond tendrils she'd favored since the first day. "Or are you afraid it'll mess up your hair?"

Maria started to speak again but Sunny cut in. "Yeah. That's it.'' She faced straight ahead while making a shooing motion with her hand. ''Now, unless you want to tell us about the bed, beat it.''

Maria chuckled. Jesse fumed. He'd never been shooed in his life...and certainly not by a woman.

''Start slowing down, Maria. Let the rest of us catch up with you before we get to Sparks.''

Maria barely had a chance to nod before Jesse turned and galloped toward the herd.

Why was it so impossible for them to have a decent conversation? She was too doggone stubborn, that's why. He let out a string of obscenities that made the horse whinny.

He'd gotten halfway back before his good sense returned and he slowed down. It was totally unnecessary to have ridden the animal the way he'd just done. Tugging the reins, he brought Thunder to a stop.

''Sorry, boy.'' He leaned forward and stroked the horse's heated neck. ''Just because she makes me crazy doesn't mean I have to take it out on you.''

Jesse twisted in his saddle and watched the wagon amble off. He ought to leave her in Sparks, is what he ought to do. She distracted him, and that was trouble.

Then that day at the spring flashed in his mind. This drive was important to her. Although he sure didn't understand her reasoning. Cash and Rainy's stake in the drive was protected. The name of their ranch was being nationally identified as a sponsor. Their advance work alone had earned them a valuable place at the table. Sunny's presence hardly seemed necessary, other than securing Rainy's spot as PR person if the drive was to take place again next year. He understood that notion to some degree.

He shook his head. He just didn't understand Sunny. Peering over the prairie, he watched the hovering cloud of dust that signaled the herd's approach. The air was so hot, the scenery seemed to melt together like some abstract painting. Jesse lifted his hat and plowed his hair off his forehead. The sun beat down on his crown.

"Son of a—" Jesse bit back the words as Thunder twisted to look at him. "I know, boy." He patted the horse one last time, then nudged him with his spur. "I'm a damn fool." As if he understood, Thunder automatically turned and headed for the wagon.

As Jesse had asked, Maria and Violet had slowed down considerably, and he caught up with them in minutes. He waved to Violet and Slim, one of the young hands riding with her, as he passed them several yards behind Maria and Sunny's wagon. Then he skirted around to Sunny's side of the wagon until he caught a glimpse of her profile. She didn't see him at first, and he frowned, watching her laugh, playing with Ana, tugging the large, frilly brown hat over the child's eyes and poking her in the ribs until she squealed with delight.

Then Sunny spotted him, and all pleasure vanished from her face...her very red, sunburned face.

Jesse exhaled loudly. They were never going to get along. He guided Thunder nearer to the wagon. Maria had slowed down when she'd seen him, so it was a piece of cake for him to get within arm's reach. He pulled off his Stetson, stretched up and tossed it on Sunny's head. Her hand shot up to catch the hat, and it ended up at an angle, stuck between her palm and her topknot.

"Put it on," he said. "It'll protect your face." When she opened her mouth, he tugged on the reins. Then he galloped away before she could confirm what a damn fool he really was.

"Now, I want you all to remember that you represent this cattle drive," Jesse was telling the entire crew as they set up camp just outside Sparks. "Anything you do here reflects on each and every one of us and the people paying our salaries. By all means have a good time, but please, be on your best behavior."

Sunny didn't appreciate the way he looked pointedly at her when he'd said the best-behavior part. What did he think she was going to do? Thanks to him, most of her time was going to be spent buying new clothes. Of course, she wouldn't admit that to him. She still hadn't given him any sign that she was ticked about her suitcases having disappeared. And if she wasn't so darn uncomfortable in the tight, short skirts she'd been forced to wear all week, she'd be sorely tempted to buy more of the same just to irritate him.

"Do you all understand? Any questions?" Jesse asked the murmuring cowboys.

She hadn't heard a word he'd said in the last minute, not that she thought he had anything important to say. She sniffed, the action making her nose burn. Gingerly she touched the tip of her nose. It was hot to the touch.

"Yeah, I got a question." Smiley stepped forward. "When are you sendin' the ol' bat packin' back to Maybe?"

Violet stepped up behind Smiley and leaned toward him, her face getting nearly as red as her hair. "I didn't hear you complain when you wolfed down my barbecued beans or my apple cobbler, you ol' coot."

Jesse let out a sound of disgust. "Will you two stop it? You've been fine all week. What's the problem now?"

"That she devil—" Smiley hitched a thumb toward Violet without looking at her "—has some dang-fool notion that she can already start gittin' people to vote for her chili at the Swing Festival this summer."

Hoots of laughter were heard from several of the cowboys acquainted with the couple's long-standing feud over the chili cook off.

Violet glanced guiltily at Maria, then glared at Smiley. "If you're gonna eavesdrop, get it right."

"I don't get it at all," Jesse said wearily.

"Ain't your moonshine good enough anymore to steal votes from my entry?" Smiley shouted.

"No one needs to steal votes from you. The taste of your pathetic chili scares votes away."

"Wait a minute, Smiley," Sunny said, remembering the one Swing Festival she'd attended. "You'll be on the trail this summer. You won't even be entering the contest this year."

Smiley frowned as the truth sank in. He raised a hand to

scratch the stray gray whiskers on his jaw. He suddenly looked old and tired.

Violet laughed. "That's right. Not that you were ever any competition."

Except Sunny saw the hint of regret that crossed the older woman's face as she lapsed into silence. The unconscious look the elderly couple exchanged was almost heart-wrenching.

Jesse put up a hand. "Do you have to argue about this now? Can we get along at least for publicity purposes?" He lowered his voice as he glanced at the approaching townspeople.

A tear sprang up out of nowhere and Sunny had to blink it back. Rainy hadn't had to tell her about their years of unrequited love. Sunny had seen the tension between them firsthand. She didn't think Jesse had to worry about them arguing right now. The fight had deserted them. Why did some people ruin their lives by being so stubborn?

"I think you ought to come with me to meet the mayor," Jesse said close to her ear. She started, then turned to look at him. A ridge marked his hair where his Stetson had been, then she remembered she was still wearing his hat. "Then we'd better go get something for your sunburn."

She pulled off the hat and stood on tiptoe to settle it on his head. "Let me worry about that."

She made the mistake of looking at him when she was too close. His eyes roamed her face, then came to rest on her mouth. She moistened her parched lips, released the hat and stepped back.

"Why do you have to be so damn stubborn?" His gaze moved from her lips to her eyes as he adjusted the Stetson in place.

Stubborn? Her? "You have enough to do. I can take care of myself."

"Sure." He grinned.

She frowned, and her whole face hurt. "Thanks for the use of your hat."

"Sure," he repeated.

Strangers converged on them. A short plump man wearing

a Western string tie, a white shirt and brand-new blue jeans identified himself as the mayor. Jesse and Sunny stepped aside with him as groups of men, women and children milled around the wagons and asked the cowboys questions.

The mayor seemed anxious to get on with his own sight-seeing and quickly gave them details on the barbecue starting at seven-thirty.

Sunny glanced at her watch. She had forty-five minutes. "I'll see you at dinner," she told Jesse as soon as the mayor stepped away.

"Wait a minute. Don't you—"

She disappeared into the crowd before he could ask her any questions. She desperately needed something fresh to wear to-night, and she needed a shower. She knew there was a motel on the outskirts of town. Maria had pointed it out on the way in. And Jesse had said something about a bed. Maybe they were actually going to have a real shower, a real bed, a solid roof over their heads. Her entire body quivered with excitement.

And how pathetic was that? she asked herself as she grabbed her purse from the wagon and hustled into town, her pink, rhinestone-studded boots slipping and sliding in her haste to make use of every minute.

But as soon as she got to the string of buildings comprising the town of Sparks, she knew she'd hurried for nothing. Disappointment coated her along with layers of dust. The place wasn't exactly booming. As far as she could tell, only three storefronts looked like possible candidates for clothes shopping. She tried the yellow, aluminum-sided building first.

The salesclerk was pleasant and helpful, but all Sunny could find were seven pairs of underwear, all pink, each indicating a day of the week in black script. She shook her head, feeling like she was in a time warp. She hadn't seen anything like it since she was ten years old. Not in a position to be choosy, she took them, and after paying the clerk she wandered to the next store where the saleswoman had assured her she would find more than underwear, socks, hammers and nails.

But not much more, Sunny soon discovered. If she'd wanted

to sew her own clothes, the store had a beautiful assortment of fabric, she thought glumly. And housecoats that were a mile wide. She was, however, able to pick up a treat for Ana and a hot tip that there was one more place where she could find T-shirts, jeans and shorts.

She left the shade of the sundry store and took another look at her watch. Twenty more minutes. She supposed it wouldn't matter if she was late for the barbecue. No one would miss her. Lord knew there were enough people who were going to be there. In fact, it seemed as though everyone had deserted the town in favor of checking out the cattle drive.

Only two pickups and a car were parked on the street. An older woman busily swept the sidewalk on the opposite side of Main Street, and Sunny didn't see another soul. Until she got to the end of the strip. Then she saw two young women near the truck-stop diner. Right beyond that stood the ugly, sight-for-sore-eyes pink motel.

Sunny wasn't sure which excited her more, the motel or the two women who looked like they had a good deal more fashion sense than to wear mile-wide housecoats. Surely they'd steer her in the right direction. As she got closer, squinting against the sun's glare, she realized that she might have slightly over-estimated the situation.

The shorter one, whose platinum blond hair hung limp around her shoulders, wore a skirt even shorter and tighter than Sunny's. When she turned around, Sunny saw that the black blouse the woman wore was see-through and that she was bra-less. If it wasn't for the woman's pink, glittering suspenders, Sunny would have seen a whole lot more than she cared to. And fishnet stockings? Pink, no less. Who wore those anymore?

Too late, Sunny realized she had gotten too close. "Hi," she offered with a tentative smile.

The blonde eyed her with a frown and said nothing. The redhead sized her up pretty thoroughly, too, and said, "How ya doin', sugar?" She pulled her skintight, stretchy top away from her body and blew into her pumped-up cleavage. "Sure is hot for April, ain't it?"

Sunny nodded. "Yeah."

"You must be new," the blonde stated.

New at what? Sunny had a sudden feeling she knew the answer to that and swallowed. "I'm just passing through."

"How quick?" the blonde demanded.

"Uh, you know that cattle drive." Sunny pointed in a direction she hoped was remotely close to the camp. She never knew where to point in cases like this. North was always in front of her, as far as she was concerned.

Both women looked off with mild interest in the direction Sunny's finger guided them. "Cattle drive?" The redhead frowned.

"All right. I've had it with you." The voice came from somewhere behind Sunny's left shoulder. All heads turned in that direction. A uniformed man with a shiny badge approached them.

"Oh, shit," the blonde muttered. "I can't afford another bust."

"Relax, you two," the redhead said under her breath. "I'll take care of this." The woman smiled. "Why, Buford, sugar, it's so nice to see you again."

"It's Beaufort, *Sheriff* Beaufort to you, Mildred." The man was as tall as a bear and just as wide, and he towered over the three of them without a hint of a smile.

Mildred? Women like her didn't have names like Mildred. Sunny shrunk back a step.

"Well, since I have such a difficult time rememberin', I'll just call you sugar." Mildred ran a long red nail down the sheriff's shirtfront. He didn't look pleased.

Sunny glanced at her own red nails and tucked them behind her back.

"Well, you see, Mildred, it's like this. If you'd stayed the hell away from my truck stop, you wouldn't have to remember my name at all." The sheriff reached behind him.

Sunny took another step back. Wrong move. Beaufort turned

his angry blue eyes on her. "Where do you think you're going?"

"Well, actually..." She laughed, the sound brittle in her ears, as she spread a hand toward the women. "I'm not with them."

"Right," he said, and slapped the cuffs around her wrists.

Chapter Nine

"Hey, your name is Sunny?" The blonde stopped chomping her gum and grinned as she, Mildred and Sunny stood in the sheriff's office being booked by his deputy. "Mine, too."

Sunny's eyes widened on the woman. Terrific. Didn't anybody have a name they were supposed to have?

"It's short for Sunshine, and I spell it with an *i*." She blew a pink bubble. "And I always put a little heart over it instead of a dot."

Sunny twisted toward the sheriff, who was unlocking the cell doors. "I really need to speak with you, Sheriff Beaufort."

He ignored her, swinging the jail door back and forth, listening to it squeak. "Earl, remind me to oil this thing, will ya?" he said to the deputy. Then he transferred his steely gaze to her. "After Earl books y'all, you each get one phone call."

"I don't need a phone call." She sighed. Who would she call, anyway? The last thing she needed was for Jesse to get wind of this. "I can straighten this out myself."

"Can you, now?" The sheriff stuck his thumbs in his gun belt and lifted both his chins.

"Yes." She sighed again, this time with some relief. This was the first opportunity he'd given her to explain. "I am not what you think." She slid an apologetic look to Mildred and Sunni with an *i*. "I'd never even seen these women before you p-picked us up."

Mildred sashayed over from being processed. "She's right,

sugar. I've never seen her before.'' As Mildred checked her reflection in the glass of the wall clock, Sunny shot the sheriff a triumphant look. Then Mildred added, ''She must be new to the business.''

Sunny snorted. ''I'm not in the business.''

The sheriff ushered Mildred into the first cell and locked the door. With a half grin, he looked Sunny up and down. ''Then what kind of business are you in?''

Sunny puffed out her cheeks. She could explain about being with the cattle drive, except that he'd probably check it out and Jesse would find out what had happened. She wasn't quite sure if her ego was up to that scenario. She eyed the remaining empty cell. At least it had a real honest-to-goodness bed. Plus, the place was air-conditioned. She craned her neck to look down the short hall past the cells, wondering if there was a shower back there.

''You can't stand there all day. Git in,'' the sheriff bellowed. Sunny jumped at the sound of his voice. He held the barred door wide, and she reluctantly moved forward.

''Okay, wait a minute.'' She swallowed. ''I'm with the cattle drive.''

The sheriff narrowed his eyes on her for a moment, took another look at her clothing, then burst into laughter. His deputy joined him.

Oh, God. They were going to check her story. ''Look, we just pulled into town. I left the group to do some shopping.'' She pointed to the brown paper bag they had confiscated. ''If you go find someone named Violet or Maria, she can verify who I am.''

Sheriff Beaufort's chuckle died down as he studied her panicked face. ''What would you be doing with that drive?''

''I'm their PR person.''

''Where are you from?''

''Michigan.''

He frowned, but when he glanced at her boots, he nodded. ''Earl, go take a ride over there, will ya? Find out if anyone knows this gal.''

"Not anyone. Violet or Maria," Sunny said.

"Sure thing, boss." Earl reached for his battered Stetson, strapped his holster around his hips and headed for the door. "Be right back."

"Violet or Maria," Sunny called again and wrapped both hands around the cold metal bars. Please not Jesse.

HE WAS going to kill her. Or maybe when his temper subsided, he'd send her back to Maybe instead. Nah, he needed to actually feel his fingers wrapped around Sunny's lovely neck, Jesse decided, flexing his hands as he sat in the passenger seat of the deputy's car.

Hadn't he just warned everyone to be on their best behavior? When the deputy had approached him at the barbecue, somehow he knew the law officer's business had something to do with her highness. The woman was a trouble magnet.

And now here he was in a cop car, of all the damn places. Just about the last place Jesse wanted or needed to be. He adjusted the cool-air vents and took a deep, steadying breath.

"Sheriff Beaufort is gonna be real surprised she was tellin' the truth." The deputy chuckled. "She don't look like she belongs on any cattle drive. 'Course, she looks damn good, all the same." The young man managed to make his voice sound like a leer.

Jesse merely smiled, when what he wanted to do was smash the guy's face in. Except someone in Jesse's position could hardly afford to antagonize the local heat. He loosened his shirt collar.

The deputy parked his car in front of the small, brick office and led his passenger inside.

Jesse spotted the two strange women first. They were standing near their cell door, filing their nails and taunting an older man Jesse presumed was the sheriff.

When the tall redhead saw him, she asked the deputy, "Where'd you find that one, Earl?" A slow smile curved her ruby lips. "Just toss him right in here with me, sugar."

Jesse ignored her. In the next cell he saw Sunny sitting on

the narrow twin bed glaring at him. He did a double take. Where the devil did she get off being angry with him?

"This is the trail boss, Jesse..." The deputy turned to Jesse. "What'd you say your last name was?"

The sheriff peered at Jesse, then glanced at Earl. "Hell, boy, don't you know who this is?"

Jesse's heart slid to his toes.

"Jesse James. The Outlaw." The sheriff grinned at him, then slapped him so hard on the back, Jesse had to dig in his heels. "I saw you break a bull at the Coon County rodeo four years back. Ain't seen nothing like it since. You were poetry, son, pure poetry."

"Thanks." Relieved, Jesse gave him a weak grin.

"Excuse me." Sunny stood and crossed her arms over her chest.

Sheriff Beaufort slowly swung his gaze toward her. "Well, son, do you know this gal?"

Jesse didn't answer at first. As the silence stretched, she squirmed. He merely rocked back and enjoyed the view.

A pretty amusing view, too, he decided. Her hair was more down than up, and whatever was left of the original pinup job hung at a comical angle from the side of her head. If at all possible, her face had grown redder in the past minute.

"Jesse?" Her voice was a thinly veiled threat.

Tough. She deserved to squirm, he told himself, but when he saw her shoulders slump and noticed that she seemed unsteady on her feet, he gave in. "Yeah, I know her."

"My, oh, my, Sunny." The redhead poked her nose between the bars and sized Jesse up more thoroughly. "None of my tricks..." Her voice trailed off and she glanced at the sheriff. She cleared her throat. "That is, none of my business associates look like him."

Beaufort gave Mildred a dry look, then turned to Jesse. "She's really with the drive, huh?"

Jesse nodded, although he was sure his reluctance showed, especially when he heard a low growl coming from Sunny's cell.

Shaking his head, the sheriff picked up a large key ring, unlocked Sunny's cell and stood back as she walked out. "For God's sake, young lady, git yourself some decent boots."

Sunny's chin lifted several cool degrees as she strolled past the sheriff. She stopped at the desk and faced the deputy sitting there. "My purse and bag, please."

Earl handed them to her with a wolfish grin, which she ignored. She started toward the door, then paused and gave the other two women a crooked smile. "Take care, Mildred. See ya, Sunni."

Jesse looked at the sheriff and frowned. *Sunni?* The sheriff grimaced and mouthed, "Don't ask."

"You, too, sugar." The redhead sighed and went back to filing her nails.

The blonde blew a huge pink bubble and wiggled her fingers.

Jesse shook his head as he watched Sunny reach for the doorknob without so much as a look back. She obviously had no intention of waiting for him. "Well, Sheriff." Jesse stuck out his hand. "Thanks for everything. Sorry about the trouble."

Sunny paused, but only for second, then she was out the door, letting it slam.

Sheriff Beaufort shook Jesse's hand. "No problem. Earl can give you two a ride back."

"That's okay." Hurrying, Jesse jerked the door open. He had a feeling a knock-down-drag-out fight was in the making, and it would be better if they walked back in private. Besides, hanging around the sheriff's office was giving him the willies. "So long, Sheriff." He touched the brim of his hat. "Deputy."

By the time he got outside, she was already half a block away. She must have been moving. Although how she covered that much ground so fast in those silly pink things he couldn't figure. He grinned, thinking of the look on her face when the sheriff had told her to get decent boots.

"Hey, your highness, wait up." He jogged up beside her.

She kept her face forward, her posture perfectly straight. She didn't even blink. She just kept moving at a clip he almost had trouble keeping up with.

He was about to head her off when he heard someone yell from behind.

"Hey, Outlaw."

Jesse turned to find Sheriff Beaufort sticking his head out the door. "You riding in the rodeo tomorrow?" the man asked.

Jesse took several quick breaths. He was used to the name Outlaw, but hearing a man in uniform say it was a little too unnerving. "Not tomorrow," he called.

"Damn shame." Beaufort shook his head and ducked inside.

Jesse let out a whoosh of air and turned to catch up to Sunny. She'd made it another half a block without slowing down.

"Come on, Sunny." He touched her arm when he finally reached her. She slid him a tentative glance. "Aren't you going to tell me the going rate?"

Her mouth dropped open. "Screw you."

He grinned. "That's what I'm talking about."

She made a low rumbling sound under her breath and kept walking.

Jesse laughed so hard he fell behind. He wiped the tears from his eyes and caught up to her. "Don't tell me you didn't expect some ribbing over this?"

She exhaled loudly. "What I expected was for you to stick up for me."

"I got you out, didn't I?"

She stopped and faced him. "Yeah. Then you apologized to them for the trouble." Briefly she closed her eyes, and her shoulders sagged. "I didn't do anything wrong. They made the mistake."

"Hell, Sunny." He shoved a hand through his hair. Why did he suddenly feel like crap? She was the one who'd screwed up. And he'd had to go to the sheriff's office to put things right. Some of his earlier anger returned. "Maybe if you didn't dress like a hooker, you wouldn't be mistaken for one. Ever think of that?"

Her face fell. She opened her mouth, then closed it again.

He'd really done it now. She looked hurt. Shaking her head, she started walking again.

Jesse hung back for a moment. He decided he preferred the old, feisty Sunny better. That he could handle. He caught up to her again. "What's the matter, your highness? No smart-ass remark?"

She blinked a couple of times, then turned on him. By the look on her face, he knew she was about to tear into him. He almost sighed with relief.

"It's called fashion, you idiot." She jabbed his chest with her finger. "But what the hell would you know? I'll tell you something else, buster. The only hooking I'm guilty of is hooking up with a bunch of hicks like you." With one last scathing look, she marched off again.

He grinned. This was more like it. "Fashion, huh?"

Without looking at him, she threw out her hands, gazed at the sky, and said, "On top of everything, this is all your fault."

Frowning, Jesse looked toward the heavens, too. "Who?"

"You."

"This ought to be good. How do you figure that?"

"My suitcases." She pinned him with a glare worthy of a mad bull entering the ring. "Where are they?"

"Gee, I don't know." He used every ounce of willpower he possessed to keep a grin off his face. "Aren't they back at your sister's ranch?"

She stopped again and crossed her arms, defeat written all over her face. "They are, aren't they?"

"Isn't that where they're supposed to be?"

"You're a real jerk, you know that?"

"So I've been told."

"Apparently not enough." She started toward the camp, but he grabbed her arm.

"Just out of curiosity, what does that have to do with your getting arrested?" he asked.

"Well, Einstein, since I haven't had a change of clothes all week, what else did you expect me to wear?"

"You mean what you have packed in the suitcases would have been more appropriate?"

She looked away for a moment. "Yeah."

"Sure."

She shook off his hold. "Besides, the only reason I was in town was to buy some jeans."

He sighed. "And the stores are closed now."

"What a surprise. Hicksville has rolled up the sidewalks for the night."

"Okay, Sunny, for the sake of the drive, if nothing else, let's put this behind us." He was genuinely sorry that she hadn't gotten to do some shopping. Especially if lotion for her sunburn was on her list. "The sheriff may have been wrong in arresting you, but you can't go around calling this place Hicksville."

"I know." She nodded, a small, sad movement. She stared at him for a long, uncomfortable minute, her lips pressed firmly together. "You're right. The drive is what's important." She sighed deeply. "So I guess you win."

This time she smiled, but somehow managed to look twice as sad. "Tomorrow I'll head back to Maybe."

A SHOWER had never felt as good as the one Sunny had just taken. She lay on the motel bed and stared at the chipped ceiling. As angry as she'd been with Jesse an hour ago, she couldn't be more grateful now for the room he'd had waiting for her.

For tonight and tomorrow night, anyone on the drive who wanted a room was free to rent one instead of sleeping on bedrolls or in the wagons as they'd done for the past five days. For Sunny the decision was a no-brainer—as if that wasn't clear to everyone. She smiled, thinking of how Jesse hadn't bothered to ask her if she wanted a room.

Then she thought about her suitcases, back at Rainy's ranch. As irritated as she was with Jesse for his sabotage, her selfishness made her cringe. The wagons barely had enough room for the supplies and cots as it was, let alone four extra pieces of luggage. Knowing that, she admitted that if Jesse hadn't discovered her stash, someone else would have.

Not that she had to worry about any of this, she considered ruefully. In a moment of weakness she'd announced that she was going back to Maybe. And it wasn't her imagination that Jesse's eyes had lit up like a damn Christmas tree. Had she really been that much trouble?

Sunny scooted back on the bed and bunched a pillow under her head. She truly hadn't been any trouble. She was certain— almost certain, anyway. In fact, Violet and Maria had both claimed she'd been a lot of help. She kept Ana busy and even tutored her when Maria was too tired.

Most of the time she'd enjoyed pitching in. She knew she was going to miss the noon scramble to get lunch ready, the nightly storytelling when each cowboy tried to outdo the other. Although visiting with Rainy would be a treat.

Oh, God. Sunny buried her face in the pillow. How was she going to explain all this to Rainy? She was probably the only person in history to get expelled from a cattle drive. Well, that wasn't quite true. She was the one who'd decided to leave. Which made matters worse. Her sister had counted on her. How could she let her down like this?

Her lids drooped for several minutes as she recalled all the times Rainy had bailed her out of jams. She couldn't do this. Even if she had to crawl. She couldn't let Rainy down.

Crawl to Jesse? Gee, what an appealing idea. She sighed. Maybe she could break her leg tomorrow instead. Then she'd have an excuse to return to Maybe.

Sunny flopped onto her stomach and immediately cringed at the friction the scratchy quilt created against her sunburned legs. It stung to high heaven, and she had second thoughts about hauling her carcass out to the barbecue as she'd been so rudely instructed to do.

Since this could be her last dinner, she really should make the effort. Although the thought of leaving the drive tomorrow didn't hold nearly the appeal it had over an hour ago when she'd felt hurt and angry. She'd sleep on it, she told herself, and worry about how she was going to straighten out this mess tomorrow.

She pushed herself to a sitting position, knowing she was already very late for dinner. She was about to sort through her meager wardrobe when someone knocked at the door.

It had to be either Maria or Violet. Both women had been fussing over her sunburn, each coming up with her own home remedy. After pulling on a green robe Violet had loaned her, she opened the door.

Jesse looked up from the pair of jeans and paper bag he held in his hands. His hair was damp, his face freshly shaved. Sunny once again noticed how devastatingly handsome he could look...when she wasn't mad at him.

She tugged uselessly at the robe, which was far too short for her. "Yes?"

"Uh." He lifted a hand, then dropped it as if he didn't know quite what to do with it. "Got something for you."

Sunny was intrigued. She'd seen many facets to Jesse. Nervous hadn't been one of them. Her amused gaze strayed to the bag.

"Can I come in?" he asked.

Bunching the shawl collar in one hand, she pulled the robe closer. Violet was at least eight inches shorter than Sunny was and probably two sizes smaller.

"Damn it, Sunny." He slapped at a mosquito. "You gonna leave me standing out here, or what?"

The thought had certainly crossed her mind. She stepped aside, holding the door. "You waiting for every bug in west Texas to get the jump on you?"

He brushed past her, giving her a hooded look.

Oh, my. She pulled the robe tighter.

He threw the jeans on the bed, and she noticed one of his shirts was folded up beneath it. "I thought maybe you could use these. Until you find whatever you need." He shrugged and reached into the paper sack. "This should come in handy, too, for your sunburn." He held out a tube of aloe.

Holy smokes. Ten minutes ago she'd been thinking about

how she'd kill for a dab of that stuff. "I take back everything I've ever said about you," Sunny said and grabbed for the tube.

He jerked it out of her reach and grinned. "Yeah? Like what?"

"You don't want to know." She rose on tiptoe, her arm extended, but the robe rode too high on her thighs. "Please," she pleaded.

"I'll go one better."

"I don't think that's possible." Bouncing like a child, she jiggled her tingling legs in anticipation of the promised relief.

Jesse watched her movement, and when his gaze returned to her face, his eyes had darkened. "Oh, yeah," he assured her. Placing both hands on her shoulders, he walked her toward the bed.

Sunny's eyes fastened helplessly on his intense ones. As soon as she felt the scratchy quilt touch the backs of her calves, her knees softened. She slipped onto the bed to keep from stumbling and losing her grip on the robe. She laughed nervously. "What are you doing?"

Jesse sank to his haunches, unscrewed the cap and squirted the aloe into his palm. With his other hand he circled her ankle, straightening her leg. "Giving you the famous Logan rubdown."

"Oh." Her mind went blank.

Very gently, he swept the cream-colored salve up the side of her calf. "Better?"

She swallowed. "I can do that myself."

"I know." He ran his palm down the back of her leg.

"I didn't get burned back there."

Jesse merely smiled.

Why was he being so nice all of a sudden? Was he that glad to be getting rid of her? That had to be it. Sunny put her hands on his shoulders and shoved.

His arm shot up in a futile effort to maintain his balance, and he landed on his rear end. Instead of being angry, he laughed. "What are you doing?"

"Me? Since when are we so chummy?"

He pushed off the floor, grabbing the bed for balance only inches from her bare thigh. "I was trying to be helpful."

Her eyebrows shot up.

He leaned closer and dabbed some salve on her nose.

She stiffened as his thumb gently brushed across her cheek. "Now don't tell me that doesn't feel good."

It felt better than good, it felt heavenly. She snatched the tube from his hand and leaned away from him. Not far enough to look like a prude, but far enough to clear her clouded senses. "Where did you get this, anyway? The stores are closed."

Jesse stared at her for a long moment, then he stood, one hand working his thigh muscle as he stretched out his leg. Unfortunately, that put her at eye level with his fly. The denim was worn and faded but the fabric was thick and bulky. At least she hoped it was the fabric. Her gaze flew to his face.

"I have my ways," he said.

"Yeah, I bet." She sniffed. "You probably irritated it out of someone."

He chuckled. "If that had been my strategy, I'd have sicced you on her."

Her? The store clerk? Figures. He'd probably rubbed *her* calf too to get the damn salve. Sunny blinked, wondering why the heck that idea annoyed her so much. "Well, however you got it, I am grateful." She twisted around and looked at the clothes he'd tossed on the bed. "Are those yours?"

"The fit may not be great, but I don't think they'll get you arrested."

She cast her gaze to the ceiling. "Don't give up your day job. I don't think the comedy circuit is ready for you."

He grinned. "Either you slop some more of that cream on you or I will."

"Your concern warms me."

"Don't get too carried away." He looked away for a moment, then steadied his gaze on her face. "I have to make sure you'll be okay to continue on day after tomorrow."

Sunny swiped the hair away from her face and stared at him. Had he forgotten what she'd said about returning to Maybe?

Surely not. He'd looked too darned excited when she'd impulsively shot off her mouth. Or maybe he'd misunderstood and thought she was returning to Maybe the day the cattle drive resumed. Although he had said continue on...

She studied his face—the whiskey brown eyes ringed with gold, his full stubborn mouth—but found no clue in his unreadable expression. Was he giving her a chance to renege and still save face? The silly thought that maybe he wanted her to stay on the drive flitted through her mind. No, that was probably stretching it. She glanced at his tanned hands, remembered the way they'd felt on her skin.

She tried to adjust the tightening collar of her robe and realized it had pulled away from her neck.

"The clothes," she said, inclining her head toward the heap but keeping her eyes on him. "I probably won't need them." Then she waited for her clue, anything that revealed her future with the drive.

"What about the barbecue? Have you decided not to go?"

She sighed, sending up a little prayer. She had a more distant future in mind. "I don't know."

He crossed his arms, a low, guttural sound of impatience coming from his throat. "Well, your highness, when do you think you'll decide? Sometime before the damn thing is over, I hope."

Sunny stood, yanking the terry-cloth belt tighter around her waist, her eyes narrowing on him. She was sick of his calling her your highness. That was one of the few things she wouldn't miss about this drive. And Maybe was sounding better by the second.

She was about to tell him so, but took a deep breath and bit her lower lip instead. Impulsiveness had already gotten her in a bind. Besides, there were so many more things she would miss. More important, there was Rainy to consider, even if he did insist on calling Sunny...

"Well, your highness?" he asked, one dark brow lifted in arrogance.

Her eyes widened. She had it. She'd get her answer and she wouldn't have to grovel to do it.

Mimicking his stance, she folded her arms across her chest. She raised her chin. And mentally crossed her fingers. "If you call me your highness one more time…" She scrambled for a breath. "I'm back on the drive."

Chapter Ten

Jesse stared at her, his arms suddenly going slack and starting to uncross. He jammed them into place. Was she testing him? Was she really as uncertain, as vulnerable as she suddenly looked? Surely not. What was going on in that conniving little head of hers?

Rainy needs me and I'm not letting her down.

Sunny's earnest statement at the spring several days ago popped into his head. Maybe she was trying to save face. Maybe she regretted her words. Maybe she'd miss him just a little.

And maybe he ought to have himself committed. He shook his head and focused more intently on her. Her brown eyes betrayed her internal battle—the one that vulnerability was clearly winning.

Jesse didn't like the softening he felt in his chest. So far she'd been trouble, a distraction, downright annoying. She'd disregarded direct orders, proven she couldn't physically stomach the elements, displayed the lack of common sense to keep from getting sunburned, for God's sake. And she'd even managed to land him far too close to a jail cell for comfort. He shuddered just thinking about that. Now was his perfect chance to be rid of her.

She shifted from one foot to the other, and his gaze snagged on her long, silky legs. His palm itched, recalling their texture.

She cleared her throat, and he raised his gaze to her eyes. Her vulnerable, anxious eyes.

Oh, hell.

He swallowed around the knot in his throat. "May I remind you, your highness, that this barbecue is considered part of your public relations duty."

She blinked, looking a little uncertain. *"Your highness?"*

God, when had he turned into such a wimp? Now he was even making sure she realized he'd taken the bait, for goodness' sake. "Get your fanny in gear."

A huge smile spread across her face.

He felt the sappy tug at the corners of his mouth. He was more than a wimp, he was a damn wuss. In the hierarchy of such things, he was fairly certain a wuss was far worse than a wimp, and he grudgingly accepted the title—then scowled at her.

She seemed to remember what this role-playing had been about, and she scowled back. "Okay. That does it." She scooped up the jeans and shirt and hugged them to herself. "Now you're stuck with me all the way to the Oklahoma border."

She looked happy about it, and damn if he still didn't want to smile.

And kiss her.

He exhaled sharply. "Okay. I'll wait outside while you get ready."

"I'm going to the barbecue. I don't need a baby-sitter."

Unfortunately, that was one of the problems. She did. "I could wait in here," he warned.

"I'll be out in five minutes."

He smiled then and flicked the brim of his hat. "Make that four."

He thought something might have hit the door as he closed it behind him and let loose an even wider grin. Life on the trail certainly wasn't boring with her around. He only hoped she'd stay clear of jails. He wasn't sure his ticker could take the excitement...any more than it could take the excitement of seeing her in that robe. Hell, that thing had been even shorter than her skirts. And the amount of cleavage it showed. Whoa. The flurry of movement in his chest reassured him that his ticker was just fine, and he took a deep, steadying breath.

He was glad, for more than one reason, that he'd thought of lending her some clothes. Besides the fact that she could wear a flour sack and make it look good enough to get arrested, he was starting to worry about what a distraction she was to the men...not to mention himself.

The problem wasn't exactly a news bulletin. It had been evident from the beginning. Only each day Jesse had expected...hoped she'd wear something more appropriate. Foolishly, it hadn't occurred to him that he'd reduced those chances by returning her luggage to the McCloud ranch. He'd traveled so light his entire life, never having had much to his name, he hadn't considered that problem.

It had turned out to be a good thing, he admitted, that Sunny was the type of woman she was and never once encouraged the men. In fact, she was so friendly and helpful that, if anything, she discouraged sexual overtures.

So why couldn't the boss start thinking with the brains between his ears? Just imagining her wearing his shirt and jeans had his body strung tighter than a brand-new fiddle. Well, they weren't exactly his jeans, but he had a feeling she wouldn't be keen on accepting something that had once belonged to another woman, a woman she didn't know.

And he wasn't keen on having to explain how he'd come by them.

He glanced at his watch. She had thirty more seconds.

SUNNY LEFT the last three snaps of Jesse's blue Western shirt undone, figuring she'd tie it at her waist once she got the jeans on. While the shoulder seams fell halfway to her elbow, rolling up the sleeves made the shirt look okay.

She was so relieved she was back on the drive she was willing to wear just about anything. Even though she had

banked on Jesse not being able to resist his god-awful pet name
for her, she'd gotten a funny feeling about the outcome. At one
point, she'd almost convinced herself that he'd used the name
deliberately. But as she adjusted the last roll of her sleeve, she
realized that was impossible. He wanted to be rid of her. And
for whatever reason, the thought made her a little sad.

She was ready for the jeans…sort of. Although the lotion
he'd brought had worked like magic, her legs still stung in
places, and the thought of rough denim against her skin made
her want to go screaming into the night. That's why she'd
decided that although the jeans would be far too large, they
were probably her best bet.

Tentatively, she picked up the Levi's and was pleased to
discover they were buttery soft from so many washings. Sitting
on the edge of the bed, she started to tug them on.

It wasn't easy going at first. The pants bunched and caught
over her knees right where the worst of her sunburn was. She
gritted her teeth, trying to slide them up as easily as possible,
but the fit seemed incredibly snug.

She checked the zipper and found that it was halfway up.
Although she took care of that, she knew something else had
to be wrong. She should have been able to get Jesse's jeans up
practically without unzipping the damn things.

Frowning, she noticed that one pant leg was twisted and
hindered her progress. She breathed a loud, relieved sigh. For
a moment, she'd thought she'd had one too many of those fat-
laden hush puppies on the trail.

She straightened out the leg and continued to pull—and pull
and pull. Panic knocked the wind out of her. They were almost
too tight to get over her hips.

She hopped off the bed, the fabric bunched around her knees,
and she bounced, baby stepped and waddled to the mirror as
fast as she could, cursing most of the way there, her hands still
gripping the denim.

Had she really gained that much weight? Fried chicken, fried
hush puppies, fried potatoes, biscuits and gravy. Heck, she'd
eaten them all. And she'd never even seen the weight creep up

Oh, God, she had to quit wearing those stretchy, waistless skirts.

She balanced herself in front of the mirror, turning sideways for a profile shot. Dropping the jeans, she stared at her reflection.

Sunny frowned. She sucked in her stomach, tucked in her butt. They didn't seem to look a whole lot different than they had a week ago.

"Except jeans don't lie," she wailed.

There was a knock at the door, then Jesse's voice. "Sunny?"

"Oh, sh-shortcake," she muttered. Why had she already started soaking her skirt? Of course, she no doubt looked like one of the cows in the stupid thing.

"Coming." She hopped to the bed and plopped down on the mattress. Lying down, she lifted her rear end and inched the denim up, sucking in her breath at the last minute and successfully tugging the waistband home. She took one more large breath before holding it in and jamming the button in place.

Only when the ordeal of stuffing herself into the denim was over did she realize her legs stung like the dickens. Carefully, she sat up and tested her walking ability.

The jeans were tight, skintight, but she could get through this evening. She grabbed the front tails of the shirt and tied a knot. The back tail she left out, hoping it would cover her hideously wide fanny.

As she started to open the door, her rotten stomach decided to add insult to injury by growling for food.

"You're late," Jesse said, tapping his watch.

"Oh, stick it in your ear." She slammed the door and marched past him, realizing too late that she'd forgotten her key.

He gave her a stunned look, then strode after her. "What's your problem?"

She snuck him a sidelong glance, hoping he hadn't noticed how fat her rear end looked. Yup, he was noticing, all right. She swore under her breath.

"What did you say?" The astonished look he gave her almost made her laugh. Then she remembered she was on a diet. As of now. And there wasn't a damn thing funny about that.

"I HOPE the smoked ribs aren't already gone," Jesse said conversationally. She was in a snit about something, and he wanted to lighten her mood. "They had the most amazing hickory sauce on them." He patted his stomach. "Of course, the apple dumplings were pretty mind-boggling, too."

She gave him a dirty look.

"I only had one helping." He frowned and pointed for her to head south of town, where the barbecue was in full swing. "I was gonna have seconds, but I waited to eat with you."

The next look she gave him would have brought a lesser man to his knees.

He scratched his jaw. "They have ice-cold watermelon, too." She slowed down and some of her hostility seemed to disappear, replaced by a more pensive look. He was finally on to something here. "And corn, too. With freshly churned butter."

Her lips thinned. "I'll thank you to keep your commentaries to yourself," she said and stomped off several yards ahead of him toward the spirals of hickory-and mesquite-scented smoke.

That suited Jesse just fine. He had no idea what the blazes had gotten into her, and he was tired of trying to be nice. Besides, those jeans fit her so snugly, he didn't mind watching her take off like a bat outa hell.

He sighed. Why did everything she wore look so...so good? Even his faded six-year-old shirt looked dynamite on the woman.

Either that or he had a major case of lust.

Jesse tried not to dwell on either possibility for the rest of the night. As much as he hated making small talk, he mingled with the townspeople who had so graciously provided their dinner, discussed the logistics of tomorrow's rodeo with the mayor and generally kept an eye on the cowboys.

He didn't know all of them as well as he'd like to, and the

earlier incident with Sunny and the sheriff was already one too many for him. He'd had several stern words with Violet and Smiley, and was no longer concerned about them. Occasionally his gaze wandered through the crowd to locate Sunny. She was usually easy to find, surrounded by large groups of men.

The recurring sight had ruined his appetite for second helpings. Now some of the townswomen were clearing the food away. Most of the people had brought their own lawn chairs, and those, too, were being gathered up and carted off. Some of the cowboys had headed to the local bar, although they all knew they had a midnight curfew. It was almost eleven now.

Jesse looked at the darkened sky, at the silvery crescent that partially bracketed a whole slew of stars. Yawning twice, he stretched and looked around.

Sunny was standing several feet away, peeking into one of the wrapped platters of food that had not yet been removed.

"I'll walk you to your room," he said softly, striding up behind her.

She jumped and released the foil wrapping. "What are you doing sneaking up on me like that?" she snapped.

He held up both hands. "Excuse me. I didn't know I had been sneaking." He shook his head at her. "What is wrong with you?"

"I'm hungry. That's what." She snatched a carrot stick off the platter, started to turn away, then grabbed two more. "Are you headed back now?"

"Didn't you eat?"

"What does this look like to you?" She chomped a carrot stick in half and started in the direction of the motel.

This was one of those woman things, he decided. It had to be, in which case there was no right answer for him to give. So Jesse did the smart thing and shut up.

He stayed with her, though, keeping several paces behind, despite the fact that Sparks's major crime threat was probably Mildred and the other Sunni's truck-stop visits.

When they arrived at the motel, she stopped in front of her door, staring at it, and sighed loudly.

He took a deep breath, fully prepared to get his head snapped off. "What's wrong now?"

She turned to face him, slumped against the door, and puffed out her cheeks. "What would you like to hear about first?"

Ignoring her sarcasm and the fact that she didn't want an answer, he said, "The part about dinner. As in, did you have any?"

She gave him a bland look and held up her last carrot stick. "I have this."

"That's not dinner."

"I don't need dinner," she said, as if it was a mantra, her lids drooping shut. "All I need is some oral gratification." Immediately her eyes flew open when she realized how that sounded.

Jesse grinned, his gaze slipping to her surprised mouth. She blinked, then stared like a wallflower who'd just been asked to dance. "Well, honey, that I can help you with." He pulled off his hat and covered her lips with his.

Her head arched against the door with the force of his kiss, and Jesse had to rein in the sudden hunger he had for this woman. Her lips were soft and mobile and starting to part under his. She brought a hand to his neck, lightly cupping his nape, and he felt her nails scrape his skin.

The last of his control nearly slipped. He kissed her hard and thoroughly one more time, then pulled back before his ability to do so was lost.

Sunny looked dazed for a moment. Her head lolled against the chipped turquoise door, her hair in disarray from having been windblown dry. Jesse forced himself to take another step back before he totally blew it and helped himself to seconds.

Three doors down, hinges squeaked. Voices flooded the still night air. Jesse took two more steps back. Sunny straightened, her dazed expression fading.

She tossed her hair. "Thanks for walking me back."

"No problem." He slid a look at the young couple stepping onto the walkway, heard their door creak shut. Fortunately he didn't know them. The last thing he needed was to fuel talk among his crew. Yet here he was, standing in front of a cheesy motel in full view, making a damn fool of himself. "Where's your key?" he asked gruffly.

She lifted a shoulder, still looking uncomfortable and definitely not at him. "I left it in the room."

He glanced toward the motel office. The blinds were slanted open, but the interior was pitch-black. Sighing, he reached into his back pocket and produced his wallet. He flipped through an assortment of phone numbers, one lone credit card, which had been issued to him by the drive's promoters, and an old, faded picture. He finally found the narrow plastic strip.

He started to nudge Sunny aside, thought better of risking contact and dropped his hand. "Move away from the lock."

Frowning, she did as he'd asked and continued to watch him with undisguised interest.

Within seconds of jimmying the lock, he turned the knob. He pushed open the door, then gestured her inside. "Don't forget your key next time."

Still frowning, she slowly started to enter the room. Just over the threshold she stopped and turned to give him a sly, amused look. "Wow!"

He didn't nibble the bait. He merely returned the plastic strip to his wallet and waited for her to close and lock the door.

A slow smile teased her lips. "What other criminal tendencies do you have?"

Jesse humorlessly smiled. If she only knew, he thought grimly. If she only knew.

IT WAS MURDER to roll out of bed the next morning. Not only did Sunny have zero desire to give up the wonderful, slightly lumpy mattress, which was actually stuffed deeper than two inches, but it was also difficult to move because she hadn't slept worth a hill of beans.

Hill of beans? Oh, jeez, now she was even thinking like a hick.

She scolded herself. Her words had been ugly and hateful yesterday, born of humiliation. These people weren't hicks.

They had all been warm and welcoming, and it wasn't their fault that Jesse Logan was a creep and that she was on a diet.

She shuddered at the thought and swung her legs out of bed. Immediately she went to the mirror, twisted sideways, pulled up her T-shirt and frowned at what she saw. After starving herself last night, surely she should have lost at least a pound.

Sighing, she dropped her shirt and headed for the shower. She had far more important things to worry about. Like trying to keep her hands off the creep.

All through her shower and her battle with pulling on the still-tight jeans, Sunny replayed his kiss in her mind. She seemed to be thinking far too often about his incredible, hot, demanding kisses...something that was getting her a little flustered right now, not to mention reducing her willpower to a pool of warm honey. What had happened to her? If those people hadn't come out of their room, heaven knows what might have transpired. It had to be the lack of food making her dizzy.

She automatically reached into her bag in search of her blow dryer and remembered she didn't have one. Then she remembered why. She gritted her teeth and left the room, recalling one of the reasons Jesse Logan was such a jerk.

The thought oddly soothed her and replaced the kiss in her mind as she headed for the rodeo grounds. She hadn't gone far before swarms of people, coming from all directions, converged on the area.

Violet was the first person Sunny saw whom she knew, but the woman was busy chatting with several of the local women and Sunny kept walking, keeping an eye out for Maria.

She didn't care where Jesse was, she told herself, as her gaze bounced from one tall, tan-Stetson-wearing dark head to the other.

"Looking for me?" his low, husky voice floated out from a crowd of cowboys.

"Now, why would I do that?" Her sarcastic tone wavered when she turned to look at him and her gaze fixed on his mouth. His lips were askew in a lopsided grin. The tip of his tongue lazily dabbed at the corner of his mouth.

She quickly lowered her eyes to the flurry of black curly hair spilling out of his shirt, which he normally kept buttoned to the top.

What was this? Torture Sunny week? She schooled her face into a bored, bland look.

"Why would you be looking for me?" he asked with raised brows. "Oh, I dunno. Maybe you needed to get into your room."

Last night. Leaving her key in the room. His kiss. Damn him for reminding her of that. "Not today," she said airily and continued toward the rodeo.

He fell in step beside her. Although he didn't say anything, she could feel him checking her out, and she gave him her best knock-it-off glare.

He blinked. "I'm glad to see you're making use of Natalie's je—" He cut himself short.

"What did you say?" She spun on him, wondering if she'd heard correctly.

By the look of sheer panic in his eyes, she knew she had. Quickly he erased the emotion. "Nothing."

She stepped closer to him. "Tell me what you were going to say."

He gave her a long, hard look as if weighing his decision. "Nothing."

"Wrong answer."

He sighed, passing a hand over his face until it covered his mouth. "The jeans," he mumbled. "They belong to a...to a friend."

Sunny pulled his hand away. "What?"

He sighed again, a long, disgusted sound. "The jeans belong—or rather belonged—to a woman named Natalie."

She realized that she still held his hand. She let him go and crossed her arms over her chest.

"And it's not what you think," he said.

"Oh?"

He shoved his fingers through his hair. "She wasn't a lover or anything like that."

The new information that the jeans weren't Jesse's after all had Sunny in such a tailspin, surprising her one instant, angering her the next, that the thought hadn't yet entered her mind.

But it did now. As soon as the word *lover* fell from his lips, the reality hit her like a stampede of enraged bulls.

And she loathed the way she felt about that. Of course he'd had lovers. Many, no doubt, and none of them any of her business. So why did she feel so...so awful?

"Why would I care if she had been a lover?" she snapped.

"She was only twenty, for God's sake." Glancing around, he lowered his voice, "Natalie is Hank's younger sister, and he definitely doesn't need to know what happened during her last rodeo visit."

Neither did Sunny. "What happened?"

Jesse shifted uncomfortably. "She practically threw herself at me."

Let it go. It's none of your business. "And you didn't accept the offer?" she asked.

"No."

"How honorable of you."

He didn't look uncomfortable anymore. He looked affronted. "I thought so."

She experienced a moment's remorse for having stuck her nose where it didn't belong—and for having treated his character with acerbity. She looked into his velvety brown eyes and saw a hint of vulnerability there. "Do you have to care about someone, Jesse," she began, swallowing hard, wanting the right answer more than she should, "in order to sleep with her?"

His expression went flat. "I didn't say that," he answered warily.

Sunny glanced away, trying and hoping to shutter her emotions. She'd almost given in to him last night, given in to herself. She'd wanted him with an intensity that had frightened her, one she had never experienced before. Had she almost made a fool of herself?

"No," he said, startling her out of her reverie. "No, I don't," he repeated, his face a hard mask.

Then he walked away as she sadly realized he'd just answered both questions.

Chapter Eleven

Five days after they left Sparks, Jesse still had barely said anything to Sunny. He didn't ride up and check on the wagons, she noticed, as he'd done all last week. She'd seen him for all of ten minutes during breakfast each morning, when it was generally too dark to really see him at all. Then she'd seen him for about half an hour each evening at dinner before he disappeared among the men.

This week she'd shared the wagon ride with Violet, while Slim drove Maria and Ana. In Sparks, Jesse and Maria had gotten word that her sister was still too ill to join them, and much to Smiley's consternation, Violet had agreed to stay on. Because of the change in plans, being without her sister's help, Maria had felt Ana was not receiving enough schooling. So Slim had agreed to drive the wagon while Maria spent time with her child. Although Violet was an amusing traveling companion, Sunny felt more lost and useless than ever.

She'd felt a little hurt that Maria hadn't asked her to spend more time tutoring Ana. Sunny had helped the girl with her studies last week and had felt she'd done a fairly good job. Propping her elbow on her knee, she let her chin drop to her palm.

"What's wrong?" Violet glanced at her, then swung her attention to guiding the wagon away from a low but treacherous precipice near the highway. "You bored?"

"Not exactly," Sunny answered. Most of their route this

week had been close enough to the road that there'd been plenty of passing cars to wave to and stares to laugh at. "I just wish I could be a little more useful."

Violet frowned. "Useful? Girl, you've been nothing but that. I bet people are still talking about that interview you gave back in Sparks. After you got done with that radio person and the reporter, we had all kind of folks asking if they could sign on."

Sunny laughed. "I hadn't meant to make it sound that fun and adventurous."

"And you had them eating outa your hand that half-day stop in Tonka."

Sunny stretched out her legs and pulled up the hem of her new khaki shorts. Her legs glistened with three layers of sunscreen. After that last burn, she'd have started wearing jeans if it hadn't been so hot. Then she recalled Jesse rubbing her legs with aloe, kissing her until her hair curled...then ignoring her like she was a pesky ant. She sighed.

Violet gave her another swift glance and asked softly, "Is he giving you that much trouble?"

Sunny blinked and kept her eyes straight ahead. It was useless to pretend she didn't know who Violet was talking about. She only hoped her funk wasn't that obvious to everyone. She briefly considered ignoring the question but knew Violet was too stubborn to back off. So instead she lied. Partially. "No. I just wish I had more to do."

"You help with Ana, you help with every meal, you..." Violet trailed off, frowning. A slow smile lit up her face. "I have a suggestion."

"What?" Sunny asked suspiciously. She had an uneasy feeling about the way the older woman was suddenly smiling. Sunny did need something to occupy herself...as long as it didn't involve Jesse.

"How about menu planning?" Violet asked. "We're almost out of supplies. We'll be buying them tomorrow when we get to the next town. But we have to know what we've got planned first."

"Menu planning?" How much more boring could that be? Besides, they had the same old biscuits, meat and hush puppies almost every day. "What's the point?"

Violet narrowed her gaze. "I thought you had some ideas about cutting fat and all that health rigmarole?"

"I did." Sunny slumped against the wooden seat and watched the hypnotic sway of the horses' tails. After her scare in Sparks, she'd decided that, weight gain or not, the whole crew could stand a better diet. "But Maria said it wouldn't work."

"Well, don't you worry about that. This go-around with supply buying and meals is up to me."

Sunny sat up. "Really?"

"Yup." Smiling, Violet hitched a thumb over her shoulder. "I got a notebook and pencil right back there."

"This is great," Sunny said as she twisted in her seat and started to crawl into the interior. "You all are gonna love macrobiotic cooking."

"MACRO WHAT?" Jesse bellowed as he stared at the piece of notebook paper in his hand. "I can't even pronounce it, much less count on liking it." He scanned the list of food items. "Tofu? Mung beans? What the hell are those?" he asked Violet, his patience as existent as a cool breeze—and right now it was about ninety in the shade.

Violet shrugged innocently. "Sunny wants to try it. I didn't think a vegetarian diet was the best thing for the men, but I couldn't hurt the poor girl's feelings." She smiled. "Maybe you should talk to her."

Talk to Sunny? He'd sooner talk to a rattler. Heaven help him, why hadn't he let her go back to Maybe while he had the chance?

She was driving him crazy, making him think things he shouldn't be thinking. Women like her flitted from one man to the next...after they made the men crazy. He shook his head. If he didn't have the responsibility of this drive in his hands and if she wasn't Cash's sister-in-law, he'd seriously think about having a hot and heavy fling with her. But that, of course, was a moot point.

He caught the cagey look Violet was giving him and frowned. "Where is she?" he growled.

"Near the wagon."

Of course she was, Jesse thought as he angrily strode in that direction. It was dinnertime, wasn't it? Time for her to pretend she was little Miss Suzie Homemaker. She'd assumed the role ever since the interview in Sparks, helping with the baking, the laundry. Wasn't she just the perfect little pioneer woman? She'd even cut her nails.

Jesse slowed down and mopped the back of his neck with his bandanna. He was a little sorry about that. Not that he'd changed his mind about her. Her assuming the homemaker role wasn't any different than rodeo clowns putting on their theatrical makeup, making children laugh, distracting the bulls. It was all for show. But as soon as the rodeo was over, they became hard-drinking rabble-rousers, just like the rest of the cowboys.

Sunny was no different. This Suzie Homemaker stuff wouldn't last forever. She'd already shown her true colors. She was a pampered little princess who cared more about her comfort than the good of the whole.

He saw her at the rear of the chuck wagon, hauling down bags of burlap. Even in her nondescript, knee-length shorts and blue tank top she looked dynamite. Her legs were no longer red, or even pink, but a silky golden brown. Her hair was pulled into a braid. Not a normal braid, but one that started at her crown, woven loose and soft, and tucked under at her slender neck. He'd heard Maria call it by some foreign name—a French braid maybe—and he was reminded once again that nothing about Sunny was normal.

She was humming when he came up behind her, the notebook paper in his hand, and asked, "What is this?"

She dropped the bag she carried and spun around. One hand flew to her chest, the absence of color at her fingertips a little unsettling to Jesse. "You about scared me to death," she said, a smile beginning to lift the corners of her mouth. When his only response was a cold stare, her gaze lowered to the paper he held.

She plucked it out of his hand, scanned the list for a couple of seconds, then looked at him, a hint of mischief twinkling in her eyes. "What is this?" she asked, mimicking him. "Well, I see you were never hooked on phonics." She pointed to the first word on the list with exaggerated patience. "This says tofu, mung—"

"Sunny." He cut her off, grabbing the paper out of her hand. "I'm not in the mood."

"What do you expect?" Her hands flew to her hips. "You come charging over here like a mad bull. You really need to work on your delivery, Logan." She turned to pick up the burlap bag.

Jesse yanked it from her hands. "Where do you want this?"

She jerked her chin toward the Dutch oven and turned away from him.

After he delivered the bag, he took a deep breath, then said, "Look, Sunny, I'm sure you're trying to help, but a vegetarian diet is out of the question."

She pulled another burlap bag past him. "Why? It's a lot healthier than the stuff we've been eating."

"Have you forgotten that this is a cattle drive?"

"Precisely my point. The men have been working up to seventeen hours a day. They need nutritious food."

Shaking his head, he helped move two more bags. "Call me crazy, but don't you think our sponsors, especially beef-related ones, may have a little problem with the crew turning into vegetarians?"

She frowned as though considering that possibility. "We wouldn't have to publicize it."

He laughed. "Having the men all go on strike would take care of that."

"You see." She sank cross-legged to the ground to root around in one of the bags. "You're assuming that vegetarian food can't be interesting. Why can't you give it a chance?"

She looked at him, her eyes wide and appealing, and he wondered how he had let his guard down for even one minute.

Hell, this entire conversation was ridiculous. They'd never be able to find the items on her list in west Texas.

He crouched beside her, knowing he should get on his horse and get to the cattle where he belonged. "We could give the men a vote tonight."

She made a face. "That's not fair. You know what they'll say."

Shrugging, Jesse began helping her stack the tin dinner plates. "I don't want to buy a bunch of groceries they aren't going to eat."

"Well," she began slowly. "Maybe when we get to Hard Rock tomorrow, I could buy enough ingredients to cook you dinner."

He glanced up. "And?"

She lifted a shoulder, her fingers trailing along the rim of a tin cup. "And we could have our own private dinner." She looked up suddenly. "Just so you can sample the type of cooking I'm talking about, of course."

He nodded slowly. "Of course."

She dropped the cups she was stacking and stood. "You'll see that it's not as scary as it sounds."

Jesse smiled. "Okay. It's a date."

Sunny's gaze flew to his and she laughed. It was a husky, nervous sound. "Maybe we should invite Violet to join us. Since this was her idea."

"What?" He stood, too, his temper rising along with him.

She frowned in bewilderment. "She suggested I try a healthier menu."

Jesse looked over his shoulder just in time to see Violet duck behind the other wagon. She'd set him up. But why? He stared angrily for a moment until some of his steam evaporated. Was he that transparent? Did the whole damn crew know how much he'd ached to talk to Sunny all week? How hard it had been for him to stay away from her?

"Look, if you don't like it after the sample dinner I make

you," she said after he hadn't responded, "I'll go back to slinging hash." She gave him a weak smile.

He grinned. "Fair enough." Her smile widened, her beautiful brown eyes touching him, making him think of the private dinner he had to look forward to, and he added, "I can live with that."

She blinked and the half smile on her lips quivered. "At least for another eleven days, huh?"

She averted her gaze, searching the horizon. When she finally returned her attention to him, her eyes were bright, sparkling, and there was a new spring to her step as she vigorously resumed her chores.

In eleven days they expected to be at the Oklahoma border. There she'd pass the proverbial torch to someone else, Oklahoma's representative.

Sunny was obviously counting the days.

And Jesse realized he should be counting his blessings. He had enough to worry about in Oklahoma without Sunny adding to the mix. But as he listened to her cheerful humming, he wondered why he felt like smashing something.

IT HADN'T occurred to Sunny that the small town of Hard Rock wouldn't carry the items on her list, which she had to admit had been pretty foolish on her part. The store clerk had stared at her as if she'd been from outer space when Sunny had presented the man with the list.

She glanced at her jeans and lime green T-shirt and chuckled. What would they have thought if she'd shown up in her former clothes?

Then she sobered. Although she hadn't been able to get the items, she was grateful for having gone to the store that day. It had to have been fate guiding her, being kind to her.

Even now, five days later, she shuddered at the thought of one of the cowboys having found that last, ancient copy of *Midnight Fantasy.* Or even worse, Jesse could have found it. This time the shudder rocked her entire body.

Violet glanced at her, the reins lying loosely in her hands as the wagon rolled at a leisurely pace, waiting for the men and cattle to catch up as they approached the next town, called Pocito. "What's the matter, Sunny?"

She smiled. "Want me to take a turn for a while?"

"Think I'll take you up on that." Violet passed her the reins and relaxed against the wooden backrest, her eyes already starting to close.

Although this was only the second time Violet had entrusted her with the wagon, Sunny couldn't help but feel a small surge of pride. She'd come a long way from the fluff head they'd treated her like in the beginning. She was becoming an integral part of the drive. She had been both flattered and saddened when Jesse had decided to keep Violet on after Maria's sister had caught up with them in Hard Rock. He'd said that the cooking duties were greater than anticipated and after they reached Oklahoma and Sunny had left, he was afraid the work would be too much for Maria and her sister.

No one knew how much Sunny's heart had sung with those words. Without saying so, Jesse had admitted that she'd been needed, that she had filled a void.

Except all that was about to come to an end.

"You're not still thinking about that magazine, are you?" Violet asked, making Sunny start. She'd thought the woman was asleep. "You look so sad, child. No one but me knows about it. And along with the coals, it made a dang-fine fire for dinner."

Sunny sighed. Violet had known about the centerfold when it had come out nearly two years ago and Rainy had been caught in the backlash. "No. I wasn't thinking about that. Although how that magazine managed to hang around for so long sure beats me."

"Out here in the country, sometimes things do," Violet admitted. "But two years is a long time, and I wouldn't be worried about any more popping up. Besides, you didn't do anything wrong, remember?"

Sunny swallowed the urge to cry. She wasn't normally a weepy person. She didn't know exactly what was wrong.

Maybe it was hormonal. Violet was being so kind. She knew the older woman had to be as tired as she was, if not more so. The drive had been the hardest thing Sunny had ever physically attempted. The days were long, the nights short, the heat stifling and the food dreadful. But it was also the most satisfying thing Sunny had ever done.

And of course there was Jesse…who she seemed to annoy just by being alive.

"Why did you come, Violet?" Sunny asked, half out of curiosity, half out of the desire to get her mind off Jesse.

Violet chuckled. "I don't know."

Sunny arched a brow at her. "Smiley?"

"You wanna tell me about Jesse?" Violet snapped.

Much to her amazement, tears welled up in Sunny's eyes.

Violet slipped an arm around her. "I'm sorry, sweetie."

Sunny shook her head and swiped at her lashes. "I'm just tired."

Her friend pushed back her hat and tried to tame the unruly red hair that sprung forward. "I'll tell you about Smiley if you tell me about Jesse."

Sunny was too astonished to respond right away. That was the first time she'd ever heard the woman use Smiley's name in a civilized tone.

Violet laughed. "Only Rainy knows about the torch I've carried for the old coot. Mind you, it fizzles out when he gets to yakking about his chili too much."

Sunny wasn't about to break it to her, but she suspected half of Maybe knew about the torch. But Violet had confided only to Rainy…and now she was telling Sunny. Other than her twin, Sunny had never had close relationships. She'd always felt different, like she didn't belong. Rainy was the good, responsible one. Everyone had always said so. Sunny was the flake. And now Violet was sharing a lifelong confidence with her. Sunny sniffed.

"Now, you wanna tell me about Jesse?" Violet asked softly.

She ignored the question. She wanted to hear more about

Violet. She wanted to bask in her new role. "Why didn't you ever marry him?"

Violet shrugged. "We're both too stubborn."

"That seems a shame." Sunny blinked when Violet narrowed her eyes on her. "I mean, to have wasted so much time and to have given up something so precious. I don't understand."

"I guess you wouldn't." Violet took the reins from her. "Apparently, neither does Jesse."

Sunny didn't say anything for a moment as Violet's words sank in. "Wait a minute. You can't liken Jesse and me to you and Smiley." When her friend gave her a bland look, she added, "You've known Smiley for most of your life. I've only known Jesse for a little over three weeks."

"Doesn't matter. I knew with Smiley the first week I met him."

"So why didn't you act on it then?"

Violet gave her a sad smile. "Because I was married to someone else at the time."

Sunny's heart convulsed. If she hadn't felt humbled enough before, she certainly did now. From the look on Violet's face, Sunny was certain she'd just been gifted with a confidence no other living soul had been given. And the information saddened her beyond belief. It haunted her in a way she couldn't explain.

She had no words of comfort. She merely patted Violet's age-spotted hand and was once again reminded that this trip was far too grueling for someone her age, yet she'd followed her heart.

"It's still different for Jesse and me. I like him...." Sunny slid a glance at the woman she could now never lie to. "I don't think I love him. I mean I don't even know what that's supposed to feel like." She shrugged, feeling helpless and depressed. "Besides, I don't even think he likes me. He ignores me most of the time."

"Oh, Sunny." Violet's laugh was short and humorless. "He's not ignoring you, honey, he's working double time."

"What?"

"The night watch. He's taking double shifts."

"I don't understand. He's trail boss. He's got other duties. Why would he do that?" *To stay away from me,* she added silently.

Violet looked around. Acres of prairie and sporadic outcroppings of mesquite surrounded them. Maria and her sister were in the other wagon several dozen yards behind. One lone redtailed hawk patrolled the cloudless sky. "You can't breathe a word of this, you hear?"

Sunny shook her head.

"Since Jesse won't let the men keep the cattle too close to camp, it causes more work. Sometimes it requires an extra man. That's why he takes on an extra shift at watching the herd."

"I hate to sound dense..." Sunny lifted a palm.

Violet turned to look at her. "For you, Sunny, he does it for you...since the first day you fainted."

Sunny swallowed. "You mean the cattle aren't normally kept so far away from camp?"

Violet shook her head.

Sunny slid a stubby nail between her teeth and nibbled. She'd heard the men grumbling about the distance of the herd at night, but she'd figured it was a matter of them having differences of opinion as to how far the cattle should be kept.

"Now, remember, not a word," Violet warned. "Jesse threatened to fire anyone who told you."

Jesse. No wonder he looked so tired all the time. If the weariness around his eyes and mouth had broken her heart before, this new knowledge all but shattered her into a million pieces.

Sunny slid a second nail between her teeth and chomped down so hard she heard a crack. Holding up her hand, she looked at the jagged edges reminiscent of her tomboy years.

Oh, God help her, is this what love felt like?

Chapter Twelve

Pocito wasn't much of a town. It did have two diners, though, and a pink brick building that doubled as a beauty shop and volunteer fire station. Beside it was a general store that sold everything from chicken wire to gourmet potpies.

That was where Sunny had been shocked yet delighted to find her favorite brand of tofu. The eccentric store owner had just returned from a trip to San Francisco, where she'd purchased a hodgepodge of unusual delicacies. Although the faded box of bulgar wheat Sunny picked up had had enough dust on it to make her a little uncertain, the thought of having dinner alone with Jesse was enough reason for her to overlook that small detail.

Sunny poked the fire beneath the Dutch oven one more time, causing the coals to erupt in a fresh burst of flame. She checked her watch. He was ten minutes late for dinner. If the little weasel had stood her up because he was too chicken to try her new menu...

Sunny took a deep breath to calm herself. She was being a twit again. He had given her no indication he wouldn't show up as he'd promised, despite the fact that the entire crew had been invited to complimentary dinners at the town's diner. So why was she working herself into a frenzy? Why was she looking to pick a fight with him?

Because you're the one who's chicken.

Sunny stabbed the hot coals again. She had to do something

with all this nervous energy. Violet had given her a lot to think about. Too much. Now her wayward thoughts were prompting emotions Sunny wasn't sure how to deal with.

Her pathetic stub of a thumbnail had just made it between her lips when she heard someone behind her. Startled, she bit down hard, her teeth clamping flesh instead of nail just as she started to turn. "Ouch."

Jesse encircled her wrist and put her thumb to his lips. He placed a soft kiss there, his eyes capturing hers. "Better?"

Hesitantly, she nodded.

He didn't let go. He drew her thumb into his mouth and gently sucked it. "How's that?"

Great. She started with only a sore thumb and now she was going into cardiac arrest. Clearing her throat, she pulled at her hand. "Fine." It came out a croak. She cleared her throat again.

He smiled, gave her hand a squeeze, then dropped it. "Smells good. Do I get a peek?" He reached for the cast-iron lid.

This time she grabbed his wrist. "Careful. You'll burn yourself."

His eyes met hers, amusement glittering from them. "Damn," he said, a slow grin forming on his face. "I think I already have." His fingers brushed her lips, seeking ministration.

Sunny tried to swallow again, except her mouth was far too dry. Quickly she glanced away while stooping to reach into the cooler. She brought out several ice cubes. "Here."

Laughing, Jesse accepted them. He popped one into his mouth and looked around the deserted camp. His gaze fell upon the low, makeshift table that she'd fashioned out of plywood and had set for two, his eyes lingering on the piece of muted floral fabric doubling as a tablecloth. In the middle sat two lighted, cranberry-scented candles.

His eyes slowly swept to her, and she felt the blood rush to her face. Two hours ago, arranging the table had seemed like a great idea. Now, watching the wariness cross his face made her want to tear everything to shreds. She bit back the excuses she longed to hurl at him, lifted the oven lid and briskly stirred the contents. Too late, she remembered the contents were not meant to be stirred.

Sighing heavily, she stared bleakly at her tofu patties—former tofu patties, now tofu goulash. Oh, hell, at least he wouldn't know the difference.

"Need some help?" he asked, peering over her shoulder.

She shook her head and slammed the lid down. Moving back, she caught a whiff of something spicy, pine soap, maybe. She darted a glance at his jaw and was surprised to see that he'd just shaved. She wondered if he'd noticed her new cologne. Suddenly she hoped not. "No, it's ready. You go sit."

"Can't I carry something to the table?"

She reached into the cooler and retrieved a plastic-wrapped tin bowl. She all but threw it at him. "Here."

"Anything else?"

"I'll bring it."

"Um…are we going to have enough room?"

She turned to see what he was talking about and saw him frowning at the thick cranberry candles taking up a sizable portion of the tiny, cozy-looking table. Oh, brother. She might as well have written "date night" across the damn tablecloth.

"Oh, shoot." She slapped a thigh as she hustled over to blow out the candles. "I meant to get rid of these. They're aromatherapy candles, you know," she said, the fib stumbling from her lips. "They relax me while I'm cooking. I'll get the gas lantern."

"I have a better idea." He'd set down the bowl and grasped her about the waist from behind just as she bent forward, about to blow out the flame. He pulled her back.

Her bottom connected with something solid. She straightened immediately and turned wide eyes on him.

"Let me see if I can enlarge the table a bit." His hands slid from her waist. "That way we can keep the candles." His mouth twisted wryly. "I could use some relaxing, too."

He crouched to fiddle with the plywood strip. A minute later, he stood, the table unchanged, and lifted a shoulder. "I vote we leave the candles and serve ourselves beforehand in order to save room."

"Fine. Bring the plates." Sunny preceded him to the goulash, snatching up the chilled bowl he'd set down earlier.

When she turned around, ready to take the plates and dish out their dinner, she realized he hadn't followed her. Then she saw him reaching behind the wagon.

He brought out a cola bottle, a spray of colorful wildflowers bursting from the top. He caught her gaze and shrugged. "I figured they'd go with the candles."

She saw that wary look again. It darkened his eyes, etched a crease between his brows. The flowers went with the candles all right. And he was as apprehensive as she was about their unofficial date. She moistened her lips. "They're beautiful."

"They don't have a florist here." He moved his shoulders, stretched his neck. Restless energy radiated from him. "I picked them right outside of town."

"Here, let me take them." Her fingers meshed with his as she tried to grasp the bottle. He didn't let go, and the warm skin beneath hers felt both soothing and frightening.

She withdrew her hand. "In fact, maybe you could put them on the table while I get our food." Her eyes met his for a moment before she had to look away. He looked different somehow, tense, keyed up. Putting some breathing space between them, she returned to the fire.

She could feel his eyes upon her as she opened the lid of the Dutch oven and stared at the lumpy concoction. Running a clammy palm down her jeans, she sighed. So much for impressing him with vegetarian cooking.

After rooting around for a tofu patty that still vaguely resembled one, she carefully flipped the lump onto a plate and flattened it out. Then she crowded it with a bean-and-brown-rice combination and a mound of tabbouleh salad.

After assembling her plate, she carried them both to the table.

Jesse sat on his haunches, a wine bottle tucked between his

knees as he struggled with the cork. He successfully yanked it out just as she set their plates on the table. He looked up and grinned.

"What are you? A magician in your spare time?" She narrowed her eyes.

"If I was, I'd have conjured up something better than this."

Her brows shot up. She couldn't believe it. He was already making cracks about her cooking.

Except it wasn't his plate he was staring at. His whiskey brown eyes glittered with amusement as he made a lazy appraisal of her flushed face, down the front of her sleeveless shirt to the loose hem she was wringing.

Sunny swallowed and dropped to her place on the tarp-covered ground opposite him. She watched him fill one of the tin cups with the red wine and pass it to her.

"I wasn't sure what type of wine went with tofu," he said, grinning wryly.

She sipped and smiled. "I think this will do just fine."

He put the bottle and his cup aside and picked up his fork. A slight frown puckered his brow as he peered at his plate. The flickering candlelight did nothing to help the presentation of dinner. It made everything look gray and pasty.

Great. Sunny sighed and picked up her fork.

Jesse glanced up. "It looks great." His wary gaze dropped to his plate. He poked at the brown rice a few times then speared one of the red beans and forked it into his mouth. "Mmm. Pretty good."

Sunny bit back a smile. No kidding. Those he ate all the time. "What about the rest of it?"

"I'm getting there."

In what century? she wondered as she watched him poke some more. She scooped up a portion of the tofu mixture and chewed thoughtfully as he inspected the clumps of food he was separating and apparently cataloging. Three weeks ago she'd have been irritated with him for being so prickly about this experiment. But, of course, three weeks ago they wouldn't have been able to sit across from one another without biting each other's head off.

What had changed between them? When had it changed? Maybe he was glad to be getting rid of her in a few days. Now there was a cheerful thought. Sunny stabbed at her salad and sent a wave of the bulgar wheat, parsley and tomato over the side of her plate.

Jesse looked up from his inspection. A slow, lazy grin tilted his lips. "Well, that's encouraging."

"Sorry." She tapped the mess under the lip of her plate. "Have you tried it yet?"

He shoveled a small amount onto his fork and slipped it between his lips. Slowly he chewed. "Not bad." He took another bite. "Good, actually."

"And the tofu?"

Fear darkened his eyes and he blinked. "I'm getting there." He peered at his plate. "What's in there, exactly?"

"Besides the tofu, there are carrots, onions, mushrooms, all kinds of seasonings. I threw in a little tuna and egg, too." She shrugged. "Obviously it's not strictly macrobiotic. I worked with what I had."

"Obviously," he agreed, his lips twitching. He poked some more, then set down his fork, picked up his wine and sipped it.

"Chicken," she accused, grinning.

"Me?" He looked thoroughly insulted. "You should have seen some of the things I ate when I lived in South America."

"Where?" She nearly dropped her fork.

He smiled. "Argentina and Brazil. I spent four years there."

"Why?"

He shrugged. "Seemed like a good idea at the time. They've got some big ranches down there. Lots of work."

"When was this?"

"Seventeen, eighteen years ago."

Sunny was amazed. She knew he'd been a rodeo champ. And she knew what the narrow-minded citizens of Maybe thought about him—the reminder making her blood simmer. But other than that, she knew so little. "You were only a kid."

"About eighteen."

"Didn't you miss home?"

"Nope." He picked up his fork again.

"Weren't your parents worried? Your mom must have been a basket case," Sunny said, thinking about how her mother still lectured her before every trip she took.

His smile was oddly cynical. "Nope."

"If you were as stubborn then as you are now," Sunny teased, "you probably scared the living daylights out of her and didn't realize it."

"Let's drop it, okay?" He raised his steely gaze to her over the flickering candlelight, telling her far more than his words had.

She was trespassing.

Sunny nodded, her eyes still held by his. She hated the sadness she saw there. Sadness warring with hostility. Sadness he never meant for her to see. It sent her imagination into overdrive.

She returned her attention to her plate, but nothing looked appetizing anymore. Glancing at him, she found him methodically forking the tofu mixture into his mouth. She grinned. "So, what do you think?"

Jesse stopped his heaping fork in midair and stared at it as if he hadn't realized he'd been eating. He put it down, chewing slowly, then reached for his wine and took a long sip. "Great," he said, barely getting the word out.

Shaking her head, Sunny erupted into laughter.

"No, really," he insisted and took another sip.

She laughed harder.

"What's so funny?" A smile tugged at his lips as he rose from the ground. "Ouch." He cupped his knee and flexed it.

Sunny laughed harder still, realizing her feet had gone to sleep under the cramped, makeshift table. Although she'd had only one cup of wine, she was a real lightweight when it came to drinking and could feel its giddy effect.

He limped around and grabbed one of her arms. "Come here," he said.

"I can't." She swatted at him and tried to wiggle life into her numb toes.

He grabbed her other arm, as well, and hauled her up, spinning her to face him.

"My feet are asleep," she grumbled, her giggles weakening the complaint.

He held her against him, her breasts pressed to his chest, barely any weight reaching her feet. "I guess you'll have to trust me to hold you up then."

Tilting her head, she gazed at him. She started to speak, started to tell him that she did trust him, even though she didn't know why. But she hiccuped instead. "Oh, my." Her hand flew to her mouth. Embarrassed, she mumbled, "The wine."

Jesse laughed. "You're a cheap date."

Sunny swallowed and moved her palm to his shoulder. "Am I?"

He didn't answer. He merely looked at her for a long time before he kissed her.

Sunny's eyes drifted closed. Her feet weren't numb anymore. At least she didn't think so. The rest of her was hotter than a firecracker, so it was pretty hard to tell.

Jesse's tongue was doing amazing things along her inner cheek and the side of her tongue, and she wasn't sure about anything at the moment.

She sagged against him and felt him harden.

Panic and the overwhelming need for self-preservation assailed her. But curiously, when her eyes fluttered open and Jesse's familiar, hooded gaze captured hers, the feeling fled as quickly as it had invaded.

She closed her eyes once more, pressing her body to his. Blood pounded and rushed to her ears. She grabbed the collar of his cotton shirt as breath left her body. His tongue dove and probed and Sunny prayed for oxygen.

When her palm slid to his chest, she felt his heart hammer against it. Desire, longing, then something even stronger pooled in her belly. She felt residual defenses splintering, shattering into small, fragile pieces. The feeling was so real it shook her.

She pulled away, breathing heavily, her chest heaving. She stared at him. Heaven help her. Was it Jesse? Was he the one? She shook her head. It couldn't be Jesse. Could it?

He stared, his breathing as labored as hers. He looked a little shaken, too. Or maybe she wanted to believe he was. Because if he was going to be the one, she had to believe that he felt the same way about her as she did about him.

She realized that her hand still lay on his chest and that it trembled uncontrollably. She slid it away with as much poise as she could manage.

He rotated his shoulder a half turn in the absence of her touch, his gaze dropping to the hands she now twisted together. When he looked up, his expression had slipped behind a hard mask. "I guess that was inevitable."

Sunny took another step back, his sudden coldness zapping her like an arctic blast. "What do you mean?"

"Us. Curiosity." He shrugged an indifferent shoulder.

She gave a small shake of her head. She didn't understand. They had kissed before. Surely he remembered. She did. To the last detail.

"Come on, Sunny," he said, giving her a feral smile and stepping closer. "Don't play coy. It's not your style."

"And this is yours?" She didn't like the cold look in his eyes, the restlessness she'd sensed earlier. This wasn't Jesse. She stumbled backward until her legs bumped the table.

His hand shot up to steady her and she flinched. The movement seemed to startle him, snapping him out of the unfamiliar role he was playing. His fingers gentled on her arm, then fell away.

Jesse sighed. "Go on to the diner, Sunny," he said quietly. "Violet and Maria want you to meet them there."

"Jesse?"

He gave her his back. "It doesn't matter, Sunny. In two days we reach Oklahoma."

She didn't move for several minutes, and neither did he. He

kept his gaze averted as she stared at the dark hair curling at his collar, the broad width of his shoulders, his slim hips. He didn't move except for the scuffed toe of his boot. It drew a jagged line in the dirt.

He wasn't going to turn around until she'd left, she realized.

Sighing softy, she ignored their half-eaten dinner, the cranberry-scented candles, the bouquet of wildflowers, and turned slowly toward the diner.

Because he was right.

After two days, she'd probably never see Jesse Logan again.

Chapter Thirteen

Jesse got up earlier than usual for a rest-stop morning, gathered up his bedroll and went in search of a shower.

Although there was no motel in Pocito, various townspeople had graciously offered beds to the crew. Everyone who hadn't pulled night duty with the cattle had accepted the hospitality. Everyone except Sunny.

God only knew what her reasoning was, but she'd insisted on sleeping in the wagon on her usual cot. And like the damn fool that he was, he'd laid out his bedroll and slept out here with her...except he'd been on the hard ground, under the stars, several feet away.

He didn't know why he'd done that. It wasn't as if it wasn't safe in Pocito, except he knew that if he hadn't stayed close enough in case she'd needed him, he wouldn't have gotten any sleep. Not that he'd gotten any, anyway.

Wearily he rubbed his eyes, then watched several men cart wood planks toward the area where the rodeo would be held. For a minute the insane thought that he should ride today struck him. He quickly discarded it. It had been quite a few months since his last and final rodeo, and he wasn't in the best of shape these days...physically or mentally.

Last night Sunny had been a temptation he couldn't afford. He'd almost blown it. He had wanted her so damn bad the obsession had nearly hog-tied his good sense. When was he going to learn that women like her only caused heartache? All these flighty beauty-queen types were good for was flirting and teasing. All they wanted was one-night stands and a life in the fast lane.

Except Sunny hadn't flirted and teased, a small voice reminded him. He wanted to believe she had. He hadn't wanted the game to change. Only Sunny had looked almost alarmed by what had happened between them.

Then he'd frightened her. And that was what bothered him most.

He replayed the confused look she had given him, how wide and vulnerable her eyes had grown. That's when she'd changed the rules of the game. The rules that should have been carved in stone. The game that kept his heart on a short leash.

He didn't understand her, he thought as his gaze wandered in the direction of the rodeo pen. She dumbfounded him. She made him crazy. She made him think about her far too much.

It was a good thing she'd be leaving the drive the day after tomorrow. For two more days he figured he could keep his pants zipped.

"DID Y'ALL HEAR the news?" Hank called excitedly as he jogged up behind Sunny, Maria, Ana and Violet. As he passed, he turned to face them, continuing to move backward toward the rodeo arena. "The Outlaw is riding today." Then he raced off toward the sound of the festivities.

"That damn fool," Maria said, shaking her head, then exchanging a troubled glance with Violet.

"Why did you call Uncle Jesse that bad word, Mama?" Ana raised her big black eyes to her mother.

Maria grimaced, then smiled. "You're right. That wasn't a nice word, *chica*."

"So why did you say it?" the child insisted.

"Because Uncle Jesse shouldn't be riding those nasty bulls." Maria patted her daughter's head.

"Why not? He always used to."

Again Maria exchanged glances with Violet, and Sunny found herself impatient for the answer. Although the thought of Jesse being bucked and thrown by some wild bull was enough to make her agree.

"Well, because…" Maria hesitated as though carefully choosing her words. "Because he's done it too long. He has too many injuries, *chica*."

"What's injuries?" Ana asked, but her attention was already waning, her gaze wandering to the penned rodeo animals.

Maria easily evaded answering and steered the child toward the crowd gathering near the bleachers. Except Sunny wanted to know more. She turned toward Violet and was about to ask her when Smiley broke through a throng of cowboys.

"You heard about Jesse?" Violet asked him immediately.

"Yup." Looking tired, Smiley shook his head. The tight braid he normally wore appeared hastily woven. "I tried poundin' some sense into him, but the boy is stubborner than a mule. I figured he'd rodeoed for the last time after that last incident. Where's Manny? Maybe he can talk to him."

"Near camp. He's got watch," Maria said. "Better grab one of the boys to cover for him. He'll talk to him for all it's worth. But I've seen Jesse hell-bent on these suicide missions before."

"Well, he ain't gonna finish this drive he's been so fired up over if he breaks his neck," Smiley said and hurried off in the direction of the longhorns.

Suicide mission? Break his neck? Sunny's heart raced. Maria, Violet and Ana had moved several yards ahead of her before Sunny realized that she stood perfectly still, staring at nothing. And feeling panic swell inside her.

When she caught up to the others, she asked Maria, "What did Smiley mean about the last incident?"

"He was thrown and gored in the thigh by a bull," Maria said, and when Sunny felt herself blanch, the other woman hurried to add, "It wasn't life-threatening or anything like that, but it could have been avoided if Jesse's reflexes had been quicker…like when he was younger. We all saw it."

"That's when he retired from the circuit," Violet said. "Although I can't say for certain he would have quit if it hadn't been for this trail boss job."

Maria nodded. "I hope he can get that ranch he's always wanted. He sure doesn't need to be on no bull's back."

A mob of people pressed in around them, and Sunny's dwindling supply of oxygen seemed to grow scarcer. Jesse's name was being murmured throughout the crowd, most of them referring to him as the Outlaw or Jesse James. They never thought they'd see him ride again, some were saying. They hoped he'd last the entire ride.

Two clowns with their funny painted faces and bright red wigs huddled behind the pens where large, angry-looking beasts awaited their potential victims.

Sunny shuddered. Why was he doing this? He'd turned down invitations in the other two towns where there had been rodeos. He'd even ignored the drunken jeers he'd gotten from some of the local cowboys. Why had he decided to ride now?

The rodeo was already in full swing and everyone had taken seats, including Violet, Ana and Maria. Sunny had far too much restless energy to sit and had waved them ahead, opting to stand near the fence where the rodeo riders entered as their turns came up. She was hoping to see Jesse in the event that Manny and Smiley had been unable to talk him out of riding. She wasn't sure why she wanted to see him. She doubted she could talk him into or out of anything, but she stood glued to her spot, waiting.

The sun was hot on her bare arms, making it feel more like midafternoon than late morning. Oily smells of movie popcorn occasionally wafted through the air from the food concession and made Sunny's stomach a little queasy. But when she shifted away, the odor of fear mixed with anger and sweat emanating from the bulls' pens made her downright nauseous.

Announcement after announcement was made. One rider after another entered through the gate. But still there was no sign of Jesse. Maybe Manny had talked him out of riding. Sunny stood on tiptoe and craned her neck over a tide of Stetsons, trying to see if Smiley or Jesse had joined the others. But today's rodeo had drawn an amazing crowd, and she could no longer find her friends.

After what seemed like hours, Sunny decided to go find Violet and Maria. She was about to turn away from the fence when the voice over the loudspeaker announced the final morning event.

Her fingers wrapped tightly around the metal pole, Sunny pressed her face against the chain-link fence and held her breath.

"And now, what everyone has been waiting for…" The announcer took a dramatic pause. "The Outlaw, Jesse James."

Although the man went on to describe the event, cheers from the crowd nearly drowned out his voice. Not that Sunny could have heard a thing anyway. Blood rushed to her ears and pounded like a stampede of longhorns.

She elbowed a tall cowboy who was in her way and stretched to see Jesse climbing over the pen of the meanest-looking bull of the lot. Jesse looked tired, as though he hadn't slept well, but he flashed a quick grin for his fans who continued to cheer him on.

Red-hot anger infused her. Anger toward these people who blithely rooted him toward danger. And anger at him for so foolishly risking his life this way. Then as he poised above the savage animal, the anger gave way to fear.

As Jesse mounted the bull, she squeezed her eyes shut and tightened her grip on the metal pole to keep herself from slipping to the ground. Seconds, minutes, hours could have passed, she wasn't sure. Even when everyone quieted for a moment she didn't look, but when the crowd once again roared to life, her eyes flew open.

By the time her gaze found the ring, the bull—minus Jesse—was charging a clown in a barrel and Jesse was hopping up and over the wooden fence. Grinning, he waved to the crowd.

Sunny stayed frozen in place, beyond grateful that he was okay. Several cowboys surrounded him, slapping him on the back, shaking his hand, as he made his way toward the open grounds.

When he got within a few yards of her, Sunny stepped away from the fence, and his gaze fastened on her. He looked away for a moment when someone spoke to him, but his eyes slowly returned to her.

She was glad he was okay because she wanted to kill him herself. No less than ten gray hairs had sprouted in the few seconds Jesse had been atop that bull, and she was certain she could feel permanent wrinkles around her mouth from jamming her lips together.

She didn't remember ever being so afraid in her life.

When he made no attempt to approach her, she started slowly in his direction. Some of the men who had been congratulating him ambled off, but many stayed clustered around him. She didn't know what she was going to say once she reached him, but that didn't stop her legs from moving.

His expression was dark and guarded at first, and she felt uneasy about not being able to read it. As she got closer, a slow grin tugged at his lips and his eyes gleamed with the thrill of victory. She didn't care about the victory part, but she reveled in the sign that he was safe. She wanted to kiss him and hug him and feel tangible proof that he was okay.

She stopped in front of him, her hands flying to her hips. "What the hell was that all about?" she snapped.

The men around him turned to stare at her but she ignored them. Jesse's smile faded and his eyes narrowed. "Haven't you seen enough rodeos yet?"

She dismissed his sarcasm with a glare, but a catch in her voice betrayed her. "You could have gotten hurt."

The other men howled at that, but something oddly tender glittered in Jesse's eyes for a moment and he broke away from the cowboys to close in on her. She stepped back, her hands falling from her hips.

He stared intently at her, raising her chin with his index finger, and asked, "Were you worried?" When she tried to twist away, his thumb shot up to help hold her chin in place. "Were you, Sunny? Worried about me?"

Her gaze lifted reluctantly to his and she was surprised to find a spark of anger where the tenderness had been. "I was worried about you being able to finish the drive."

His dark, wary eyes searched her face. "Good," he said, his expression tight. "Don't waste your concern on me."

Only Sunny knew it was too late. She edged away and twisted her chin from his touch, her eyes never leaving his. She'd been concerned, all right. Too concerned. Far more than she wanted to be. Sighing, she figured there was only one thing left to do about the strange knot in the pit of her stomach, the way her heart beat quicker these days.

She had to go condom shopping.

THIS WAS her last chance, Sunny told herself as she circled the cramped aisles of Pocito's small general store for the third time. In a day and a half they'd be at the Oklahoma border and she would be returning to Rainy and Cash's ranch. As much as she was looking forward to spending time with her twin, she was incredibly sad about leaving the drive...and most of all Jesse.

"Are you sure I can't help you?" the elderly store clerk asked for the fourth time.

And for the fourth time, Sunny nearly jumped out of her skin. She blindly picked up a tube of hemorrhoid cream and smiled. "No, thank you."

The afternoon rodeo activities would be winding up soon, and if she was going to get her shopping done in private, she'd better hurry. Just thinking about what she had to do made her ears burn. But she squared her shoulders, her gaze darting behind the counter, past the store clerk, who stared at her over his reading glasses.

Sunny spotted what she hoped were packages of condoms. She'd never bought them before but she recognized the brand name. Now all she had to do was point, she told herself, flexing her index finger. She didn't even have to say the word. This entire process would have been far easier in a city pharmacy, but by early tomorrow morning they would be out of here, she reminded herself. And she would be closer to leaving Jesse. Swallowing the last of her pride, she stepped to the counter.

Her finger made it to midair when the bell over the door

tinkled. Out of the corner of her eye, she saw Violet enter the store. Sunny's arm dropped to her side.

"Did you want something?" The clerk frowned at her.

"No. Just this." She set the hemorrhoid cream on the counter.

"Hey, Sunny. Where have you been?" Violet asked, heading for her. "You missed the best part." The woman's gaze strayed to the hemorrhoid cream just as the clerk started to sack it. Her brow puckered.

Maria followed Violet. "No cooking again tonight. The town is giving us a send-off barbecue." She looked from Sunny's anxious face to Violet's frown. "What's wrong with y'all? That's supposed to be good news."

"Great," Sunny said, and paid for her purchase. Her hand shook slightly as she digested this new information and how it would affect her plans for the night.

Plans? Who was she kidding? There were no plans for tonight. She was horrible at this sort of thing. Her heart was beating like a jackhammer, her palms were itching and all this was in response to just buying the damn condoms. Which she'd also failed to do.

She grabbed her package off the counter. "I'll see you later," she said to her two confused friends, and hurried away.

Outside the store, she stepped off the wooden boardwalk and ran into Jesse.

"Where's the fire?" he asked, his hands shooting up to grab her upper arms. Although he'd managed to stop the collision, his fingers remained wrapped around her bare skin. There was a hint of a smile in his voice, and when she looked at him, she saw the corners of his mouth tilt in amusement. He needed a shave again. It looked like he hadn't bothered in a couple of days.

"I heard there's a barbecue tonight," she said and was surprised that it came out so breathless.

His grin widened. "Not for several more hours." His thumb stroked her warm flesh a couple of times. A strange expression crossed his face and he seemed to realize that he had no reason to continue touching her. He lowered his hands. "You've been shopping?" he asked conversationally.

Sunny followed his gaze to the bag. Her cheeks flamed. "Sort of," she mumbled.

"Me, too." He blinked when she frowned. "I mean I gotta pick up something, too."

Sunny had never seen Jesse James Logan disconcerted. But he certainly was edgy now. He fumbled with the top pearl snap of his Western shirt and took a deep breath.

Violet and Maria stepped out of the store behind Sunny, their voices floating ahead of them.

"You two are going to the barbecue, aren't you?" Violet asked once they'd gotten closer. "Unless Sunny hooked you with her macrobiotic cooking." Both women laughed.

That wasn't a bad idea, Sunny thought. She could lure him away under the guise of trying out a new menu.

"I'm not sure I'm going," Jesse said.

Maria frowned. She leaned closer and whispered, "I'd stay clear of the diner, if I were you. The food is awful."

"Yeah." He laughed nervously and glanced at Sunny.

Neither Violet nor Maria seemed to notice and meandered off toward camp. But curiosity rooted Sunny in place as she considered asking him what he intended on doing tonight. When she looked into his eyes and watched his gaze slip to her mouth, then darken before meeting her eyes once more, her breath caught in her throat. She thought—no, she hoped—she'd found her answer.

"Well, I'd better get my shopping done and go get cleaned up," he said, blinking and breaking the spell. He removed his hat and hit it against his hand. Dust filtered through the air.

When he hesitated a moment longer, Sunny realized that he was waiting for her to leave before he entered the store.

"Yeah, me, too." She gave him a tight smile and turned away. After she'd taken several steps in the direction of camp, she heard the store door open behind her.

Out of nowhere the absurd notion came to her. The odd discomfort she'd witnessed, the secret looks Jesse had given her, his evasiveness about tonight. Could they possibly have the same thing in mind? He'd been sensible last night, but Sunny wasn't so stupid that she didn't recognize the chemistry that existed between them.

Sneaking back to spy on him was insane, nervy and rude, she told herself. So she did it very carefully. She'd worry about the guilt later, but right now she had to know if they shared mutual shopping lists.

It took all the nerve she had to sidle up to the store's window, position herself on the side and turn her head just enough to peek through the red painted letters proclaiming to everyone that this was Humphrey's General Store.

Between the thick *H* and the *U* Sunny spied Jesse standing at the counter. He had nothing in his hands, nothing on the counter in front of him. He said something to the clerk, who smiled and grabbed a package off the shelf behind him.

She immediately drew back and slumped against the rough wood siding. Her pulse leaped into the next century. Although she didn't actually see it, she knew exactly what Jesse had bought.

SUNNY OPENED her compact and checked her lipstick. It was almost six forty-five, and in another fifteen minutes she'd have to light one of the lanterns.

Poking her head outside the wagon, she noticed that almost everyone had left the camp to go to the barbecue. With the exception of several cowboys exchanging shifts to watch the cattle, she knew the camp would soon be totally deserted. Would that be when Jesse came to get her?

She started to drag her damp palms down the sleek black leather miniskirt she wore, then caught herself and rubbed her hands together instead. Blowing into her palms, she snuck another look around.

In her head, she did a mental checklist. She'd used her best herbal shampoo, had borrowed a blow dryer from the woman whose shower she had used. And with as steady a hand as she could manage, she'd applied the makeup she'd given up on nearly two weeks ago.

Now, waiting was the only thing left for her to do. She flipped open the compact once more and dabbed the smoky gray shadow at the outer corners of her eyelids. Her face had been exposed to far too much sun this last month, despite her efforts to protect her skin. She knew her agent was going to have a royal fit when he saw her, but she didn't care in the least. In fact, the thought of returning to the camera in another two weeks held zero appeal.

She wanted to stay with the drive. She wanted to be near Jesse. And after tonight, after she knew what it was like to love him... She shuddered, realizing that her skin's exposure was the least of her problems. Her heart had suffered far greater damage.

She snapped her compact closed and picked at her pathetically short nails. This was only going to be a one-time thing, she reminded herself, so if she couldn't handle it, she'd better back out now. In forty-eight hours, she'd be back in Maybe. And Jesse would be well on his way to forgetting he'd ever met her.

Sunny swallowed hard. She had no choice. Her decision had been made weeks ago, she realized, when Jesse had touched her. Somehow, deep down inside, she had known he was the one and she had fought it, fought him every step of the way. Except tonight she was ready. Ready to admit, at least to herself, that she cared about this man.

For some reason, the acceptance calmed her and she tucked her compact away for the last time. In another few minutes, she'd have to break down and light the lantern, but for now she swung her legs over the back of the wagon and breathed in the crisp twilight air.

It was at that moment that she saw him, standing near the other wagon. She smiled and started to lift her hand when she saw the petite, sultry brunette familiarly sidle up to him. Tilting her head to gaze into his face, the woman wrapped her arms around his waist.

Jesse smiled at her, then they turned and walked off.

Chapter Fourteen

Jesse was tired and hungry, and his muscles ached from his ride today. Although he felt a lot better since he'd bought a tube of painkilling ointment this afternoon.

At least the store clerk had been discreet, and Jesse had been grateful. Now his shoulders and ego had both been soothed, but there was still no way he was going to the barbecue, now in full swing, and risk running into Sunny. It didn't look like he was going to get any sleep tonight, either, he realized grumpily, thinking about how sweet Sunny had looked when she'd tried to pretend she hadn't been worried about him. He liked her better when she was a wildcat. He was far better off being irritated by her.

He sauntered toward the chuck wagon wondering if Maria had any ready snacks he could fill up on. Going to the diner was another dead end. The pretty little waitress, Kathy, whose sexy invitation he'd turned down a half hour ago, wouldn't be happy to see him. Although she'd assured him at one point that she had all night, Jesse wasn't taking any chances that she'd gone back to the diner. Kathy had been madder than any bull he'd ridden when, in the middle of her eager advances, he'd called it a night.

He didn't blame her for being mad. After all, he had led her on. But he figured she'd be a whole lot madder if she knew that all he could think about was Sunny. When he'd tried to make himself kiss Kathy, he'd realized that he'd made a big mistake in trying to use her to get his mind off Sunny. He hadn't fully realized what he'd been doing until the unsuccessful kiss.

It was then he started replaying all of Sunny's kisses in his head, seeing her almond-shaped brown eyes looking soft and vulnerable. When he'd caught himself nearly calling Kathy the wrong name, he'd put a stop to the phony intimacy, which not long ago would have suited him just fine.

He sighed as he fumbled for a flashlight in the back of the wagon. In another day, he wouldn't have to think about Sunny anymore. *Right, pal.* He snorted with disgust and felt the cool metal cylinder beneath his fingertips. He flipped on the light just as he noticed the soft glow coming from the back of the second wagon.

Frowning, he turned to see if anyone was around. If he'd been anyplace else, he would have been concerned about looting, but here in Pocito, the problem was more likely that Sunny had forgotten to turn off her lantern.

Shaking his head, he pointed the flashlight and walked toward the wagon. It was a safety hazard to leave the lantern on, and although the entire crew knew that, he wouldn't expect Sunny to cooperate.

Jesse stopped himself. He was being a jerk. He wanted to find fault with her. Sunny wasn't the prissy airhead he'd first taken her to be. He'd known that from the minute he'd figured out that Sunny had given Ana her hat to protect the child's face from the sun. Sunny hadn't shunned the hat in favor of her hair, as she'd let him believe.

Or maybe she hadn't let him believe anything at all. Maybe he'd chosen to believe that of her. Because it was safer. Because their worlds were solar systems apart. Because after tomorrow, they'd have nothing in common.

Jesse hopped up on the back of the wagon and parted the privacy curtain. The lantern was near the opening, turned down very low, and everything appeared in order at first glance. Then he saw the mass of tousled blond hair cascading over the edge of the cot and grazing the wagon floor.

He stepped in, picked up the lantern and moved to gaze into Sunny's sleeping, tearstained face. She'd put on makeup—something he hadn't seen on her in quite a while. It was smudged and streaked near her eyes, and a long strand of honey-colored hair wove through her lashes and rested across her flushed cheek. Crouching beside her, he gently lifted the hair from her face, wondering what had upset her so badly and feeling an unnerving fury toward anyone or anything that would hurt her. He noticed the black leather miniskirt—the expanse of long tan legs—and quickly pulled back his hand.

Too late. Sunny's lashes fluttered but didn't open completely. He thought about running while he still could, but something held him there, watching her, watching over her, wanting to comfort her.

Slowly, her eyes opened. She looked at him, her gaze unfocused, before she blinked several times. As if she suddenly realized where she was and who he was, she propped herself up on one elbow.

"What are you doing here?" she asked angrily, shoving the hair away from her face. Her fingertips swiped at the tear marks on her cheeks.

"I saw the light on," he said softly and rose to give her room.

"Does that mean you can barge in on me?"

"I thought the wagon was empty. That you had forgotten to turn off the lantern before you left."

She tugged at the hem of her skirt and started to sit up. "So, you thought you could use my cot for your little rendezvous." She sniffed haughtily, except Jesse thought he saw fresh tears shimmering in her eyes.

He held up the lantern for a better look at her face. "What's wrong, Sunny?"

She swatted at him and turned away.

"Sunny, talk to me. Did someone hurt you?" He tried to keep his voice calm but he felt his hackles rise at the thought of anyone harming her.

"Go away."

He grabbed her wrist, keeping his hold as gentle as possible, yet demanding her attention. "I'm not going away until you tell me who hurt you."

She turned her face toward him. "You did."

Then her eyes widened in horror as if she'd give anything to take her words back. She tried to twist away from him, but he continued to shackle her wrist until he set down the lantern and sank to the cot beside her.

"Please, Sunny," he said, when she gave him the back of her head. The pleasing scent of honey and almonds drifted from her hair, her semi-bare shoulders. "Honey, will you please talk to me?"

"Don't you call me honey." She did turn her head then and gave him a scathing look. "Save it for..." She sniffed loudly, which he could tell angered her to greater heights, and she clamped her mouth shut and gave him her back again.

Jesse slipped his arms around her, imprisoning her arms at her sides, until his palms cupped the front of her shoulders. "Go on. Finish what you were going to say."

She delivered a well-placed elbow to his ribs. Jesse groaned and blinked the stars from his vision. His hold had slipped a little, and when she tried to get up, he slid his arms lower, tightening them in order to protect the rest of his ribs. In this new position, he felt her soft breasts press against his forearms. Gasping, she sank against him to create distance between his arms and her breasts. He held her tighter, against his chest, his chin resting in her hair.

"Do you get the feeling you aren't going anywhere until you tell me what's going on?" he asked.

"Why don't you go find your playmate and leave me alone?" She squirmed, twisting and writhing, testing his strength, then with a deep breath relaxed against him.

She felt good in his arms, too good, and he wasn't thinking all that clearly. But as her last words sank in, the fog started to lift from his brain. Playmate? Could she be talking about Kathy? Had she seen them together?

Jesse smiled. Sunny was jealous.

"If I let you go, will you promise not to elbow me again?" he asked, loosening his arms ever so slightly.

"I'll have to think about it." Her chin went up and her head nearly bopped him in the nose.

Laughing, he moved his head back. "Does that mean you like me holding you?"

This time when her body gave a sharp twist, she caught him off guard and he was forced to let her go. She spun to face him while trying to get up at the same time and nearly stumbled onto his lap. "In your dreams." She teetered over the cot, and he reached out a hand to help her. She slapped it away.

"Can we discuss this like reasonable adults?" he asked, holding his palms up.

"There is nothing to discuss. Either you leave or I do." One hand went to her hip. Her face was flushed with anger, hurt, indignation.

"Nothing happened," Jesse said.

She stared at him for a moment, then her hand left her hip to rub her other arm. "What are you talking about?"

"Kathy, the waitress from the diner. We went for a walk and nothing happened."

"Why would I care about that?"

"No reason. I'm just babbling." He put a hand out to her. "Sit with me."

"Did you go to the barbecue?"

"No. We took a walk, then we were going to have dinner at her house. But we didn't do that, either."

A smug grin tugged at the corners of Sunny's mouth, and her chin went up a few more degrees. "She dumped you?"

He shook his head. It would be easy to agree. Then he could accept Sunny's teasing and everything would go back to normal between them. But it didn't seem right for her not to know, to allow her to think she'd taken the back seat to another woman.

"No, Sunny. I left," he said and watched her eyes narrow, presumably mirroring her opinion of his ego. "I kept thinking of you."

She blinked, and the hand that flew to her hair trembled. He caught it and kissed her palm while tugging at her arm, coaxing her to sit beside him.

He kept her warm hand sandwiched between his until she sank down onto the cot, her bare thigh lightly touching his denim-clad one. In this new position, the shadows danced across her face, obscuring her eyes. Only her mouth was bathed in the soft orange glow of the lantern. When her tongue darted out to moisten her lips, his breathing faltered.

"Why did you come back?" she asked.

He removed one of his hands from hers to shove his fingers through his hair. She still clung to his other hand, and he wondered if she even realized it. "Because it wasn't fair to Kathy."

"Is that the only reason?" She brushed the inside of his wrist with the pad of her thumb, and he knew for certain that she knew exactly what she was doing.

"What do you want, Sunny?" He drew in a sharp breath. "What do you want to hear?"

Her chin and lower lip quivered. "The truth."

Except Jesse knew the truth could hurt them both. Only one more day, he told himself. One more day and temptation would be removed. Then he would spend the rest of his life wondering. "You. I came back for you."

Jesse saw the shiver that controlled her shoulders. Her hand grew slightly cool in his. "Will you kiss me, Jesse?" she asked softly.

Would he? Jesse briefly closed his eyes and drew in a deep breath before he let go of her hand and circled his arms around her. As he pulled her forward, her face slipped out of the light, but not before he saw her lips part ever so slightly.

He was going to regret this. He knew that without a doubt, but as he pressed his mouth to her soft lips and felt her tiny whimper vibrate against him, he also knew that any choice had been removed. Jesse wanted her with such burning intensity, it scared the hell out of him.

His hands were none too steady as he drew them back to cup her face. He tried to keep the kiss gentle, but once his mind processed the reality of having a willing Sunny in his arms, his lips grew hungry and urgent.

He teased her lower lip with his tongue. At first she seemed timid about opening totally to him, then her mouth fit more confidently with his and she received the thrust of his tongue against her silky recesses.

She didn't hold back anymore. She leaned into him, pressing her soft breasts against him, her hands languidly on his shoulders, receiving his kisses with both trust and longing.

Jesse felt himself getting so hard he thought he'd explode. Days, weeks had been building up to this moment. From the time her silly pink boots had hit the dry Maybe dirt and she'd opened that sassy mouth of hers, he'd been hooked. But that had been pure physical lust, and what he felt right now he couldn't put a name to. For now, it was enough that she was in his arms and kissing him like he was the most important man on earth, not that rotten Logan kid who'd never amount to anything.

Shifting on the cramped cot, he drew back from her for a moment. He needed to slow down, temper his response. He wanted their time together to be slow and thorough, but it felt like his hormones were entering a second childhood. His entire body was already protesting the slight distance he'd placed between them.

And so was hers, he noticed. The lantern's glow lit her exposed throat where a pulse throbbed wildly and visibly. The light bathed her flushed cheeks, stopping short of her eyes, and he could see traces of her earlier tears. Extending his thumb, he stroked a path through the dried salty tracks. She turned her face and drew his thumb into her mouth.

Watching her pink lips pursed around his thumb sent his libido into overdrive again. Erotic visuals that had nothing to do with his thumb pelted his brain.

"Sunny?" he whispered.

Slowly, her mouth released him. When she turned to face him, dipping her head slightly, one of her eyes caught the light. It was so wide and vulnerable it startled him.

"Sunny," he repeated, because the way she looked made him too afraid to voice his original thoughts. But he had to. "Are you sure about this?" He put a hand to her hair and brushed it from her face.

She nodded. The lantern spotlighted the long swallow she took.

He pulled her toward him so that he could see both eyes. "Say it."

Her lashes fluttered, but she kept her gaze steadily on him. "I want you to make love to me."

Jesse released the breath he hadn't been aware he held. Her eyes were so warm and trusting, and he wished she hadn't used the word *love*. She could have said any number of things that would have told him it was okay. That she wanted him as much as he wanted her.

But it was just a phrase, he told himself. Meaningless, other than conveying what she wanted. That was why he wasn't reacting adversely to it.

He looked again into those trusting brown eyes, then swore silently at himself. "I wish we had someplace else to go," he whispered. "This isn't very…"

"Romantic?" she asked, finishing his sentence when he couldn't. "I think so. This keeps in sync with how we met." A shy smile tugged at her mouth.

He felt himself smile, too, even though he didn't particularly like the tone of the conversation. This was a one-time deal, he reminded himself, not something to tell the grandkids. The fact that the thought even occurred to him sent him to his feet. Sunny stumbled with the sudden movement, confusion shadowing her eyes.

He should go. He should jump down from this wagon right this minute and leave Sunny just as he found her. He gazed at her parted lips, her questioning eyes. "The privacy curtain," he said, "I've gotta snap it shut."

She nodded and the relief that flooded her face made him feel ten feet tall. Then he shrank back down to two inches. He shouldn't be doing this. He had no right. She was Cash's sister-in-law, he thought, as he snapped the curtain. She should be off-limits. Then he turned to her.

She was also beautiful, and she hadn't cared that he was some hotshot rodeo champ. She hadn't been trying to snag the top cowboy in the rodeo today, who'd aced all his events. Sunny had been worried that he could've been hurt.

Smiling, he reclaimed his place beside her and buried himself in her soft arms.

Sunny didn't know what kind of internal war Jesse had been fighting. By the parade of emotions across his face, it was obvious a battle had ensued. She was only concerned with the outcome. And what a sweet outcome it was, she thought, as she cradled him in her arms.

She was comforting him for something, though she didn't know what. But she gladly held him for those few moments when comfort was more important than raw need.

When Jesse stirred, she felt his lips at her neck, soft and pliant, working their way to her jaw, the side of her ear. Moisture coated her flesh as his tongue traced the shell. His finger tunneled deep into her hair as he moved her head to expose her throat.

Taking tiny nips, then soothing them with soft kisses, he worked his way down to the deep V of her shirt. He stopped where her breasts began, took one last lick, then brought his gaze to meet hers.

She couldn't see his eyes very well. The lantern was turned down low and sat too far past his shoulder. She trusted him though, and waited for him to resume the lead.

He didn't keep her waiting long. Slowly, he began slipping the small buttons of her blouse out of the tiny holes. His long tan fingers should have looked clumsy with buttons so small, but he handled the task with efficiency and ease, and not for the first time Sunny worried that she was too far out of her league.

She was so far out, she realized giddily, that although she'd planned his seduction, she hadn't even been savvy enough to choose an easier blouse. A small, nervous giggle escaped her

Jesse looked up. Then a wide grin spread across his face, his teeth looking all the whiter against his darkened face. "Ticklish?"

"A little," she admitted, skipping the real cause of her little outburst.

"Don't worry, honey," he said, pushing the blouse off her shoulders. "Tickling is not what I wanna do to you."

A thrill shot through her, and she felt the night air caress her flesh where the blouse had been parted. The fabric scampered down her back, and all that was between her and Jesse was a piece of black lace that should have covered more than it did.

Her hands jerked toward her body. Instinctively, she wanted to hide herself. A swarm of insecurities enveloped her. He'd expect her to be more experienced. What if she disappointed him? What if she was wrong about him? What if...

But this was Jesse, whose hand suddenly shook ever so slightly as he cupped her shoulder, whose sharp intake of breath she heard. So instead of covering herself, she reached out and tugged his shirt from his jeans.

He leaned back slightly, but that was the only help he offered. When she gave the final pull, she heard a snap disengage and realized that his Western-style shirt had no buttons. Before she could chicken out, she ripped open the shirt. The sound of popping snaps filled the quiet, and even as Sunny's breath stalled in her throat, the heady sense of triumph quickened her pulse.

Shrugging out of his shirt, he flung it to the floor, his gaze remaining on her face. He returned his hands to her shoulders, pressing his palms to her skin, warming her, teasing her until he lowered them toward her breasts. Only he hovered near where the flesh started to swell, trailing his fingers lightly over the peaks and valleys while he captured her mouth once more with his.

So absorbed was she in his urgent kiss, Sunny didn't realized he had released the front clasp of her bra until his mouth left her lips and he started kissing his way toward her breasts. From her tensed arms, the black lace hung limply behind her as she clutched his shoulders. Trying to force herself to relax, she straightened first one arm and then the other until she was free of the fabric.

Before she could find his shoulder again, his mouth found her nipple. He sucked gently at first, using his tongue to outline and trace, and when he moved his mouth to her other breast, his fingers took over the pleasure he'd abandoned.

Her body went boneless and Sunny knew she was about to die from the exquisite feelings that mushroomed through her, leaving her moist and ready to burst.

Tuning out the small voice of insecurity that had kept her hands rigid, she tentatively moved her palms to follow the tight muscles of his chest. As she pressed into him, feeling the firm ridges and contours, his nipples hardened and she experimentally rubbed the distended nub between her thumb and finger.

She felt his slow grin, his hot ragged breath against her breast, and her confidence grew. Urging his face to hers, she tasted his lips, pressing her nakedness against his bare chest. His shudder echoed her own before his hand started massaging her thigh.

Her leather skirt had ridden up, and Jesse's warm palms went higher still. His fingertips grazed the string bikini panties she'd worn especially for him, then his hand retreated slowly, his fingers trailing down her thigh and leaving raised flesh in their wake. Wanting to tease him like he had taunted her, she reached for his thigh.

Only his leg was not what her hand came into contact with. She flexed her fingers a fraction and was left without a doubt that she was cupping his fly...and the hardness beneath. Jesse moaned low in his throat.

This was not the sort of teasing she'd had in mind. But he'd already accepted the challenge and started stroking his way under the leather skirt until one roving finger dipped underneath the elastic of her panties.

Sunny jumped. *This is Jesse,* she told herself again.

"Are you okay?" His hand froze. She heard the elastic snap into place.

"I'm okay." She pushed her face into the hollow near his throat.

"Hey. No hiding." Removing his hand from under her skirt, he drew back and nudged her chin. His chest rose and fell rapidly, his breathing unsteady. He ducked his head to look at her. "You'd tell me if there was something wrong?"

Her gaze roaming his familiar face, she nodded, smiled.

He smiled, then, watching her closely, he pulled her to him. She let her head loll back, enjoying the slightly rough texture of his jaw against her neck, her chest. "Jesse?"

His tongue flicked a nipple as he reached around and tugged at her zipper. "Hmm?"

Sunny forgot what she was going to say. She fell silent and listened to the teeth of the zipper slowly disengage. When the sound stopped, he gently urged her back. She lowered her body to the cot, supporting herself with one elbow and a hand around his shoulder, then slipped to a fully reclined position. He followed her down, and as she took a large, steadying breath, her nipple disappeared into his mouth.

He continued to lave her with his tongue as he skimmed the leather skirt down her hips, past her thighs. At the last minute his mouth broke away and he flung the skirt to the side, leaving her in a string of black lace.

Leaning back, he splayed a hand across her belly, then let it trail away. "You're beautiful," he whispered, "absolutely beautiful." He was looking at her face when he whispered the words, not at her body, and Sunny felt a little more at ease.

Jesse wasn't like the others. She already knew that. She didn't believe for a minute that he was any kind of saint, but she knew he would never hurt her. She'd waited her whole life for him.

When she pulled him down for another kiss, his fingers strayed to the top of her panties. Her stomach muscles clenched in response, and Jesse's hand slipped under the elastic, his fingers unerringly moving toward the center of her heat. She squirmed reflexively, but his soft whispers and gentle hands calmed her, and she relaxed against his expert touch.

Then she couldn't relax anymore. She was wet, slick, arching toward him, astonished at how her entire body was magnetized to his touch. Her thoughts spun out of control, and a tiny tremor shut her brain down altogether. Then another tremor, larger this time, and another, until her body convulsed and she twisted her head, bringing a fist to her mouth to keep from crying out.

"God, Sunny." Jesse's lips moved against her throat. She felt his low growl vibrate against her skin as her body slipped into a languid state. She fisted her hand in his hair, wanting to keep him close, but he was pulling away, smiling, his breathing labored, his hands at his jeans.

In a daze, she watched him fumble with his zipper, her mind and eyes unfocused. "I'm glad I waited, Jesse," she said, with a small, sluggish smile. "I knew you were the one." She reached a limp hand out to help him.

Jesse blinked his way out of his own fog. It took several seconds for her words to register. His hand froze. "What did you say?" When her hand jerked closer to his fly, he grabbed her wrist to stop her. "What did you say?"

Sunny closed her eyes and breathed a contented sigh. "It's okay," she whispered. "I know you're the one."

She was a virgin. Stunned, he released her hand and backed out of her reach. Slowly he zipped his jeans against the painful hardness, which had already begun diminishing.

Damn. How could he have known? Why hadn't she warned him? His thoughts disjointedly skipped to all the times he'd been surprised by her reactions to their chemistry. He shook his head.

Sunny blinked, and he could tell by the way her eyes grew wary, and the way the hand he'd stopped from touching him drew protectively against her breasts, that the shock of her climax was wearing off.

"It really is okay, Jesse," she said softly, her voice catching on his name. "I know you're the one."

His laugh was harsh as he grabbed his shirt. "You don't get

it, do you?'' Shaking his head, he jerked into his shirt. ''I'm not the one, Sunny. Don't you understand?'' His voice lowered to a brutal whisper, and without snapping his shirt, he savagely ripped open the privacy curtain and prepared to hop off the wagon. He looked at her one last time. ''I am *not* the one.''

And damn her for making him believe it...if even for a moment.

Chapter Fifteen

The next day Sunny went numbly through the motions of saying goodbye to the people of Pocito and packing up camp before getting on the trail again...the trail to Oklahoma, where she would part company with the drive—and Jesse.

Just thinking about him and what had happened last night made her eyes glaze over with tears. She sniffed loudly, which netted her a quick look from Violet before the woman returned her attention to the reins and keeping the wagon from getting too close to the highway.

When Maria and Violet had noticed Sunny's gloomy mood at breakfast, they'd automatically chalked it up to the fact that she'd be leaving the drive tomorrow. They'd urged her to ask Jesse if she could stay on, but she'd lied, telling them that she already had modeling commitments. She hadn't told anyone, including Rainy, that she'd decided to leave the business. She'd been unhappy with the work for some time, but she'd been unsure where her university marketing degree would get her. Now she didn't care about that. She merely had to have faith that she'd land on her feet.

And hope that her professional life wouldn't so grimly mirror her messed-up personal one.

She hadn't seen Jesse since he'd walked out on her last night. Oh, she'd seen him from a distance, but he'd made it a point to stay clear of her. He'd even skipped lunch.

Had she been wrong in not telling him ahead of time? she

wondered. She hadn't meant to keep the detail of her virginity from him. She'd made the decision to maintain that small modicum of control over her life so long ago, she simply didn't think about it anymore.

Having started modeling at an early age due to her mother's coaxing, Sunny had found the business to be cruel and daunting. Men had become a problem early on, when she'd been far too young to handle the attention. In trying to keep herself above the indecent proposals, the flaunting of casual sex, chastity had seemed the simplest solution.

And now Jesse made it seem like something dirty.

Sunny sniffed again, and this time Violet kept her eyes straight ahead. Sunny had already run the gamut of emotions, going through the hurt stage, then anger, back to hurt. But anger was gaining when she thought about how humiliated she felt when he left her there, in only her panties, having just had the most incredible experience of her life.

Maybe her virginity wasn't the issue, she suddenly considered. It was when she'd told him that he was the one. Then he'd really gone off on her. Maybe he'd misunderstood. Maybe he thought she was trying to trap him into a relationship. If that was the case, how stupid could he be? She knew that their involvement would have been limited to last night. They were parting tomorrow, for goodness' sake.

A fresh wave of sadness swept through her at the thought. She could almost hate him if she hadn't already fallen in love with him.

This time her sob at the sudden realization was too audible for Violet to ignore. The woman turned sympathetic blue eyes on her and, as if reading her thoughts, asked, "When are you going to tell him?"

Sunny swiped at the tear that had made it to her cheek. She thought about feigning ignorance over the question, but just as quickly dismissed the idea. She didn't have the energy. "I'm not."

"Sounds like a dumb idea to me."

"Tell that to Smiley," Sunny said nastily, immediately regretting it. She laid an apologetic hand on Violet's arm.

The older woman only chuckled. "Oh, you may be surprised about what I've told Smiley."

Sunny squinted suspiciously at her. The older couple had been unusually chummy the last few days. Enough that when they'd strolled off together this morning for a short walk after breakfast, Sunny had been childishly envious. Then she'd gotten mad all over again at Jesse.

"It doesn't matter, Violet." Sunny shook her head sadly. "He's never really liked me, you know. I think it was a lust thing."

Violet laughed again, and Sunny figured too late that she probably shouldn't have been so blunt. But her friend merely asked, "Do you really believe that?"

Sunny started to confirm that she did, but kept her mouth shut. The answer wasn't that simple. For the past week or so, she'd believed he had come to like her, but today she didn't know. But if it were a lust thing, why had he stopped last night? She had given him the green light.

There was an important answer to that question, she knew, only she couldn't grasp it right now. She was too tired, hurt and raw. And she still had one more night to go.

JESSE'D HAD better days. By the time they stopped to camp for the night, two incidents had sorely tested his sour mood. A bunch of ostriches from a nearby farm had spooked the horses, resulting in two runaways, which had to be chased down. Then, since they were sticking close to the highway until they got to Oklahoma, trucks had been distracting the longhorns, causing the entire drive to lose time.

He knew the men were ready to string him up, and rightfully so. His temper had been short and he'd pushed for an extra few miles in order to make up for lost time. As if he was anxious to reach Oklahoma, he thought wryly, which, for all he knew, was right where they stood. That idea alone gave him the willies. Although it was hard to tell where the border was in this part of the country, he'd expected to have seen a sign on the highway.

And to top everything off, he couldn't keep his mind off Sunny.

To say he'd been stunned last night when she'd shared her secret with him was putting it mildly. A bolt of lightning couldn't have shocked him more. The woman was a damn walking contradiction. What with her sexy clothes, her come-hither smile, alluring eyes, her incredible body...

As he roughly tethered his horse, a spear of shame stabbed his chest. All those attributes were external. She couldn't help the dynamite smile or sexy eyes. And she certainly didn't pay too much attention to keeping in shape, no matter what she spouted about a vegetarian diet. He'd seen her eat. He smiled at the thought. The skimpy clothes he couldn't quite figure, although she seemed just as comfortable in the jeans and shorts she'd taken to wearing soon after they'd left Maybe.

Her internal workings were something else entirely, he'd started to realize. She was kind and gentle, loyal and hard-working. Her only real flaw, he figured, was that she hadn't learned how to play by life's rules. Those rules that allowed for short-term pleasure without endangering your emotions, your sanity. The kind of rules that kept you detached and didn't remind you how easily a person could snap your heart in two and discard it with no more thought than she would a used paper bag.

That way, both parties knew the score so that when one walked away, the other wouldn't crumble, his dignity pooling like mud at his feet.

Just like his father had.

The man had been a far better example to Jesse than most people had given him credit for. Watching the tough ex-rodeo champ slide from his saddle into a bottle of booze when Jesse's mother left had been the best example of all. It had taught Jesse not to need. He'd seen firsthand how much needing someone could hurt you.

That's where Sunny had blown it last night. She needed

something from him, whether she was willing to admit it or not. He'd seen the look in her eyes, heard the message in her soft, pleading voice. She wanted him to care about her, to cherish the gift she'd been ready to give him, to make promises he could never keep. Promises she couldn't keep, either.

Heading for the campfire, Jesse sighed wearily, because he knew that he'd blown it, too. He should have stayed away. Deep down he was afraid that he just might need her, too.

THE MEN on the second shift were in the middle of dinner when Hank said he'd seen the Oklahoma border sign about a mile back. As soon as Jesse heard the news, apprehension returned to scrape like spurs against his nerves.

He dropped his fork and it clanged against his tin plate before rolling onto the dirt. Maria got up to get him a clean one, but he waved her to sit. His appetite was gone, anyway.

He was stupid to be nervous, he told himself. It had been nearly twenty years since he'd been in trouble with the law here. More important, he hadn't been guilty. He had been as much a victim as the guard who'd been shot during the robbery. Only he hadn't made it to court to prove that fact.

"Hey, Jess." Hank finished his last bite of stew. "Me and the guys think we ought to give Sunny a going-away party before she goes back to Maybe tomorrow. Maria and Violet think so too."

The fact that she was leaving tomorrow should have cheered him, only it didn't.

"Yes," Maria said, confirming her agreement. "She's worked really hard. I don't know what I would have done without her."

"Yeah," Hank added. "She's helped all of us with one thing or another. We're gonna miss her." Shaking his head, he added, "No way can the next woman compare."

When Jesse saw one of the other cowboys open his mouth to extol more of Sunny's virtues, he cut him off. "How do you plan on arranging a party?" he asked dryly. He was sick of hearing about her. Hadn't it been bad enough having to think about her all day? Even though he'd managed to stay farther from her than a country mile.

"When we get to Hobby, we thought we'd—"

"Shut up," someone cut in. "Here she comes."

Immediately Jesse tensed. His back was to her as she approached. He was glad he didn't have to look at her, see the hurt he'd put in her eyes last night. *It wasn't my fault,* he reminded himself. But it didn't do any good. He still felt like the same heel he had all day.

"You ready for some of my stew and biscuits?" Maria asked as she smiled over Jesse's shoulder at Sunny.

Jesse already knew she was directly behind him. He could feel her heat...smell the vanilla, the almonds. He shifted and pretended renewed interest in his food.

"Thanks anyway, Maria." Her voice sounded small. "I'm going to start on the dishes."

Maria jumped to her feet. "You haven't had a thing all day. You have to eat something. Violet has already started cleaning up. I'll dish you up something, then help her."

"No, really—" Sunny began.

"Sit," Maria ordered. "Hank, you help me take these plates back. Jesse's still eating, Sunny. He'll keep you company."

As soon as Hank got up, half the men followed. Jesse glanced at the cowboys, and when Hank gave him a sly wink, Jesse's suspicion slid into fear. Did the whole damn drive know about...

Sighing, he realized that they probably intended on planning her party. He exhaled. Then he remembered Sunny was still behind him and Maria expected him to keep her company.

"I'd better check on the horses," he said, and started to get to his feet.

The few men who were still eating were quite a distance away, but they heard his inane comment and gave him funny looks. He ignored them and was about to walk off without so much as glancing at Sunny when she laid a hand on his arm.

Slowly he turned to her, reluctant to look into her eyes. Finally he raised his gaze to hers.

Beneath her lower lashes, dark semicircles marred her delicate skin. Her eyes were a little bloodshot, as though she hadn't had enough sleep…or had been crying. Tension thinned her normally full lips. It took all of his willpower not to turn away from his own painful creation.

"I'm not a baby. I accept your…I accept what happened last night," she said softly so that no one else heard. "You don't have to run away because of me."

He opened his mouth to deny her claim, but she looked wounded enough and he wouldn't insult her that way. Shaking his head, he said, "I won't run away."

Her accusing eyes told him he already had. Then she quickly looked away. "Let's put last night behind us."

"Okay," he agreed quietly.

She nodded, forcing a smile. Jesse averted his gaze, doing all he could to keep from pulling her into his arms. She was hurting because he had hurt her. She had trusted him. And he'd thrown that trust back in her face.

Better now before you get involved, he reminded himself. *She's leaving tomorrow. Let's keep this civil.* The thought did nothing to cheer him. Sighing inwardly, he forced his gaze to her sad face.

Only it wasn't sad anymore. Her face was lit up, literally. He blinked. Her eyes widened, then she blinked, too, at the beam shining in her face. He turned to see where the light was coming from.

Two cars had left the highway and were bouncing over the uneven terrain, their headlights cutting a jagged path in the dusky evening air.

Jesse squinted at the cars, trying to figure out what the drivers were up to. As if in answer, blue and red lights flashed from one of the cars.

It was the police.

Jesse almost dropped his plate. What the hell were they doing here? It had been nearly twenty years since he'd set foot in Oklahoma, and now his past had all boiled down to this? His mouth went dry. His heart hammered in his chest.

How was he going to explain this? How was he going to withstand the humiliation of being arrested in front of everyone? He glanced at Sunny.

She grinned. ''They're here to welcome us, aren't they?''

Jesse stared dumbly at her. The explanation was so simple, he had to stifle the urge to laugh. They were here because of the drive. Not him. He grunted softly, tamping down his unease.

The officers pulled up near one of the wagons and got out of their cars with big grins on their faces. They introduced themselves and immediately confirmed Sunny's explanation.

After some small talk with Jesse and the cowboys satisfied their personal curiosity about life on the trail, the police officers turned to business.

''Tomorrow we'll lead you into town,'' Officer Muldoon said. ''The spot we've set up for your camp is on the other side. You'll have to use the road part of the way, but we're gonna divert traffic for you.''

''Wonderful,'' Sunny said. ''How can we ever repay you?'' she asked teasingly.

''Well...'' Officer Muldoon exchanged glances with his partner. ''How would you like to stay on the drive?''

''Me?'' Sunny looked around. Everyone straightened.

The young officer lifted a burly shoulder. ''Miss Creek County was supposed to take your place and represent Oklahoma. Only she broke her leg yesterday practicing her runway turns for the Miss Oklahoma contest.'' He shook his head, then added, ''They're gonna find a replacement. They just don't know how long it'll take, is all.''

Cheers erupted from behind her. Maria and Violet hugged each other. ''Of course she'll stay on,'' Maria said.

Longing and excitement flitted across Sunny's face, then she glanced at Jesse. The tension returned to tighten her mouth. ''I'm sorry,'' she said.

"What?" Maria stepped forward. "Sunny?" She turned to him. "Jesse?"

Jesse didn't answer right away. He couldn't move. He couldn't think. Silence stung the air. He couldn't let her go, and he couldn't ask her to stay. "We'll talk her into it," he said finally, his eyes fastened on Sunny. When he saw the hope trickle into her gaze, he turned away.

He had too much to think about. Too many demons to battle. His life had changed the moment he thought the police had come for him. Hell, if he was honest, he'd admit his life changed the moment he met Sunny. But right now he had his past to settle.

He called Smiley and Manny over and quietly asked them to take over for him once they settled in town tomorrow. Wisely, they asked him no questions. He promised to return in a day and half…and prayed he could.

EXCEPT FOR a brand-new gas station, its red-and-white sign taller than anything else around, and a small modern grocery store, the town didn't look much different than it had nearly twenty years ago. Jesse wondered if that was some kind of omen. He wondered if it meant that nothing had changed, that what he was about to do was make the biggest mistake of his life.

Except Jesse had changed, and facing the past was something he knew he had to do. Something he owed himself. And for some incredibly far-out, crazy reason, he believed he owed it to Sunny.

But at the moment, as he faced the drab, gray brick sheriff's office, he felt sixteen again, full of fear and false bravado.

He rubbed the fatigue from his eyes. Hobby was so isolated, it had taken half of yesterday just to get a rental car, which meant he'd had to drive most of the night, on miles and miles of country roads, to get here. And he'd be driving all night to get back, assuming he'd be free.

Jesse took a deep breath and pushed open the front door. A third desk had been added to the crowded room, and a water fountain had replaced the watercooler he remembered. Nothing else had changed. Then he heard five distinct beeps of a microwave coming from the back room, and he knew that was new, too.

He pulled off his hat and waited for the microwave user to appear.

Seconds before the man appeared with a steaming plate, Jesse smelled the sticky sweetness of a cinnamon roll. Startled, the uniformed man's gaze swept Jesse as he set the plate on his desk. "What can I do for ya?" he asked.

Jesse recognized the kind blue eyes immediately.

You keep runnin' and don't look back. And stay out of Oklahoma, ya hear? Can't afford to have you messin' with my pension, son.

The twenty-year-old words flashed through Jesse's mind as if he'd heard them just yesterday. He stared at the familiar face, aged by several lines and slack jowls. Then his gaze slid to the sheriff's round belly where the tan uniform shirt gapped over years of added pounds.

The man laughed aloud and unselfconsciously patted his extra girth. "Figured there's no use in gettin' a new uniform at this point. Being as I'm retirin' next month."

A little embarrassed that he'd been caught staring, Jesse lifted a shoulder and tried to smile. Then he stopped. Retiring next month? God, he hoped he was doing the right thing.

"So, mister, tell me what's on your mind." The sheriff motioned him to take a seat across the desk. As Jesse obliged, the man settled into his own chair, leaning forward, resting his elbows on his desk.

Don't mess with my pension. Retiring next month. Jesse's brain scrambled for a moment until a solution became clear. "Well, Sheriff Mason." He took a deep, discreet breath. "I have sort of a hypothetical question and I need some advice."

The man blinked, looking confused for a moment, and Jesse realized that he'd used the man's name without having been introduced.

Sheriff Mason peered more closely at him, while Jesse

calmed himself, mentally pointing out that it wouldn't be unusual for anyone to know who the sheriff was without being introduced. He swallowed hard around the tension clogging his throat.

Frowning pensively, the sheriff said, "Okay, you go ahead and ask me this hypothetical question."

"Well, actually it's not that hypothetical. I've got this friend. He's a kid. Only sixteen. Actually he's the son of a friend." Jesse had to stop to collect his thoughts. He couldn't blow this. "And he got himself into trouble. For something he didn't do. Only the law didn't believe him and he did something kinda foolish."

Sheriff Mason leaned back in his chair and locked his hands behind his head, his frown deepening.

"Hey, don't let me stop you from eating." Jesse motioned to the cooling cinnamon roll, hoping for a moment of respite, hoping to shore up his faltering confidence.

Mason shook his head. "Tell me about your friend."

Jesse shoved a hand through his hair. "The thing is, the kid didn't…I mean he doesn't have a mother. She ran out on him when he was about five, and his father…" He threw up a hand. For a moment he wasn't sure he could go through with this. The memories were suddenly gusting in, storming his composure, his ability to sound dispassionate.

Like quicksand, the hurt sucked at his heart, his defenses, and he felt like an abandoned five-year-old again.

Out of nowhere, unbidden, Sunny's sweet serene smile flashed through his mind. She'd offered herself to him because she'd thought he was worthy.

He took another quick breath. "The kid's father's a drunk, you see. After the mother left, the drinking started and he kind of emotionally abandoned the kid, too." Trailing off, he lifted a shoulder. Sheriff Mason was looking at him funny again.

When Jesse started to speak again, the sheriff held up a hand. "I think I get the picture." He rubbed his flabby jowls, his eyes narrowed. "But just to make sure I got it right, let me tell you about a similar story. A real-life case I had here...oh, about twenty years ago.''

Jesse nearly dropped his hat under the sheriff's intense gaze. He rubbed a clammy palm down his thigh and nodded.

Mason smiled. ''There was this kid. Two kids, actually. Sixteen and seventeen, if my memory hasn't failed me. Now, these two boys were hitchhiking across the country when they got picked up by two guys. Problem was, the kids didn't know these two guys had just robbed a bank. The robbers figured they'd pick these kids up to avoid suspicion in case there were roadblocks. Figured they'd look like they were on some kinda father-and-son outing. Are you followin' me?''

Jesse nodded. That was the best he could do.

''Well, to make a long story short, I had just made sheriff at the time, and it was me and my deputy who picked them up.'' He scratched his gray head and stared off as if remembering. ''Funny, we initially picked them up for speedin', then news of the robbery came over the radio and we detained them. Anyway, it was pretty plain to me after a spell that the boys were innocent. Scared out of their tennis shoes, they were.'' He laughed nostalgically.

He glanced at Jesse. ''Problem was, only the one boy's parents showed.'' He frowned again. ''Cash, I think his name was. Only his parents showed up. They posted bail, got him a fancy attorney, who proved what I already knew. The kids were innocent.''

Jesse remained silent for a moment and then asked the expected question. Even though he hardly needed the answer. ''What happened to the other kid?''

''He ran.''

''Ran?'' Jesse repeated.

''Yup.'' Sheriff Mason leaned forward again. ''Didn't see any point in chasin' him, though. I knew he wasn't guilty. Figured I'd save the taxpayers a few bucks.''

Jesse's breath came out fast and ragged. Mason had forgotten part of the story. The only reason the boy had been able to run was thanks to the help of a kind sheriff. A man who'd risked his job and reputation to give a young, stupid kid a break. A man who knew the kid's father didn't give enough of a damn to help his only son.

"So," Jesse said. "What happened to the kid?"

The sheriff shrugged. "Went on to have a good life, I hope."

"What about his files?" Briefly lowering his gaze, he fingered the brim of his Stetson. "I mean, the kid must still be wanted."

Pursing his lips, Mason shook his head. "There ain't no files left. We had a fire." When Jesse frowned at him, the sheriff quickly added, "It wasn't a big one. Just one of them little wastebasket ones, ya know?" Laughing, he shook his head, his eyes trained on Jesse. "I had a damned-fool habit of smokin' back then. Gave it up shortly after that." He paused. "My brother-in-law is the local D.A., and we decided that since the kid was underage and his file woulda been sealed or destroyed anyway, we wouldn't bother to try and reconstruct it."

Jesse nodded, feeling suddenly very emotional. "Well..." He drummed his fingers on his thigh.

The sheriff picked up his cinnamon roll. "Did I answer your question?"

"Yeah." Jesse gratefully took his cue and stood. "Yeah, you did." He headed for the door and put his hat on. His hand on the knob, he hesitated. How could he ever thank this man? A stranger who had done more for him than his own father had done.

"Son?"

Jesse's head jerked at the unfamiliar title.

Sheriff Mason smiled, his kind eyes wrinkling at the corners. "Tell Jesse I said to have a nice life, will ya?"

Unable to speak, Jesse nodded. Then hurried out of the office while his legs still worked.

Chapter Sixteen

"Smiley, you've got to tell me when Jesse's coming back." Sunny pushed a shaky hand through her tangled hair, exhausted from another sleepless night. "The mayor wants us to participate in a parade and I don't know what to tell him." She didn't give a damn about the parade. It had been twenty-four hours since Jesse had disappeared, and all she could get out of anyone was that he'd be back. She had a feeling that Smiley knew where he'd gone. She wasn't sure about Manny or Maria. No one was being cooperative. And Sunny was a wreck.

"When's the parade?" Smiley asked, seemingly unconcerned as he continued to comb his horse.

"This afternoon," she said impatiently to his back. "They would've given us more notice but they hadn't expected us to stay this long," she added, hoping for some scrap of information that would tell her what had been so urgent that Jesse had delayed their departure half a day.

Smiley's hand stopped for a moment. She moved to his side and saw the worried frown he tried to hide. He immediately grinned and resumed his combing.

"Come on, Smiley. Don't do this to me." When he didn't respond, she stared across the open prairie. Although most of the crew had checked into the local motel, Sunny had stayed at the camp they'd set up north of town. She figured this would be the first place Jesse would stop when he returned. If he returned.

She shuddered at the thought. *There's no reason to think he won't,* she reminded herself. Jesse would never desert the drive. Besides not being an irresponsible person, he had far too much at stake. He wanted to buy his own ranch so bad he could taste it. Sunny knew that without a doubt. Heck, everyone knew it. No. Jesse wouldn't desert the drive.

Not if he could help it.

The irrational idea that something awful could prevent him from returning sent her fragile emotions into panic mode. Oh, God, she was far too exhausted to cope with the unknown right now. Weariness made her feel sappy. She choked back a sob.

Smiley stopped what he was doing, reluctantly glancing at her.

"Please," she begged, swiping at the renegade tear that slid down her cheek.

He set down the currycomb and put an arm around her. He had a sad look on his face that did nothing to reassure her. "He's gonna be back. I can't tell ya where he is, but he's gonna be back."

Another tear rushed down her cheek and landed on Smiley's shoulder. She blinked another one away as he roughly put his other arm around her, too. Did she have anything to do with Jesse leaving? Sunny wondered. Why hadn't he said anything to her? She had so many questions. "But why did—"

"Hey, am I interrupting something?"

His voice came from behind, cutting her off. She froze, staring at Smiley's surprised but smiling face. He gave her a wink and dropped his arms from around her. She blinked her eyes dry and dabbed at her cheeks before slowly turning around.

Clearing her throat, about to give him a piece of her mind, she stared at his tired face. His jaw was stubbled with at least two days' growth. The Stetson shadowed his eyes, but tension and weariness showed in the lines bracketing his faint grin.

He opened his arms to her.

Sunny flew into them, vaguely surprised that he'd greet her this way. But she was too happy to see him to wonder about that, or about how this looked to anyone else.

He hugged her tight and pressed a light kiss to her temple. She hugged him back, stretching her arms as far around him as they would go, cradling him reassuringly against her. As his hand stroked her back, urging her impossibly closer, she got the feeling that she was comforting him as much as he was comforting her.

His chest expanded. Inhaling deeply, he murmured, "You smell so good." Then he let her go, brushing the tangled hair off her face as she stepped back to make room for Smiley.

Jesse's gaze switched to his old friend, and he put his hand out to him. As they shook, a meaningful look passed between them that Sunny was helpless to understand.

"Everything okay?" Jesse asked.

Smiley grinned at Sunny. "It is now. You wanna tell him about the parade?"

She blinked. Tell him about the parade? Everything was back to normal, just like that? Now that the shock of seeing him was wearing off, Sunny's temper sparked. He had a lot of nerve leaving the way he had.

"Since we were inexplicably delayed," she informed him, "they've asked us to participate in a Memorial Day parade this afternoon."

Jesse grinned, presumably at her haughty tone, and succeeded in turning her anger up a degree. "Sure," he said. "That is, assuming we have interest among the crew."

"Hank said he and Chester would drive a couple of the longhorns. Three of the other men volunteered to ride. And Maria said she'd drive the wagon with Ana."

"Good. Glad to see everything went well without me." Jesse smiled when she glared at him. "You can use my horse if you want. If not, Manny will get one of the guys to lend you theirs."

"Me?" Sunny laughed, glancing at Smiley then Jesse.

"Sure." Jesse paused. "Your highness, you still are our public relations person, aren't you?"

Your highness? Everything really was back to normal. She

felt a modicum of comfort in that fact. "That doesn't mean riding a horse."

"Can't you ride?"

"That's beside the point." Her voice rose a notch.

"I best be gettin' back to my chores," Smiley said and started to slink away.

"Smiley, can she ride?"

The older man sighed loudly. "Not too good."

"I've ridden twice at Rainy and Cash's ranch." She lifted her chin. "And I sat on a horse once for a vacation advertisement I did."

Jesse laughed. Smiley scurried away. "Well, that's all you gotta do. Sit on that horse," Jesse said. "It's a parade. You won't be going fast. You can handle it."

Sunny nibbled at her fingernail. She wasn't crazy about the idea at all. What she had neglected to mention was that one of the times she'd tried riding, she'd fallen off. She frowned, wondering how she was going to get out of this gracefully, when Hank rode up.

"Hey, boss." The young man nearly tripped out of his saddle in his haste to shake Jesse's hand. "Glad to see ya back."

Jesse frowned. "Anything wrong?"

"No. The way you just up and left had us all worried, is all."

Sunny watched a dull flush climb Jesse's neck and face. His mouth tightened for a moment, then relaxed. "Something personal came up. But it's over now." He slapped Hank's back, a slow grin erasing the last of his tension. "It's all over. Now, help me give Sunny a quick riding lesson."

She was so fascinated by the parade of emotions that had crossed his features she'd almost forgotten about the other parade. "I'm not going to do it," she said flatly.

Jesse shrugged. He looked too tired to argue. "Okay. There are enough people willing to ride already."

"Well…" She made a face. "Not exactly. They want someone to ride alongside the mayor." He shrugged again. Her conscience rallied and she decided to give him the rest of the news.

"The parade might be a little bigger than you think. It's also getting a lot of local media coverage."

Jesse crossed his arms over his chest. "You know what the promoters would say to that."

She nodded miserably. She knew they were never to turn down free publicity if they were at a stop along the trail.

"You *are* public relations," he reminded her.

Great. Now she could fall off a horse in public. She folded her arms, too. "My contract became void once I entered Oklahoma."

Sighing, Jesse removed his hat and swept his too-long hair off his forehead before settling the Stetson on his head. She noticed how bloodshot his eyes were. "When does it start?" he asked. "Can I grab an hour of sleep first?"

Wishing he'd hollered at her, she uncrossed her arms. "Hank'll give me a refresher course." She glanced at the agreeable young man before turning to Jesse. "You go rest."

He frowned. "Are you sure?"

Not in the least. She smiled. "Positive."

"Okay." He passed a hand over his face. "Spread the word we'll leave first thing in the morning so we don't leave everyone hanging. I'm only gonna sleep for an hour. I promise I'll make the parade."

Sunny told him what time it would start and urged him toward the motel. He hesitated for a second, giving her a look that made her knees as stable as grape jelly. She gulped back unexpected desire and watched him walk off.

Then she turned to Hank. "I'm going to level with you. I really stink when it comes to riding. I don't know what we can do in the next two hours to change that, but I'll give it a try if you will."

Hank scratched his head, his black Stetson bouncing with the motion as he squinted in concentration. "Hey, I know," he said finally, his blue eyes widening. "We can use Velcro."

"Velcro?" Sunny laughed.

"Yeah. To keep you in the saddle. They use it at dude ranches all the time."

"Yeah?" She frowned, not totally convinced.

"My uncle has a summer camp for kids at his ranch. He uses it."

"So…" Her hope nosedived. "You're telling me they use it for kids."

"What's the difference?"

About a zillion inches around the butt, she thought. "I don't think that's such a good idea."

"We only got two hours." Hank tapped his watch. "You got a better one?"

He had a point. She let out a huffing breath of air. "Have you ever seen them do this?"

"Sure. Tons of times. They rig the Velcro to the saddle."

"And you think you know how—?"

Hank rolled his eyes. "They gotta have everything I need back in town."

"Okay. We'll try it." She barely got the words out of her mouth when Hank started to race toward town. "Wait a minute," she called after him, swallowing a gulp of pride. "Remember, you might need a little extra Velcro."

He waved and kept on going.

Sunny watched him disappear with a combination of dread and anticipation. She hurried to the wagon to pick up her bag. She was ready to check into the motel for a long, cool bath now that Jesse was safely back. Humming, she glanced at her watch and calculated how much time she had to get herself together.

She had a special outfit that was going to knock his socks off.

FROM BEHIND DARK GLASSES, Jesse watched the colorful floats, cars and horses go by. Although he'd managed to sleep for an extra hour, his eyes still burned from lack of sleep and too much night driving. He felt a hell of a lot more comfortable on a horse than he ever did in a car.

A bright blue pickup with a ranch logo on the door drove by, its bed adorned with streamers and balloons in red, white and blue. Two little blond girls sat amid the decorations and waved to the crowd.

He was going to have all that soon, he realized with a jolt of shock. Well, the ranch and pickup, anyway, minus the kids. This time next year, he'd be working on his own spread, raising his own cattle, finally putting down roots. His mind strayed to Sunny. He wondered where she was going to be in a year.

No use wondering about that. Jesse slapped at the cloud of dust kicked up by a passing convertible. It didn't matter where Sunny would be. Because she wasn't going to be with him. The thought should have consoled him. It didn't.

A squeal rose above the crowd's murmurings, and Jesse saw several kids across the street pointing toward the rear of the parade. He followed their gazes and saw the wagon. With Maria's guidance, the horses plodded slowly behind a red pickup, haphazardly decorated to resemble a giant American flag. Ana sat beside her mother, her face wreathed in a smile, waving to the crowd.

Several yards behind them, Sunny sat stiff and straight atop a white mare. Jesse recognized the horse and knew Hank had done a good job picking out the gentlest animal available. Only Sunny looked scared out of her...

Jesse squinted behind his dark glasses. What the hell was she wearing? Her light brown leather pants were so tight that he'd almost mistaken them for bare skin. And her blouse... Smiling sadly, he shook his head. He eyed the pink, frilly ruffles, remembering the first time she'd stepped out of the cab in Maybe. Nothing much had changed in the last month, and he'd be a fool to think otherwise.

Not that he had, he assured himself. In a few months he'd be on his ranch and Sunny would be... Hell, he didn't know where she'd be. On some exotic Caribbean island, no doubt, wearing sleeveless, pink frilly blouses and skintight leather pants and passing out smiles that made a man's mouth water.

Jesse continued watching as first the wagon, then Sunny passed by. He realized she wasn't offering one of those smiles now. To anyone.

One hand clutched the saddle horn so tightly he could see the tension in her forearm. The other hand she waved stiffly at the onlookers. When a stray breeze lifted her long hair away from her face, he saw the fear in her eyes.

He cursed under his breath and started walking, dodging around people to keep abreast of her. He should never have insisted that she ride. She'd been such a good sport along the trail, doing anything anyone had asked her to do. But he now saw that he had pushed too hard by asking her to ride.

She was still as stiff as a board by the time she reached the end of the line.

Someone had led Maria and Ana off Main Street to a spot where people could look at the wagon and ask questions. Several horseback riders had dismounted and exchanged their reins for ice-cold colas.

But when it was time for Sunny to dismount, she wouldn't budge. As Jesse approached, he heard the young man trying to coax her down.

"I'll just ride on back to camp," she told the frustrated young man.

"You can't do that, miss," the freckled-face teenager explained, his hand wrapped stubbornly around her reins. "We'll return your horse."

"I'm not getting off this animal." Sunny tried to tug the reins from his hold.

Jesse tapped the young man on the shoulder. "I'll take care of this."

Looking relieved, the boy handed him the reins and trotted off to help the next person.

"Come on, Sunny." Jesse raised his hands, ready to guide her. "Get down from there."

"I can't."

"What?"

"I can't," she repeated. Her hair fell forward as she leaned toward him, and she shoved it roughly out of her face. "I'm stuck," she whispered.

He frowned. "Stuck?"

"I think it might be the glue."

"What are you talking about?"

"Don't use that tone with me. It's not my fault. It was Hank's idea."

Wearily rubbing his jaw, Jesse noticed that the rest of the procession was beginning to back up down Main Street because of them. He clamped his hands around her waist. "Let me help you."

Her body strained upward, but she didn't leave the saddle. She wiggled and squirmed, and still nothing. Her bottom clung firmly to the saddle.

"What the hell did you two do?"

"Velcro and glue," she said, as if that explained everything. Panting from all her wiggling, she added, "Obviously it was the wrong kind of glue." She glanced over her shoulder at the impatient people waiting for her to move, then turned panic-stricken eyes to him. "I'm going to have to slip out of these pants."

"What?" He too looked over her shoulder at the curious strangers. "Come on."

Grabbing the reins from her, he pulled her and the horse off the street. The freckled-face kid he'd relieved came running toward them, hollering, "You can't ride through town like that."

Jesse ignored him. He continued past the incredulous stares and headed for the motel. He heard Hank and Smiley yelling at them from across the street, but he ignored them, too, and carefully dodging gawkers, he kept a steady path toward the outskirts of town.

Sunny had wisely said nothing the entire trip to the motel, but as soon as he stopped her horse in front of his room, she started to squirm again. "I don't know why you're so mad at me. I only did what Hank and Smiley told me to do."

Jesse peered at the strip where her pants met the saddle. The adherence was so tight, the two leathers seemed to melt together. He could barely see the Velcro between them, and tried to wedge his finger into the tight seam between her bottom and the saddle.

"Hey." She stiffened and looked around. Everyone was at the parade. They were alone. "What are you doing?"

"What the hell kind of glue did they use?"

She shrugged helplessly. "I was desperate."

He frowned. "Desperate? If you honestly didn't think you could ride today, why didn't you tell me?"

"Because you would have taken my place."

"So?"

She blinked, then her eyes anxiously roamed his face. She lifted a hand close to his cheek, but dropped it before she touched him. "You were too tired."

Jesse swallowed. He stared at her, into those earnest brown eyes, at those lips that lured thousands to the pages of magazines. Those same lips that quivered into a tentative smile for him. "I, uh…" He took a quick breath. "I need to get you outa here."

He transferred his gaze to the saddle and tried to concentrate on the problem of unsticking her. But his mind wandered, and the heat he was trying to ignore crawled up his spine and fogged his brain.

They were different, he and Sunny. They came from different worlds, wanted different things. But she cared about him like no one ever had before or probably ever would again. She made him care about her, too. Sunny had even made him care about himself.

He reached in front of her and found her zipper. Her gasp hid the sound of the metal teeth pulling apart. He was a selfish bastard for what he was about to do, but he couldn't help himself. Sunny had offered him part of her goodness and light, and he was afraid that if he turned it down, he'd live the rest of his life without sunshine. He had too many regrets already, nearly a lifetime of them. He couldn't afford another. Especially not with this woman.

"What are you doing?" Sunny pushed at his hands as he

first pulled off her boots, then peeled the tight leather down her hips.

"You suggested it. It's the easiest—and maybe even the only—way to get you out of this mess."

"Well, you don't have to look so cheerful about it." She took one last swat at him before she grabbed his shoulder for balance.

His smile widened. "Lift."

She gave him a dirty look but raised her bottom while he rolled the leather partway down her pink panties.

"Now, hold on to me while I hoist you out of this contraption." He anchored his hands at her waist, and she slid an arm around his neck. On the count of three, she wriggled and he tugged until her hips broke loose from the leather pants. In a few more seconds, she shook free of the legs.

Their positions were awkward, and being unsure that he could get her feet safely to the ground, Jesse twisted until he could throw her over his shoulder in a fireman's hold.

Sunny shrieked. Swinging her leg in an attempt to reach the ground, she just missed maiming him for life. "Put me down this instant." She arched, and he swatted her bottom.

It was then he noticed the writing across her panties and chuckled as he fished in his pocket for his room key. "It's Monday, Sunny, not Tuesday."

She stilled for a moment and said, "Oh, God."

Then she bucked, trying to get out of his arms. But he held tight while fitting the key in the lock, then pushing the door open. A blast of cold air hit them and she gasped, tensing her bare thighs. When he turned his head and took a light nip through her panties, she went totally still.

"Jesse?" Then she clawed at his back, trying to lever herself, trying to look at him.

He kicked the door closed. Using the light streaming in where the curtains didn't meet, he walked to the bed and gently lowered her onto the mattress.

Propped on one elbow, she shoved the hair from her face and stared wide-eyed at him.

He smiled and undid the top button on his shirt.

Chapter Seventeen

Sunny watched his fingers move to the second button, release it, then tackle the next one. When he got to the last button, he yanked his shirt out of his jeans.

Slowly, her gaze skimmed his chest where the shirt hung open. His skin was taut and tan over a lean stomach, a nicely muscled chest. Dark hair swirled around brown nipples that were beginning to bead.

She raised her eyes to his, and her breath shuddered at the raw need she saw there. She scooted back on the bed, not sure whether she was making room or running away. He caught her ankle.

"Tell me, Sunny," he whispered. "Tell me what you want."

She shivered. She didn't know for sure what she wanted. Except she did want Jesse. Sunny wanted him to be her first. She wanted him to be her only lover. But she was prepared to accept the fact that that probably wasn't possible.

Keeping her gaze steady on him, she reached for her own buttons. Only there were so many silly pink ruffles and her hands shook so badly that she couldn't find them.

Releasing a ragged breath, Jesse shrugged out of his shirt and joined her on the bed. He kissed her hard and fast before showering her jaw and neck with tiny nips. His hand trailed up one of her bare legs until he reached her hands and took over the job of unbuttoning her blouse.

A smile tugged at one corner of his mouth as he slid first one tiny button out of the hole, then another.

"What?" she asked warily, uncertainty tightening her shoulders.

He shook his head, the grin winning. "You have the smallest buttons I've ever seen." He ripped the last two off and pushed the material aside. "I owe you a blouse."

Her heart slammed against her chest. Excitement roared through her like a hot west Texas windstorm. She fell back on her elbows and Jesse followed her down, his mouth hot and wet through the thin silk of her bra.

His fingers fumbled for the front clasp as he continued to press his lips, his tongue, to her nipples as though he couldn't wait to touch her.

Her elbows gave way just as her bra clasp did, and she fell back onto the mattress, silently cursing her shyness. She wanted to touch him, too, but she was afraid her inexperience would turn him off…again.

Jesse pushed the silky cups away and slid his arm under her back. He lifted her enough to free her of the blouse and bra. She was left with only the crazy pink panties she'd bought that day in Sparks. The day Jesse had brought her lotion and rubbed it into her sunburn. The day, she realized now, that she knew for sure Jesse would be the one.

Is that why he'd angered her so? Because her mind had been fighting something her heart had already accepted?

He must have felt her stiffen when she realized that truth because he raised his head to look at her. His hand stilled over her breast. "Are you afraid?" he asked softly.

"A little."

"Me, too."

She smiled. "No, you aren't."

He smiled, too. "Wanna bet?"

"Oh, no. Not again." They both laughed, and she wondered how he'd put her at ease so quickly. "Why would you be afraid?"

Uncertainty eclipsed his face. His thumb brushed restlessly against her nipple. "I'm afraid you'll be sorry we made love."

She strained for his touch, pulsing her breast instinctively into his hand. "I won't be."

"God, Sunny." He dragged his mouth down her throat, his breath hot and ragged against her skin. "I hope you're right." He took the nipple into his mouth and suckled her. One hand massaged her other breast while the other followed the curve of her hip.

Swallowing the last of her fear, she reached between them. His mouth suddenly stopped the sucking motion. She barely felt his touch, only his lips skimming her nipple, his fevered breath rasping against her skin as he took unsteady gulps of air. Then he pressed his hips forward and she felt rock-hard denim fill her palm.

Slowly, his tongue began circling her nipple again. But when she flexed her hand, his ministrations faltered. Sunny smiled, liking this new power she'd discovered.

But her smile quickly wavered when he pulled away from her, taking her panties with him. His gaze drank in her naked body as he shoved off his jeans and underwear. He stood for a moment, hard and ready, looking at her before he eased down on the bed beside her.

Sunny knew she shouldn't be staring. She'd seen naked men in magazines before, but seeing one in person was so much more overwhelming. Especially when that man was Jesse. A hot thrill shot through her, and she raised her gaze to his.

He was watching her, smiling, his hands doing wonderful things to her thighs and breasts. Then he bowed his head at the juncture of her thighs. Immediately, instinctively, she clamped her legs together. He pressed a soft kiss on one thigh and quickly brought his mouth to her breast.

"Jesse, I—"

"Shh." He kissed her mouth. "I'm sorry I went too fast for you." His hand stroked her thigh near that secret place. "Is this okay?"

She nodded and allowed her legs to relax.

Kissing her tenderly on the mouth, he slipped a finger into her. When she moaned, his kiss deepened and she felt her hips automatically rising to him. She wanted to feel the way he'd made her feel before. That time in the wagon when his fingers had found her heat and the world exploded around her. The thought had no sooner entered her head when the fireworks began.

She twisted and writhed beneath his hand while his mouth swallowed her surprised gasp. She called his name over and over as gusts of pleasure stole the earlier shyness she'd felt. When the spasms subsided and she looked through the haze at his solemn face, she knew she'd made the right decision. Tentatively, she reached out to touch him.

He was already swollen beyond belief, his sex hard and hot in her palm, and Sunny wondered if she could possibly make him feel as good as he had her. He closed his eyes, his head falling back, the muscles around his neck bunching and cording. Opening his unfocused eyes, he brought his head up. "Wait a minute," he whispered. "You gotta wait..."

When she ignored him, he muttered a curse and pulled away. Reaching for the jeans he'd discarded on the floor, he pulled a small packet out of the pocket. After slipping on protection, he eased himself on top of her, nibbling her jaw, her neck, her ear. He kept most of his weight off her, but she could feel his shaft resting heavy on her belly.

She shifted, wanting him closer, inside her, branding her. He adjusted to her new position without making any attempt to enter her. So Sunny rearranged her body until she was in a more compromising place.

His lips left her throat and he moved his head back in surprise. His eyes looked briefly wary, then confused. He studied her flushed face a moment before a slow smile lifted his lips. "Okay, baby."

He knelt between her thighs, brushed a tangle of hair from her face and kissed her urgently on the mouth.

He entered her when she was busy kissing him, but as soon as she felt the foreign invasion, she tensed. He stopped for a few moments, gently nibbling her lips, whispering reassurances, and as she relaxed, he slid in until her body's barrier halted him.

"You'll feel a sting," he said, stroking her hair.

"I know," she whispered and hugged him. She wanted to tell him that the pain wouldn't matter. That she loved him and that she knew he'd never really hurt her. But instead, she merely braced herself and surged toward him.

Jesse moved instinctively, then moaned when he unexpectedly broke through the barrier. Although she'd done most of the pushing, he stilled his body and peered into her face. "You okay?" He dragged his thumb over a tear seeping from the corner of her eye.

"Better than okay." She smiled.

He smiled back and started moving over her again. When her fingers dug into his buttocks, his pace became frantic, and with a low, guttural sound, he emptied himself inside her.

As soon as he was able to breathe semi-evenly, he flipped onto his back, taking her with him. She lay atop him, her breasts flattened against his chest.

Her hair was a tangled mess as she gazed at him, and he brushed it away, massaging her scalp at the same time. "Hi," he said with a widening smile, then kissed the tip of her nose.

"Hi." She started to duck her head as the heat blossomed in her cheeks.

He nudged her chin up, his eyes shadowed with concern. "I'm sorry—"

"No." She looked him directly in the eyes when she realized he thought she already regretted their lovemaking. "Don't think that. I..." She bit her lip. "Thank you, Jesse."

He grimaced as if he'd been stung. "For chrissake, honey, don't thank me."

Sunny stiffened. "I didn't mean it like that. I'm glad you..." She glanced away. "I'm glad we made love."

Sighing, he hugged her to him. "Me, too."

She wondered if she'd be pushing it to ask when they could make love again. Idly, she dragged a fingernail over his flat nipple. When he shuddered, she smiled, knowing she'd just gotten her answer. She lifted her face for a kiss, and he dipped his head to oblige just as a loud bark of laughter sounded from outside.

Sunny's gaze flew to the window. "The festivities must be over." She looked at Jesse. She hoped it wasn't regret she saw shadowing his eyes. "I need to get to my room before everyone starts coming back."

Jesse nodded. He gave her a brief kiss before leaving the bed. He pulled a pair of jeans out of his bag and tossed them to her. "Use these."

As she scrambled into the too-big jeans, she stole looks at him pulling on his pants. In his haste, he'd ignored his underwear, and she watched with renewed excitement as his buttock muscles flexed and relaxed.

He caught her watching and grinned. Heat flared in her cheeks. He fastened the top button. "Come here," he said.

She carried his shirt to him, clutching the pink ruffles of her blouse together.

Jesse tossed his shirt over his shoulder, then removed her hands from her blouse. He parted the fabric a little and kissed the valley between her breasts before fastening the first button. Then he dipped his head lower, kissing and fastening as he went.

"This is not the way to get rid of me," she whispered between labored breaths.

He shrugged into his shirt, smiling at her. "Darlin', who said anything about getting rid of you?"

Sunny exhaled, mentally fanning herself. "Okay. I'm leaving now."

He went to the door, opened it a crack and peered out. His expression tightened at what he saw. Then a deep, rumbling laugh erupted from his chest.

"What?" she asked, cautiously creeping beside him.

He opened the door wider, his shoulders shaking with laughter.

Between two parked cars, Sunny's mare stood tethered in

her own parking stall. Even odder looking, the leather pants remained glued to the saddle, the brown legs hanging limply off either side of her white, riderless body.

Sunny covered her mouth. Quickly, she glanced around. Seeing no one, she looked at Jesse and burst out laughing.

"How far down is your room?" he asked, still chuckling.

She glanced at the number on his door. "Three."

"I'll take care of the horse and see you in a half hour?" He drew his hand down her arm and smiled.

She nodded, happy in the knowledge that he wasn't going to bolt from her. She stretched up to kiss him, no longer caring who saw them.

A second before her lips met Jesse's, she saw the man over Jesse's shoulder. Startled, hoping fervently she was seeing things, she pulled away to get a better look.

Her mind wasn't playing tricks on her. She felt the weight of the man's evil stare, making her feel dirty and ashamed. She recognized his oily smile immediately. It was imprinted in her brain forever, and sadly she realized she would be the one to bolt from Jesse.

SUNNY'S HAND SHOOK as she brought her fist to the orange door and started to knock. The fact that the slime was staying only two rooms down from her was enough to give her the shivers.

As soon as the door swung open, his creepy smile was in place. He seemed to have a touch of gray in his blond hair that wasn't there two years ago.

"What do you want, Robert?" she asked acidly before he could say anything.

His pale blue eyes took in her face, then traveled leisurely down her body, and his sleazy smile widened.

She thought about slapping him. She had nothing to lose. He couldn't hurt her any more than he already had.

"Come on in." He stepped aside.

"We'll talk right here. Not that I believe we have anything to talk about." So why was she putting herself through this?

If Violet hadn't seen what an emotional wreck she'd been only ten minutes ago and hadn't convinced her to see what the man wanted, she probably wouldn't be here. But Violet already knew about Robert and the magazine, and she was right. Sunny would be a basket case until she knew what the photographer was up to.

Robert shrugged. "I don't think you'll want to discuss my proposition out here."

Proposition? The man was insane. Sunny swallowed. Actually, he was unethical. And she wasn't sure she should hear anything he had to say in public. Stiffening her spine, she stepped through the doorway. "Leave the door open."

He laughed. "Don't worry. This is business."

"Business?" She whirled on him. "You took and sold my pictures without my permission. That isn't business."

"You signed the waiver, doll."

"Not for the kind of smut—" Sunny stopped herself. She'd had this argument with him before. She'd had it with his lawyer and with hers. Arguing and pleading hadn't done any good. Two years ago, her pictures had still made it into the May issue of *Midnight Fantasy*.

"Yeah, well, those pictures made me a bundle of money, and had you cooperated, they would've made you a bundle, too." He smoothed his greased-back hair. "But I'm gonna give you another chance."

"You're crazy." Sunny backed up a step. The lampshade on the cheap, walnutlike dresser was crooked, and she had the irrational urge to straighten it.

"I saw some pictures in the newspaper of you on this cattle drive." He made a clicking sound with his disgusting mouth. "You looked hot as ever. We could do quite a pictorial of you out in the desert, like it was part of the drive." He stared at her breasts. "Figure we could sell them to someone even bigger than *Midnight Fantasy*."

She choked back a laugh, astounded by his audacity, yet relieved that she held the cards this time. How had she been naive enough to have trusted this man? "Besides being stupid, you're a pathetic excuse for a human being." She shook her head, stopping briefly at the door. "Go to hell."

Robert laughed, unconcerned. "By the way, did I tell you they wanna buy your old pictures in South America and Asia?"

Sunny's breath fled her lungs as she blindly stumbled out of the room. Was this nightmare never going to end? What the hell was she going to do?

JESSE WAITED for Sunny one hour too long, he decided, as he headed for Violet's room. Sunny hadn't been in her room at the agreed time, or if she had, she wasn't answering.

He'd had a bad feeling when she left him an hour and a half ago. Her whole attitude had done an about-face when they parted. At the time, he'd attributed her jitters to being worried that someone had seen them. But now, with her sudden disappearance, he was getting a funny feeling in his gut. A feeling that told him something wasn't right.

After replaying their last ten minutes together several times in his head, he couldn't figure out where he had gone wrong. Maybe he should have told her how he felt about her?

Right, Logan. He raked his hair before he brought his hand up to knock on Violet's door. Exactly how did he feel? God help him, he didn't know. Sex had always been a simple, primal act for him in the past. But there hadn't been a damn thing simple about making love with Sunny. Her beautiful, vulnerable face unfolded in his mind. *Forget it,* he told himself. *She has her life and you have yours. Remember the ranch.* Recalling that his longtime dream was close to a reality calmed him a little. Very little. His fist pounding Violet's door drowned out his curse.

The older woman seemed especially tired and frail when she opened the door. She didn't look surprised to see him, but when she pushed the door wider, Jesse was surprised to see Smiley sitting on her bed.

"Come on in, son." Smiley rubbed his weary face.

Jesse's bad feeling got worse. "I'm looking for Sunny."

"I know that." Smiley motioned to the room's only chair. "Shut the door, Violet."

For probably the first time in her life, the woman did what Smiley asked. That fact alone made Jesse uneasy. He moved into the room but skipped the chair.

"I don't know if I feel right telling him," Violet said as she skirted Jesse to sit beside Smiley.

"He ought to know. I'll do the talkin'." Smiley patted Violet's hand, and she nodded, looking miserable.

"Damn it. Somebody better start talking. Where's Sunny?" Jesse's patience was so far stretched that he barely noticed he'd made Violet jump.

"I ain't sayin' a word till you sit down and calm yourself, boy." Smiley's tone was stern, and Jesse knew if he didn't listen he wasn't going to get anywhere.

Ignoring the torn yellow vinyl seat, he straddled the straight-back chair, gripping the top of the backrest.

"Now listen, boy," Smiley warned. "I don't want you blowin' your top. You need to listen and you need to listen good. With no interruptin'."

Jesse nodded, his temper warring with fear. What would he do if something had happened to Sunny?

"Sunny's leavin' the drive." Smiley held up his hand when Jesse started to push up from the chair. "You ever seen a magazine called *Midnight Fantasy?*"

Jesse's gaze flew to Violet. She sat calmly, waiting, her brows raised. He shrugged and nodded at the same time.

"Two years ago," the older man continued, "Sunny got her picture put in one of them issues."

Jesse's patience bottomed out. "What?" he bellowed.

"Sit down. She didn't pose for the dang thing. She was tricked."

"Tricked?"

"You shut up, Jesse Logan." Violet brought up a warning finger at his sarcastic tone. "That poor girl *was* tricked. Everyone knows that. You haven't heard talk of it, have you? No. Because it never should have happened. She was taking lingerie pictures to play a joke on Rainy when that sleazy photographer snapped pictures of her undressing behind a screen."

The older woman's face was bright red but she continued, "Sunny had arranged a modeling trade with him for his fee, so she'd already signed the release form allowing publication of any pictures he took of her." She shook her head, her face creased in anger. "The poor girl did everything she could to stop the magazine from using them."

It wasn't easy listening to what they had to say. Jesse remembered the magazine, all right. He'd seen it plenty of times when it had first come out. He'd been a kid working in Argentina at the time, and the men down there went nuts over the blond American girls. He hated the thought of Sunny being ogled by strange men.

He took a couple of deep breaths. "I still don't get it. You said this happened, when? Two years ago?"

Smiley and Violet exchanged glances. "That's right. Although the dang incident had been put to rest, that photographer fella saw her picture in the paper because of the drive," Smiley said. "He's here and he wants to take more pictures."

Jesse blinked. "Of Sunny?" Over his dead body. He stood and the chair crashed to its side.

"Of course she wouldn't do that," Violet quickly added. "The problem is that he says he's selling the old negatives to a company in Asia and South America. She's worried that an American publication might pick up on it, and the last thing Sunny wants to do is to hurt the drive. That's why she's leaving. The poor child was just getting her life back."

Jesse paced the small room. If he'd ever thought he was capable of murder before, he was sure he was capable now. His hands clenched and flexed. He ached to strangle the scum for having degraded Sunny. God, how awful the publication must have been for her. He remembered how shy she'd been the first time he'd seen her naked, how uncertain and vulnerable she'd been with him—even though she loved him.

Damn it. He scrubbed his eyes with his palm. He knew her feelings toward him were more than casual, he could tell by the way she looked at him, yet he'd ignored that and made love to her anyway. Hell, was he any better than that other bastard?

His gaze found Violet's shadowed eyes, and he knew his pent-up anger was frightening her. What was he going to do short of killing the guy? he wondered as he headed for the door. He couldn't let Sunny leave, and he couldn't let this idiot continue to harass her. Although not sure what, he knew he had to do something.

He turned the knob, then looked over his shoulder at the older couple, his grip so tight he thought he might break the fixture. "Don't let her leave. I'm counting on you." He glanced heavenward. "Please don't let her leave."

EVEN IF HE HADN'T KNOWN what a slime Robert Westin was, Jesse wouldn't have liked the man. He instinctively recognized the snake as soon as he slithered into the dingy bar with his slicked-back hair and fake smile. Jesse wondered how Sunny could have ever trusted the guy. A month ago he would have figured she'd asked for the trouble. But now, Jesse knew better. Not his Sunny.

That's why, after an hour of racking his brain, he'd come up with the only solution. The only way he could help make up for all her hurt...some of which he might have caused. He wanted to keep her from getting hurt again.

And after a quick call to Robert Westin his plan went into action. It hadn't been difficult to get the underhanded photographer's attention. The scent of money had been enough.

Jesse took a long pull of his beer and grimaced. It had gotten warm. In the past four hours, he'd moved heaven and earth to come up with a plan to get this guy off Sunny's back. He had threatened, cajoled, begged. The local banker had tracked down his own banker in Houston. He'd called in favors, promised his soul. In the next few minutes, he hoped it would all be worth it.

"Jesse Logan?" Robert Westin stuck out his hand.

Jesse did everything he could not to punch out the guy's big white teeth. "Yeah. You got them?"

"I don't know why this couldn't wait until tomorrow." Westin's hand fell to his side. "You have any idea how much it cost me to get—"

Jesse stuck an envelope in his face. "I think this will more than take care of your expenses," he said in a low, dangerous voice. "Do you have them, or not?"

Westin smiled. "I've got them." He reached into his jacket. "Bet you can't wait to see these puppies."

"The negatives," Jesse warned, his control slipping. "I want the damn negatives."

Westin's smile made Jesse's knuckles itch. "Consider the pictures a bonus." He laid a large manila envelope on the bar. "Everything is in there."

Jesse took a deep breath. Reining in his anger, he laid his envelope beside the larger one. When Westin reached for it, Jesse slammed his hand down on the man's wrist. His painful gasp made Jesse grin. "I have something for you to sign before we make the exchange."

"I didn't agree to sign anything." Westin rubbed his wrist.

"If you intend to honor our deal, you don't have a thing to worry about. All this does is make sure that if her pictures ever surface again, she can sue the pants off you."

"That won't happen." Westin produced a pen, read the brief statement, then scrawled his name. "Hell, you're paying me enough." He snatched up the smaller envelope and peered inside. "Cashier's check. Look at all those zeroes." He glanced at Jesse and smiled. "A pleasure doing business with you."

Jesse cast a cursory glance at the negatives in the manila envelope. Satisfied that he'd gotten what he wanted, he slid off the bar stool and started to walk away. "Oh, yeah." He turned to Westin. "I got a message for you from Sunny."

The photographer lifted a cocky brow.

Jesse would have preferred a better target. But what the hell...

His fist smashed into Westin's surprised face. The man staggered to the floor, his hand flying to his nose.

Jesse grinned and touched his hat.

"I'M NOT LEAVING without saying goodbye." Sunny sniffed as she sat on her overnight bag and jammed the lock closed. "I want to be ready as soon as Cash gets here. He's driving six hours as it is, I don't want to hold him up."

"It ain't like you to run from your responsibility like this," Smiley said, glancing at Violet, who stood at the open door running her hands down her denim coveralls.

"You know why I have to leave." Sunny tried not to look at Violet. Tears welled in the woman's eyes, and Sunny was close to bawling, herself. "I'll do the drive more harm if I stay. I don't trust Westin. He'll use my association to his advantage."

"Jesse will fix it," Violet said. "I know he will."

Why did Violet have to mention Jesse? A tear slipped down Sunny's cheek. She quickly dashed it away. "He can't, Violet, nobody can. Anyway, he's got enough to worry about."

"He ain't gonna let you leave, ya know?" Smiley said.

"I'd be leaving in a couple of weeks, anyway. I've got modeling jobs," she lied. "He's got the drive to finish."

She paused, taking a deep breath. Smiley eyed her cynically. Violet's blue eyes swam in tears.

She shrugged and tried to smile. "He has his life and I have mine. This was a job. Now it's over for me. And when he's done with the drive, he'll be busy looking for land for his ranch. End of story." She turned to busy herself with her overnight bag, hoping they didn't see the fresh wave of tears welling in her eyes. Because that summation held more truth than she could handle right now.

After a long silence, Smiley said, "There ain't gonna be no ranch."

She carefully kept her back to them and blinked her eyes dry. "Of course, there is. That's been his goal. Everyone knows that."

"Yeah, but he don't have enough money."

Sunny turned her narrowed gaze on him. Violet had finally stepped into the room and had slipped an arm through Smiley's. She gave him a nudge.

"He will after the drive is over," Sunny said. "He's even checked on land prices along the trail."

Smiley shook his head. "Seems things have changed."

"What things?" She stepped away from the suitcase. She could feel the heat from the open door cutting through the air-conditioning. It was uncomfortable, hitting her back and making her shirt stick to her, but she was too interested in what Smiley was talking about to give it much thought.

Smiley shrugged. "You gotta ask him that yourself."

Sunny looked at Violet. Her friend averted her eyes. "What's going on?"

"Ask him," Smiley urged.

"Violet? Please tell me."

"It's true," Violet confirmed. "It's going to be a long time before he can save that much money again. And without his rodeo career, he—" She shook her head.

Smiley snatched off his hat, looking more sad than angry. "Gosh dang it, woman. Don't say another word."

"But why? Where did—" Fear clutched her heart. They had to be mistaken. Jesse had been saving for the ranch his whole life. He'd sacrificed everything. He wouldn't give up his dream now. "You're wrong," she said, shaking her head.

But when she looked into both pairs of bleak eyes, she knew better. She turned away, not wanting to see visible evidence of the truth. It hurt too much because she knew Jesse had to be hurting, too.

Her thoughts tangled and scattered, wondering how this could have happened. What had he needed the money for? Was he in some kind of trouble? What could possibly have changed in only a few hours? Why did life have to be such a mess?

She couldn't imagine Jesse not having his ranch. Even worse, she couldn't imagine how he'd come up with the money to get it. God, would he even think of returning to the rodeo? An image of him atop a bull flashed in her mind.

"I can get it," she said, surprising herself as much as Smiley and Violet. They both frowned at her. She took a deep breath. "The money for his ranch. I can get it."

The couple frowned deeper.

Sunny had to steady herself. The mere idea of what she was about to say made her light-headed. "I'll pose for Westin." She cleared her throat. "He said the pictures were for South America and Asia. I'll have an attorney make sure they can't be sold in the United States." She paused for a breath. She had no idea what she was saying, only what she had to do. "I'll take them and—"

"No, you won't."

Jesse's low, angry voice came from behind her. She spun around to find him tensed at the door, his broad shoulders nearly filling the frame.

"Jesse?" Her hands shook from the thought of posing as she tucked a lock of hair behind her ear.

He gave Violet and Smiley a quick glance, and the couple scrambled past him out the door. "You're not posing for that snake."

"How do you know…" Her eyes widened, then narrowed at the empty doorway. Her gaze returned to him, her chin lifting. "Not that it's any of your business."

He slammed the door closed. "It is."

"Really?" She put a hand on her hip.

He reached for her.

She dodged him, wondering how much of the conversation he'd heard. "Don't mess with me on this. I appreciate your concern. But if I pose, it would be none of your business."

Jesse watched her shoulders tremble at the thought of posing for the degrading pictures. He sidestepped a chair and caught her around the waist. His heart pounded with her nearness, pounded with what he was about to say. "It would," he said, pulling her to him. "If you were my wife."

She gazed at him, her almond-shaped eyes growing rounder by the second. Her lips quivered and she moistened them. "What are you saying?"

"That I…" He closed his eyes. He didn't have a thing to offer this woman. What *was* he saying? That he wanted—no, *needed*—her in his life with an intensity that was burning a hole in him. That he wanted her beside him because she was funny and smart and made him feel like doing honorable, sappy things. And that, in exchange, he could give her nothing.

He had no right to ask anything of her. He wasn't worthy. How had he ever thought she was like his mother? When life had gotten rough, Sunny hadn't walked out. She'd been ready to sacrifice herself for him. How could he repay that kind of loyalty?

"Jesse?" Sunny looped her arms around his neck, her face tilted to gaze at him. "I love you."

He looked at her tearstained face, at the smile that was shyly lifting her lips. There was only one thing Sunny wanted. He smiled shakily. "I love you."

When a sob broke from her, his throat constricted. He knew he should tell her that he wasn't worthy, but he wanted too badly to be her hero. So he hugged her tightly and promised himself he'd spend the rest of his life being everything she wanted.

Blinking back the emotion welling within him, he pulled away and lifted her chin. "If you say yes, I have a wedding present for you," he teased.

"Yes." A small laugh caught in her chest.

He swallowed and gave her another quick hug, then pulled the manila envelope out of his shirt and handed it to her.

She peeked inside. As realization dawned, her eyes widened. "Jesse? Can we get married today?"

Jesse's heart soared as he kissed her.

Epilogue

Sunny watched her niece toddle off the blanket toward the open pasture. She tensed, ready to scramble after the small tow-headed child. But Sabrina stopped and bent to pick a yellow wildflower. Her other niece, Cybil, Sabrina's twin, charged her sister, grabbing for the pretty prize.

"No." Sabrina waddled as fast as her short, chubby legs could carry her to Sunny, nearly trampling their picnic lunch, and handed the flower to her aunt. "You."

"Thank you, Sabrina." Sunny accepted the offering and smiled at the toddler, reveling in her role as baby-sitter.

Not to be outdone by her sister, Cybil pulled a flower out by its roots and hurried to Sunny just as Jesse rode up on Thunder. Both little girls turned at the sound of the hooves pounding the ground, their mouths forming small Os.

"Am I in time for lunch?" he asked, sliding from his saddle and giving each of his nieces a hug.

"Is food all you care about?" Sunny pouted. "I bet Smiley cares about more than that after only fifteen months of marriage."

"Fifteen months, three weeks and four days," Jesse corrected and reached down to pull her into his arms.

She couldn't stop smiling even as he kissed her, remembering the double wedding they'd shared with Violet and Smiley. They still saw a lot of Smiley, even though he'd moved into Violet's place. Especially now that Cash was heading this year's drive. It wasn't that Smiley didn't trust Jesse to run things. He was thrilled beyond words when Jesse had accepted partnership of the McCloud ranch in order to free up Cash. It was just that some habits were too old to break, and Smiley had been a fixture for so long.

Sunny had never told Jesse that Rainy had all along hoped Cash would take a shot at one of his dreams by heading the drive. And that had been one of the main reasons Sunny had agreed to substitute for Rainy.

When their nieces' giggling prompted them to break the kiss, Sunny said, "I was thinking about taking the twins to Pocito to see Cash and Rainy this weekend, instead of Rainy coming home."

Jesse frowned. "Did Rainy ask you to do that?"

Sunny studied her husband's face, knowing he sometimes worried that she felt tied down. "No, but it's hard for her to be away from the girls for more than a week, so I thought I'd surprise her and save her some traveling time. I think half the reason she's letting us watch them is for practice."

He grinned, his gaze straying to her still-flat belly. He placed his hand there. "Is he kicking yet?"

She laughed. "It's too early. And who said it's a he?"

"It's gotta be, honey. Cash and I are outnumbered here."

"Poor you." She kissed him.

He grinned. "Yeah." He followed her down to the blanket, and both girls hopped on for a piggyback ride.

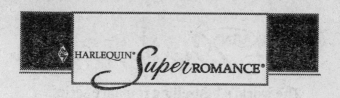
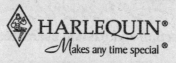

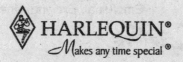

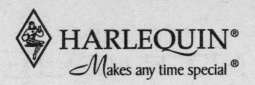